Catch Me if you Cannes

Lisa Dickenson

sphere

SPHERE

First published in ebook in 2015 by Sphere
This paperback edition published in Great Britain in 2017 by Sphere

1 3 5 7 9 10 8 6 4 2

A CIP catalogue record for this book
is available from the British Library.

ISBN 978-0-7515-6517-1

Typeset in Caslon by M Rules
Printed and bound in Great Britain by
Clays Ltd, St Ives plc

Papers used by Sphere are from well-managed forests
and other responsible sources.

MIX
Paper from
responsible sources
FSC® C104740

Sphere
An imprint of
Little, Brown Book Group
Carmelite House
50 Victoria Embankment
London EC4Y 0DZ

An Hachette UK Company
www.hachette.co.uk

www.littlebrown.co.uk

Dedicated to you lot

Now go and have a holiday, you deserve it

'We are all of us stars, and we deserve to twinkle.'

Marilyn Monroe

Part One

Once upon a time Jess accidently stole
a superyacht from Cannes marina,
but we'll get to that . . .

Jess was awoken by her best friend punching her in the back of the head.

'*Get off me please, I have a knife and I will kill you to death!*' she shrieked, rolling over and remembering in the nick of time that she was three bunks up. In the opposite bed, Bryony lay face down, fast asleep, a long arm stretched across the gap between them like a rope bridge with her clenched fist on Jess's pillow. Jess exhaled in relief and pushed her friend's hand off her bed.

Bryony lifted her head, her face painted the colour 'grump'. 'Jess, I love how bubbly you are at any God-given hour, but could you keep it down a bit? I *just* got to sleep.'

'If you're going to sleep-punch me I'll fight back, you know.'

'You're a lover, not a fighter,' Bryony yawned.

'Where's everyone else?' Jess rubbed the back of her head and peered over the side of the bunk at the empty beds below.

'The Scot with the earrings declared at two a.m. that he couldn't sleep, and that they should all go to the bar instead. I haven't seen them since. Did you say you have a knife?'

'I thought you were a robber. I was just warning you that I'd kill the hell out of you if you tried anything.'

Bryony raised an eyebrow. 'You couldn't kill a robber.'

'I could, I'm feisty. I do boxercise. And Zumba, if that's relevant.'

'You said "please".'

'Huh?'

'You definitely said, "Get off me *please*." Even when you think you're being attacked your manners are impeccable. Anyway, you don't have a knife with you. Did you mean your plastic spork?'

'If you'd been a robber you wouldn't have known that.' Jess sat up as best she could when the ceiling was less than two feet above her bunk, pulled on her glasses and cracked open the curtain, letting bright Riviera sunshine flood into their compartment of the sleeper train. 'Wow!'

'Urrrrgggghhhh, what time is it?' Bryony pulled the covers over her head, exposing her feet, which dangled off the end of the bunk anyway.

'Nearly seven.' Outside the window, glittery turquoise sea whizzed past. White sails shook like elegant swans waking up, while yachts the size of houses gleamed lazily in the early-morning sun.

A beam of happiness and hope pushed its way across Jess's face. It was happening, and this was exactly what she needed: two weeks of fun somewhere different, somewhere out of her comfort zone. She reached over and yanked the blanket off Bryony. '*Look.*'

Bryony scrunched her eyes closed. 'It's beautiful.'

'Bryony, *look*! We're in the South of France, the Côte d'Azur.' She pulled down the window as far as it would go and pushed her face up to the gap, breathing in the Mediterranean air. '*Bonjour la France!*' she yelped into the breeze.

Chuckling, Bryony pulled her back inside. 'Okay, Édith Piaf, I'm awake. Let's go and get you a croissant and me some strong coffee before we arrive.'

Jess couldn't drag her gaze away from the window as she and Bryony sat in the restaurant car munching their way through a basket of flaketastic croissants. The sea was a never-ending turquoise ribbon, and every thirty seconds Jess would point out yet another beachside eatery she wanted to try.

'We're still half an hour from Cannes,' said Bryony. 'I'm sure there will be plenty to eat there. Now answer the question; I need to know the protocol should this happen.'

'It'll happen, I can feel it. So if Mr DiCaprio makes eyes at me across the marina and says, *"My love, come to my yacht,"* I will warble, "I'LL NEVER LET GO" and you'll know I want you to skedaddle.'

'And you'll do the same if Zac Efron invites me for a Cannes-Cannes-Cannes? Only my code word will be *"cougartown"*.' Bryony stuffed in another croissant.

'Sounds perfect. But George is off-limits – he's a married man now. I shall be content to be just friends with him, and perhaps be the recipient of a good-natured Clooney prank.' Jess's phone buzzed with a text message. 'It's Mrs Evans. She says, "Havv a NICE tIME swetie" – she's just learnt texting.'

'From you?'

'Yep.' Mrs Evans was one of her regulars at the café, ninety years young and obsessed with gadgets.

'How will those villagers cope without you for the next fortnight?' Bryony smirked.

Excitement fizzed like popping candy in Jess's chest. 'They'll be fine. I can't wait to be in Cannes. Sunshine, red carpets, rosé wine, celebs everywhere ... Thanks again for letting me tag along.'

'My pleasure. Any time you want to muscle your way onto one of my trips suits me fine – this would be my idea of hell without my short-stack. Besides, when we spoke about it you were a right grump. You were practically *me*.'

The unlikely friendship of Jess and Bryony had begun the day after Bryony moved to Cornwall and joined Jess's secondary school in year nine. The personality and height differences back then were even more pronounced than they were now: Jess was the tiniest girl in their year, while Bryony towered above most of the boys, her chunky canvas high heels adding to the effect. Bryony didn't speak to anyone on her first day, just stared straight ahead among a sea of whispering teenagers. Jess had felt for this serious new girl, so made her a welcome pack of Rimmel Heather Shimmer lipstick, some Impulse O2 body spray, a copy of *Bliss* magazine and a homemade map of the school that showed which toilets to avoid and the best places to sit in certain classrooms. Bryony, who'd felt trapped in a lonely, awkward body, painfully and angrily aware that – at the time – she was the only black girl in the year, that hers was one of the only black families in the village, instantly felt a fondness for this funny, petite ray of sunshine.

They were as different then as they were now, with Bryony honing her sharp mind on crime and mystery books as she grew up to become a fiercely intelligent journalist – though not the type she yearned to be, yet – whose heroines were *Scandal*'s Olivia Pope and C.J. Cregg from *The West Wing*. Meanwhile, Jess had clung onto her *Sweet Valley* novels until the bitter end, before moving on to feel-good fiction and travel writing, all the best of which now lined the bookshelves of her very own café; she ran a homely, happy place that was like having everyone in the village come into her living room for a cuppa.

They bonded that first school lunchtime, over the pages of that *Bliss* magazine, and although life took them along different paths after school, they still got together as often as possible.

One rain-soaked Saturday evening back in April, Bryony had been visiting for the first time in weeks, and she dropped the following over a bottle of their favourite wine . . .

'Guess what? I'm being sent to the Cannes Film Festival.' Bryony reluctantly worked for *Sleb*, a highly disrespected gossip magazine with a readership of close to zero and morals at about the same level.

Jess, uncharacteristically not in the best of moods, had dragged herself back to the present, forcing herself to engage in the conversation. She had to make the most of Bryony while she was here, feeling low and lost wasn't an option. She knocked back some more wine. 'Shut the *fridge* up – really?'

Bryony shrugged. 'Apparently *Sleb* needs me there. To see, in the words of the ever-eloquent, never-misogynistic Mitch, "which stars are shagging each other and get the skinny on who's actually a fat chick."'

'Urgh, he makes my skin crawl and I've never even met him. What a penis.'

'There's literally no point in me even going; he'll Photoshop fat onto everyone anyway, regardless of what I say ... I know, I know, I shouldn't complain: a magazine job is bloody hard to come by and a free trip to the South of France isn't exactly the crappest thing in the world. But one day, Meems, *one day*, *Sleb* will magically turn into *Marie Claire* and he'll actually take me up on one of the current affairs features I keep begging him to publish.'

'Exactly.' Jess swirled her wine, racking her brain for something more insightful to say, but she was all over the place.

'So how's everything with y—'

'Maybe I could come?' Jess said, desperately interrupting Bryony. But as soon as the words were out of her mouth it was as if a pinprick of light had formed behind her eyes. *Maybe I could go to Cannes.*

'What?'

'Can I come?' The pinprick grew larger, the light seeping in like a sunrise. She sat up straighter. Jess's one true love had always been Marilyn Monroe, to the point that Bryony even started calling her 'Meems' as a nickname years ago. From the safety of her little seaside village, through reality TV and old films, Jess dreamed of what it would be like to go to golden Hollywood and live like a movie star.

'Can you come? To Cannes? *You?*'

Jess nodded and gulped some more wine, colour coming to her cheeks and a non-faked hint of happiness coming back through. *Hello again, old friend.* Maybe it was the alcohol, maybe it was the tail end of the shittiest week she'd ever had, or maybe it was that this was the live-a-little-more chance she'd been looking for, but she really wanted to go with Bryony. Jess didn't hate a lot of things, but people who moped and moaned without doing anything about it was one of them, and she realised she was being exactly that sort of person. Her words tumbled out: 'I won't get in the way, and I'll pay for my half, of course. Yes, it's time for me to get out there and explore the world. Starting with the country closest to us.'

'Are you okay?' Bryony looked at her carefully, the transformation of her friend from hunched, wine-gulping misery-guts back to her bouncy, excitable self not going unnoticed.

'I'm fine, I'm really fine. This is good; we're still youngish and should take advantage of not having any responsibilities, right?'

'Um, right?'

'Besides, Bry, I'm a bit worried you'll throw yourself under a yacht out of sheer career frustration if you go by yourself.'

'This'll be pretty different from a relaxing package holiday—'

'I know, but that's what I like about it. It'll be completely different. It'll be busy and glitzy, and all over the place there'll be people richer and fancier than us. But you have to experience how the other half lives when you can, huh?'

Bryony nodded and went to pour herself another glass of wine but the bottle dripped out nothing more than a few crimson dregs. She peered at Jess, who waited with bated breath.

'Pleeeeease.'

'You'll keep me sane?' Bryony asked.

'Trust me, you'll be keeping *me* sane. Now let's get you some more wine, you've drunk the lot,' Jess countered with a real smile.

'Well I think it looks brilliant,' said Jess, following a thirty-minute slog from the station to the outskirts of Cannes, dragging their bags behind them through the hot streets. They stared up at their hotel's façade, 'Hôtel du Bliss' emblazoned on a chipped, sun-faded sign above the entrance. 'And we're not *that* far from the sea. Look, if you peer down that road you can see a dot of blue in the distance. So technically it is a sea-view hotel, and you can't go wrong with that.'

'I knew Mitch wouldn't be putting me in the InterContinental Carlton, but ...' Bryony went to chip a bit of snot-like sludge off the tarnished address plaque, then thought better of it.

'But it's free, and we won't be spending much time here anyway.'

Bryony slapped on a smile. 'You're right. Sorry, I'm being a grumpy old cow as usual. I think work can wait a while. How about we wake ourselves up with a trek down to the marina for some French-roast coffee and a nose at the Richie Riches of the world?'

'Yes! That sounds perfect. You can have one day of holiday, right, before all that celeb scandal and fat-shaming begins?'

'Absolutely. The film festival begins tomorrow.'

'It starts *tomorrow*! This is so exciting,' Jess babbled as they walked inside. The receptionist refused to speak anything but French to them, which would have been completely fair enough had Jess not heard her on the phone, yabbering about council tax in a thick Brummie accent, when they'd first entered the lobby. Eventually they established where their boudoir was and crammed into a tiny lift, then squeezed along a tiny corridor and into a room with a tiny double bed.

Jess took Bryony's hand. 'Happy honeymoon, darling,' she breathed in a sugary Marilyn voice.

'Thank you, lover. It's just exquisite, isn't it?' Bryony heaved her suitcase onto the bed and plugged in her dead phone, while Jess pottered about opening drawers and pressing all the buttons on the air-con remote control. After a moment Bryony's phone lit up, coming back to life with the buzz of a voicemail.

'It's Mitch,' Bryony mouthed.

Jess checked her emails to find one from Barry, a salmon-trouser-wearing lothario of seventy from her village, wishing her a happy holiday and warning her not to fall in love with a 'Frenchie' and forget about him. There was also a short one from Anthony, asking if she'd be around next week. *Nope.* She looked up at Bryony, just in time to see her repeatedly smacking her phone against the pillow.

'Whoa, whoa, what's wrong?' Jess asked, putting down her phone.

'I'm sick of this! I'm sick of this job! I don't want to do this any more.' Bryony's face was pink with rage as she paced the tiny room, pinging around like a pinball. 'He makes me hate myself. Every day it's "Expose *this* celebrity, dig some dirt on *that* soap star, source some fat photos of *that* singer," when that singer is blatantly struggling with anorexia. Well guess what, Mitch? *I'm* fat. You wanna expose me? You want me to shame other women when there's a big ol' muffin top right here!' She yanked up her dress, grabbed a red lipstick from her open suitcase and drew a huge circle on her hip. '*Look how gross I am! Let's point and laugh!* Oh bugger, this is one of those twenty-four-hour lip stain things . . . '

Blimey. Bryony was always so deadpan despondent about her life that people got used to her dry manner, and it was rare that she flipped out like this. Jess stepped forward and gently slid Bryony's dress back

16

down. She had lovely knickers on – big comfy-looking mint shorts – but this was not the time to ask where they came from. 'Okay, crazy, calm down, it's okay,' Jess soothed. 'You're overtired right now, but it's okay, I'm here. Let's get you through these next two weeks and then you can hand in your notice. You shouldn't be this unhappy.'

'How come *you're* always so happy?'

'I'm not.'

'Maybe I should have just stayed in Cornwall too. No drama, just an easy, simple life.'

'I mean, I do have some dramas . . .' Jess protested. Just because she wasn't in London didn't mean she didn't have things going on.

'Besides, it's not that easy,' continued Bryony. 'Journalism is so hard to get into, and it's not like I even have a decent portfolio of cuttings because all I've been allowed to write about over the past seven years is how many wrinkles so-and-so has, followed by how ridiculed they should be if they dare to have Botox.' She sat on the floor, her head in her hands. 'I just need a good story, a story that means something, that people read and go, "Huh, well that actually taught me a thing or two about the world." Do you think if I can get something like that here Mitch would start to take me seriously?'

'Do you think he'd print it?'

Bryony shrugged and looked up at Jess. 'This'll be the last time I try.' She pulled herself to her feet with a sigh. 'Sorry I had a paddy. It just gets to me sometimes.'

'Don't apologise: it's good to unleash.'

'You never unleash. What is it you do? Flip a switch or something?'

'If I'm having grumpy thoughts I just try to turn them off, but it doesn't always work.' Sometimes Jess wondered if she turned off her feelings too much. 'What did Mitch actually say? Does he want you to do something?'

'Apparently he's heard from a source, which is his way of saying I'm not on the ball enough, that there are two Z-listers – married, but not to each other – having a very indiscreet humpathon over at the Luxe hotel pool. I have to get over there immediately. Like a pervert. So I guess that's our fun ruined for ever.'

'Not at all, it's just for a couple of hours. And, um, which Z-listers?'

'Some *Made in Money* star that has a naked cameo in one of the indie movies this year, and that guy ...' she clicked her fingers in thought.

'Which guy?' Jess salivated.

'Mitch just told me and the name's gone already.

18

You know, the one from the film with the things. The robots. Or was it aliens? Or alien robots. Big beardy man … Hang on, that's someone else … Anyway, looks like I have to dash. I'm so sorry.'

'It's fine, go. I'll have an explore, and assuming some movie star doesn't invite me back to his hotel for a festival-long love-fest, could we meet for dinner?'

Bryony was trawling through her suitcase for her biggest, darkest sunglasses. 'Absolutely. I'll be done in a few hours – let's meet back here mid-afternoon then have that big, start-the-holiday night out.'

'You okay?' Jess asked, her hands on her hips as she looked up at her friend.

'Yep. I'm glad you're here, though. If you weren't I probably would have spiralled into some naked mess lying on the carpet, scribbling on myself with red lippy and sobbing.'

'As if I've never seen you do that before.'

Jess stepped out of the hotel in her most nautical of day dresses and big Audrey Hepburn shades so she could stare at people without them noticing. She felt *so* "Riviera Life", and in her mind a big band was playing some jolly ditty while she swayed down the street like Ginger Rogers.

The air was warm, a refreshing change from back home, and although she doubted she'd actually dropped any pounds since leaving England yesterday evening, the closer she got to the seafront the lighter she felt. The air buzzed with an opening-night anticipation: the start of summer, the start of the film festival, the start of ... well, she'd see.

Film-festival posters decorated the windows of shops and restaurants, and banners on street lamps waved in the breeze. As she neared the Promenade de la Croisette, the road stretching alongside the Mediterranean in front of the exquisite hotels, the scooters turned into supercars and the regular-sized people became towering supermodels. As she wandered near to the Palais des Festivals et des Congrès, the vast white convention centre hosting most of the goings-on at the Cannes Film Festival, she could see swarms of people scurrying back and forth over the immense red carpet, tweaking lights, sweeping steps and making a thousand minuscule adjustments so that it was perfect for the big stars who would be descending upon it from the following day.

Jess watched, heart and energy levels full, a world of excitement and intrigue before her, knowing this was to be her home for the next two weeks. What had taken her so long to start exploring the world?

Yes, she could live here. She could own a Ferrari and dine out in wildly overpriced restaurants every night before retiring to her yacht. Yes. Even the air was fabulous, smelling of salt, money and chocolate, which was frankly an amazing combination. Her stomach growled, and she looked around her until she realised where the chocolate smell was coming from.

She walked up to a sea-facing kiosk, thinking the man inside had one of the loveliest views a chef could have.

'*Bonjour, Monsieur. Je voudrais une crêpe, s'il vous plaît,*' she said carefully, with an awful accent.

'Nutella?'

'*Oui, s'il vous plaît.*'

'*Crème?*' he asked, making the motion of squirty cream with his hands, though how he knew she wasn't French was beyond her.

'Oh, *OUI, s'il vous plaît!*'

The seller whipped up her crêpe in record time, and as he handed it to her Jess felt the happy smugness of one doing whatever they wanted, and jolly well treating themselves to a fat, gooey slab of indulgence for lunch if they wanted one. Marilyn would have approved. Jess chomped into the crêpe,

Nutella oozing out of the edges, spilling warm gloop over her fingers and dotting the end of her nose with chocolate. With an audible '*Mmmm*' she took another large bite and breathed in the aroma of blissful-chocolatiness-meets-summer-holidays.

What a view. Standing in the middle of the Croisette, she had the sparkling sea and ridiculous-sized superyachts in front of her, towering posh-pants hotels behind her, an expansive red carpet to her right and, mmm, a delicious man jogging down the promenade like some kind of a slow-mo scene from a romantic comedy.

Hang on, was he running *at* her? She glanced around – no muggers about to slit her throat from behind, no person standing with some bottles of water or a plate of orange slices. The closer he got, the more obvious it became that he really did seem to be heading straight towards her. Jess backed up against the fence and held her crêpe up over her eyes.

A shadow passed over her and she peeked up. The man stood, tall and lightly tanned, and sweating profusely, but not in an altogether unattractive way. He yanked out his earphones, wiped a big hand across his eyes and panted at her. She gawped back at him, unsure what was about to come next. She held her crêpe close.

'*Bon matin?*' he queried, still panting.

'*Bon matin.*'

'Um, *où est la crêpe?*' His pronunciation was just as awful as hers, but she still wasn't sure what was happening.

'*Ici . . .* ' She held her crêpe in the air, briefly, before pulling it back under her protection in case he was some kind of a crêpe thief.

'Um . . . '

'Are you English?' Jess asked.

'Yes!' He beamed, relief shining out of his smile. 'Are you?'

'Yes,' she laughed.

'Phew! You just made my day – I just assumed you were French, and I am *so* awful at French.'

'What made you think I was French?' Whatever it was, she'd gladly do more of it.

A blush tiptoed over him and he fumbled his words. 'Your dress, I guess, you look all nautical and pretty and things; you fit right into all this,' he gestured to their Riviera surroundings.

Yeah she did! 'Why, this old thing?' she joked, fluffing out her frock.

'It's nice.' They stood awkwardly for a moment, looking from one another to the view, and back again. Her shades allowed her to peer sideways at

23

him without it being obvious, and she quickly took in his open, friendly face dusted with shyness, and his sun-kissed hair. And his extreme tallness. Suddenly he seemed to remember that it was his move. 'Sorry – your crêpe. It looks way better than jogging.'

'Oh, it is! It's much better.'

'Can I ask where you got it?'

Jess pointed behind her, at the large kiosk with CRÊPES written on it. He put his hands on his hips and stared at the kiosk. 'Where? Where on earth can I get a crêpe around here? Come on, France, you had one job.'

He smiled at her, an infectious, dopey, sexy beam that she couldn't help but mirror, and lifted his T-shirt slightly to mop his face, revealing a dash of delicious stomach and even more sweat. Jess found herself fighting a primal urge to lick him. Urgh, what was wrong with her?

'I'm so disgusting,' he laughed. 'I just interrupted your happy moment by blocking your view, breathing heavily and making you smell my sweat. I swear I'm not a sex pest.'

'Good to know. How was the run?'

'Rubbish. I don't know what I was thinking – it's so hot. Then I saw you.'

Jess's heart ba-boomed.

24

'I mean your crêpe,' he clarified, chuckling and covering his face with his hands. 'I'm really not a sex pest. Nor am I a very good flirt.'

This was flirting? He was flirting with her? Well . . . all right, that was nice. 'You're doing okay, for someone who's said "sex pest" twice in the first two minutes.'

'I'm going to make a big effort not to say it again, I promise. Um, so do you come here – no, that's crap as well . . .' He sighed and stuffed his phone and head-phones into the pocket of his shorts, then looked back up at her, his eyes crinkling at the edges. 'I tell you what: how about another crêpe? It's the least I can do.'

In the spirit of seizing life a little more, and the desire to hang out with this strange, awkward and charming man a little longer, she accepted. 'I shouldn't, but yes please. They're so good, I really want another one.'

'Brilliant; with the works?'

'Yes please.' She walked with him back to the kiosk and watched him as he placed their order. Where did he come from all of a sudden? 'I'm Jess.'

'I'm Leo. Nice to meet you, Jess, hope it hasn't ruined your day meeting me.' For a millisecond Jess's heart leapt – Leo DiCaprio? – but no; even covered in sweat she knew he wasn't *that* Leo. The sandy-coloured waves to his hair, the English accent and the lack of a Victoria's Secret model by his side gave it away.

Jess sunk her teeth into the second squidgy crêpe and watched as Leo did the same. Another yummy-moan escaped her but she didn't care. 'This is the best day ever. I thought the first crêpe was good, but now it's like having a *really* good dream and waking up to have the same thing happening in real life.'

'You are so right, this is amazing. I'm definitely having another one after this and you should too.'

'No, I shouldn't.'

'But then it would be like having a great dream, waking up and it still being there, all delicious and moreish, then going back to sleep and falling back into the exact same dream.'

Mmm. 'But you've been jogging, you've earned it.'

'No, I really haven't. I've only been going for about five minutes; I'm just this sweaty because I'm so out of shape.'

Jess begged to disagree, but only in her head, and he didn't need to know what was going on in there.

'We could just keep going round in circles,' he continued, polishing off his crêpe in a few more giant mouthfuls. 'It would be so good, think how happy we'd be. People would talk it about it for years: *"Remember when Jess and Leo ate all the crêpes in France . . ."'*

She smiled. How come there were just some people in the world you felt immediately comfortable with? There was none of that just-met-someone, pick-at-your-food-in-case-you-get-some-on-your-face worry; he was just joining her in her big, messy, delicious happiness.

He checked his watch. 'Right, guttingly, duty calls and it's back to work I go. It was good to meet you. Catch you later, I hope?'

'I'm sure I'll see you around.'

'Cannes isn't that big – I'll find you. Not in a sex-pest kind of way.' He lobbed another massive grin her way and took off, jogging down the promenade towards the marina. She watched him go, until the jingling of her phone brought her back to reality.

'Hi, Mum,' said Jess, leaning against a railing and gazing out at the Mediterranean, a smile she couldn't control playing on her face.

Patty responded by belting out 'There's No Business Like Show Business'. 'How is it, honey? As marvellous as we remember?'

'Hey, girlfriend,' her dad, Jeff, said, coming in on the other landline.

'Hi, Dad.' Her parents weren't your average OAPs. In fact, Jess was convinced that when they looked in the mirror they still saw a couple of twenty-somethings, touring the world and living life like there was no time limit.

'Jeff, do you remember that yacht party we went to in Cannes, with the dancing girls and the tequila?'

'Like it was freakin' yesterday. But it was off Saint-Tropez, not Cannes. Don't you remember, "Crazy crazy Saint-Tropez-y"?'

'Move those hips like Patrick Swayze!' Patty tittered. 'Just kidding, honey,' she said, addressing her daughter again. '*Dirty Dancing* came out years later. I added that last bit, but it worked right? And it would have been very apt that night—'

'Anyway,' said Jess. 'I've arrived, and it's beautiful and classy, and I can see them setting up the red carpet for the film festival from where I'm standing.'

'Heeeeeey,' drawled Cameron, her big brother, coming on the line as well.

Really? She was away for twenty-four hours and he was already skulking about, probably eating their Jaffa Cakes and messing up her old bedroom, sitting on her blow-up chair and whatnot. 'You're at Mum and Dad's again?'

'They have Sky. I like to watch National Geographic

28

in case they have any programmes about places I've been.'

Jess rolled her eyes. 'Any luck so far?'

Cameron paused, then decided to ignore her question. 'So, whatcha doing?'

'Walking along by the sea in Cannes, looking at all the celebrities.'

'No you're not.'

'Yes I am,' Jess said, as smug as a teenager who'd got a better Christmas present than her brother.

'Who can you see?'

'Ryan and Blake,' she said, looking through her shades at an elderly couple on the beach. She shifted her gaze to a blonde woman selling ice cream. 'Scarlett Johansson.'

'Shut up, no you can't.'

'And it is *hot* here, much hotter than Cornwall. How's the rain?'

'It can't be as hot as when I was in Nicaragua . . .'

Here we go. Patty and Jeff, back in the seventies, had been in a place of unadulterated hippiedom when Patty had fallen pregnant. Being enamoured of anything that involved adventure or fun, they saw having a baby as just another piece of the big, crazy puzzle of life: someone to share their explorations with and to show what a magical place the world was. So for six years after the birth of Cameron the three of them, along with a lot of hemp nappies, kept on travelling, kept on living, living, living.

Then Patty became pregnant again, and out popped baby Jess. And bam! The fun stopped for everyone, as Patty and Jeff decided that two kids, along with the backpacks and the good times, were too much to handle and settled down by the seaside for a quiet life. Jess felt like the biggest party-pooper ever.

Nowadays, Cameron liked to think of himself as incredibly well-travelled and worldly-wise, though he'd been just six years old when he returned to Cornwall, and other than a few orienteering trips to Scotland with his uni friends, Jess hadn't seen him leave England since. Jess was determined, now more than ever, to make sure she experienced life outside the village.

'How are you doing, sweetheart, are you okay? *Go away, stupid boys*.' Her mum came back on the phone and Jess could hear herself being carried through the house to the bay window in Patty's office.

'I'm fine, it really is lovely here.'

'You're not feeling too ... I don't know ... '

'No I'm *fine*. It feels good to be out and about.'

'It does, doesn't it?' Patty sighed, and Jess felt that twinge of guilt she always felt when her parents mooned about their past and what could have been.

'Just come home if it gets too much, or if anyone wants you to do anything you're not comfortable with.'

'Mum, I'm with Bryony, and this is Cannes, not Magaluf. And I'm thirty-two.'

'Well I still like to protect you, so there. Is Bryony with you now?'

'No, she's stalking some celebrities who are having an affair.'

'That's nice. Are you finding the people friendly?'

'Very,' Jess said with a smile.

'The language not too difficult?'

'Thus far I've mainly spoken English, to be honest, or just said "yes" and "please" a lot. How's the café?' Jess had left her business in the hands of Cameron while she was away.

'It's doing fine. Cameron's got Manpreet in charge today.'

'But—'

'And you know how experienced she is.'

'Okay, but don't let him keep closing early just to hang out at yours and pretend he's reminiscing.'

Patty ignored her and steered the conversation back to Cannes. 'Now, what are you doing for the rest of the day?'

Jess breathed in and looked around her. 'Well ... I feel like I could do anything.'

♥

'You met a bloke,' Bryony said accusingly as soon as Jess opened the door to their hotel room. She jumped off the bed, pushing aside her laptop and sniffed the air. 'And you ate Nutella with him, you dirty girl.'

'How did you know? Were you stalking *me* by accident?'

'I was right?' Bryony whooped. 'I'm such a Derren Brown. I guessed the man bit because you look all pink and happy – though it could have easily been a bit of sunburn – and the Nutella bit, well, there's a big blob of it on your dress.'

Jess stuffed the fabric in her mouth and sucked. 'How was your celeb-spying?' she asked afterwards.

'Dire. How was sightseeing?'

'Brilliant. I met a boy!' Whoops, that had just burst its way out there, hadn't it? 'Tell me about yours first.'

'My day was spent almost entirely drinking coffee after coffee like Billy No-Mates, sitting behind a pot plant in the hotel foyer. No sign of the supposed lovers, no sign of anyone else noteworthy. Sometimes I think Mitch just makes these things up to keep me on my toes and see if I'll do anything he says.'

'Oh no, so you didn't see a single famous person?'

'Not a peep. I thought I saw George Clooney, but

it was just a cardboard cutout. Back to real-life boys; who did you meet?'

Jess bypassed Bryony's question, too caught up with the possibility of being star-struck. 'Can you imagine if we're out in a restaurant and at the next table are George, Amal, Brad, Angelina, Kim and Kanye, Beyoncé and Jay-Z and Jennifer Aniston?'

'I don't think Jen would be there with Brad and Ange. I don't even think Brad and Ange would be there together.'

'But wouldn't it be great if they all were? Imagine the eavesdropping!'

Bryony laughed. 'You should work at *Sleb*, not me.' Bryony was completely unfazed by celebrities, her feet firmly in the 'they're just people' camp, which only went to prove how ill-suited she was to her current role. Jess, however, whose only celebrity encounter came from going to a taping of *Deal or No Deal* in Bristol, was ready to have her tiny world lit up by a thousand stars.

'So you haven't seen any of Cannes yet?' Jess asked.

'Just the inside of two hotels. How was it?'

'Just beautiful – the sun is warm, the sea glitters, there's a buzz in the air that makes me think Marilyn could glide by any minute. Have you ever had a simple change of scenery make you feel a million miles away from home?'

Bryony thought about it. 'Not really. Most of the time that I'm away it's for work, and that makes me feel more stuck at home than anything. But that's how I want to feel, one day, when I'm going undercover in exotic or life-changing places.'

Jess put on her wisest face. 'That's deep. Shall we have some wine? The supermarket on the other side of the motorway was jam-packed with amazing cheap local plonk – mostly rosé – so I brought us back a few bottles to sample, along with some of these . . . ' Jess pulled out a large packet of crisps. 'Now, I think they're basically own-brand Frazzles-flavoured-Wotsits, but they seem to just be called "Bacon Goût", which sounds delightful – I had to try them.'

Bryony grabbed at the bag. 'Yum. Let's take these up to the roof terrace and you can make me loathe my own pitiful life even more by telling me about this man you shared a tub of Nutella with.'

'We ate crêpes,' said Jess, settling back on a white plastic sun lounger, a far cry from the plush taupe-cushioned ones that lined the private beaches of the Croisette, having poured them each a plastic cup of rosé. Leo was dancing about in her mind like the remnants of a dream – she wanted to think about him, and talk about him, but he'd come and gone so quickly and unexpectedly that she didn't know what she could piece together out loud. 'I don't know who he was, actually. His name was Leo – not DiCaprio – and he was just a nice friendly guy out for a jog and we got chatting.'

Bryony stuffed a handful of Bacon Goût into her mouth. 'Were you jogging?'

'God no, I was eating.'

'What did he look like?'

Jess mused, staring at their view of the back of a lot of hotels and a sliver of turquoise sea in between them. 'A little bit like Benedict Cumberbatch when he has lighter hair, when his hair is like honey. And very, very tall. A bit sweaty, but with this huge smile you can't help but smile back at.' She rolled onto her side and lowered her voice. 'Like, do you remember that fake scene in *Sherlock*, when Benedict and Moriarty are on the rooftop, laughing, and they grin at each other before going in for a kiss?'

'You mean the hottest scene ever on television, that I watch on repeat while eating ice cream?'

'That's the one. Well his grin was like that: kind of fun, and delicious, and like there were only the two of us there.'

'Whoa. You are in trouble.'

'I was just like, bloody hell, I would so be the hot gay Moriarty to your hot gay Sherlock right now. But maybe it was all the sunshine and Nutella. Chocolate's an aphrodisiac, right?'

'Chocolate, and Mr Cumberbatch. Is he French?'

'No, English.'

'Is he in showbiz, or just part of the playboy rich crowd?'

'I don't know.'

'Are you going to see him again?'

'I don't know—'

'Did you get his number, or Twitter handle, or whatever it is the kids do these days when finding a mate?'

'No, it was nothing really, just passing chit-chat.' Jess settled back down, unable to wipe the smile from her face.

'Passing chit-chat that made you need a cold shower. What did you chat about?'

'Stop being such a journalist!'

Bryony smiled and side-eyed Jess. 'I'm just saying ... Cannes is not a big place, and I like seeing your smile back. You've been a little down recently, and when *you're* down, Little Miss Sunshine, I worry that the big ol' Technicolor musical that is your world is about to end.'

Jess sipped her wine. Part of her wanted to tell Bryony what had been wrong, but another part wanted to submerge herself in the happiness she was just beginning to soak back into, and not drag it up again. Right now, under the sun with wine in hand and Bacon Goût in mouth, was not the time.

'I know. Sorry I was a grump. I *will* talk to you about it, but at the moment there are more important things to decide.'

'Like what?'

'Like where can we go tonight that has the highest likelihood of me being able to ogle celebrities?'

'Do you think I look okay? Can you see the lines of my Spanx on my thighs? I swear they keep rolling up.' Jess ducked into a doorway and reached up underneath her pencil skirt to unroll them. At that moment, a group of girls at least three foot taller, with cheekbones at least three times as sharp, glided past.

'You look stunning, just like Marilyn.'

'*You* look stunning. That dress is amazing on you.' Bryony was in navy sequins and silver heels with ten million tiny straps. 'You will definitely fit in with the glitterati tonight.'

'Like I care; they should want to fit in with *us*. But I'm telling you – people are going to mistake you for a movie star.'

'Well, it happens all the time in Cornwall, you know, *dahhling*.' Jess linked arms with Bryony and they sashayed around the corner of the InterContinental Carlton, pausing to admire its iconic façade in the coppery, evening light. Standing there, wearing an outfit that made her feel as glamorous as Miss Monroe and looking up at a place that had been home to countless stars from the golden era of Hollywood through to present *Forbes* Celebrity 100, Jess felt a tingle she hadn't felt ... ever? She needed this; it was going to be amazing, a great night that she and Bryony would talk about for years to come. Who would they see? Who would be there? Would Leo be there? It was the tiniest of possibilities, but one that shook her heart about like a snow globe.

'At some point in the next two weeks, can we go in here? Just for one drink?' Jess asked, peering at a menu on the wall of the terrace restaurant. 'Maybe even just for an Earl Grey, as that alone is eleven euros ...'

'We can go in now, if you like. This is your big, blow-out, start-the-ball-rolling, don't-look-at-the-prices night out. Whatever you want tonight, let's do it.'

Jess's stomach growled and she dragged herself away from the hotel. 'First, let's eat. Then let's see where the night takes us.'

They crossed the street to the Croisette, where a series of fancy restaurants lay upon the slim stretch of pale yellow sand. 'Look at this one,' Jess enthused, gawping up at a sign licked by two flaming torches that read 'Noix de Coco'. It was decorated like a Polynesian tiki lounge, with tables under pink canopies and a long pier extending from the beach out into the water, containing more secluded tables.

'Is this the one?' Bryony asked, looking at the excited awe on her friend's face. She would do anything for this girl.

'According to *Lonely Planet*, this is the hottest restaurant in Cannes. And they don't take bookings, so we should have no problem getting a table. THERE MIGHT BE CELEBRITIES.'

Jess and Bryony descended the steps to the beach, their eyes darting back and forth as they looked for familiar famous faces in the crowd. At the foot of the stairs, behind a hostess desk, stood two women with cat-like eye make-up who glowered at them.

'*Bonsoir*,' purred one of them, sounding as if she didn't mean it for a second.

'May we help you?' the other pouted.

'Do you have a table for two, please?' asked Jess, nerves ridding her of any plans to speak French all evening. She pulled on her biggest grin and sucked in her stomach.

The first hostess side-eyed the other. 'We are fully booked.'

'Oh, I'm sorry. I didn't think you took bookings.'

They both shrugged.

'But you have all these empty tables. . .'

'*Oui*.'

'Could we use one of them for a while?'

'*Non*, we are expecting many VIPs tonight and the tables must be kept free for them.'

'We're VIPs – I'm press,' interjected Bryony, flashing her dog-eared *Sleb* business card. 'I didn't think I'd need my film festival pass just to get a bite to eat.'

'*Sleb*? I don't know this,' said the hostess, barely glancing at the ID. She flicked her braid over her shoulder and turned to the other. 'Do you know this?'

The other hostess was distracted by her iPad. 'No. You don't work for *Vogue* or *Elle*?'

Braid-hostess turned back to them. 'We welcome

a lot of *Vogue* and *Elle* journalists. I'm afraid we have not heard of *Sleb*.'

Bryony's temperature rose. She could practically smell the pool of disdain that these women were dipping her magazine in. She hated not being taken seriously, especially when deep down she knew she wouldn't take her seriously either. 'Let me get this straight,' she said, glaring at braid-hostess. 'What you're saying is the tables are free, but we're not good enough to sit at them?'

iPad-hostess snickered and hid her mouth behind her bony hand. Jess pursed her lips. This was their big night out, and these mean girls weren't about to ruin it. 'Come on, let's go somewhere else.'

'No,' said Bryony. 'You liked the look of this place. And we have just as much right to be here as anyone else.' She turned back to the hostesses and stood a little taller, so that she was now looking down on them. 'I am a journalist, and would love to know more about your segregation policy.'

'You could sit at the bar and have sushi,' sighed braid-hostess.

'HEEEEEY!' cried a man of about fifty, with a neckerchief and an inviting beam of a smile. He leant over to Bryony and Jess and gave them both a swift kiss on the cheek. 'Glad you guys finally arrived. Pull two more chairs over to our table will you?' he told the hostesses, who immediately scampered off down the end of the restaurant and fussed over chairs and table settings. He turned to Bryony and Jess, his eyes creased with mischievous twinkles. 'Don't let the bastards get you down,' he said in a chummy, Sloaney voice. 'Come and sit at our table, there's plenty of room.'

Jess raised her eyebrows at Bryony, who shrugged. Dinner in an exclusive restaurant with a group of strangers? Well, wasn't this the kind of adventure she was after? They followed the man, who introduced himself as Richard and seemed to know everyone in the place.

'Everybody,' he boomed when they reached a circular table dripping in bejewelled revellers. 'This is Jess and Bryony. They need a place to sit and we need a bit more fun at this godforsaken table, so let's make them welcome.'

Jess laughed as they were greeted with a loud cheer and round of applause. The woman to her right hugged her as she sat down.

'*Yes!* Thank Christ you're here; you have to be on my side. These fucking losers think Cara Delevigne's eyebrows are here to stay, but I think it's a fad. What do you think?'

'You just think it's a fad because you can't let go of your perfect little arches,' Richard piped up, pointing at her face with his fork. 'Cara's eyebrows are the new JLo's arse. They are trendsetting, game-changing little bastards and you need to get on board.'

'Fine, fucking *fine*.' She wrenched an eyeliner out of her clutch bag and, to the whoops of the rest of the table, drew two thick lines over her current thin brows. 'I'm Bea, by the way. A make-up artist who is evidently soon to be out of business.'

'Jess. Good to meet you.' It really was, she thought, as she looked around the table in amusement.

'Let's get oysters!' roared Richard and motioned to the hostess with the braid, who deliberately refused to look directly at Bryony or Jess when she approached. Within moments a silver tray was placed on a stand in the middle of the table, with twenty-four pearly oysters on ice upon it.

'I've never had oysters,' Jess whispered to Bea.

'YOU'VE NEVER HAD OYSTERS?' she shrieked.

'Me neither,' said a glossy-haired man from across the table, who looked like a Burberry model.

Bea started banging her hands on the table. 'Drumroll . . . '

The man stood up and motioned for Jess to do the same, then held her hand across the table. Okay, so

43

she was about to try an oyster. They each picked one up in their free hand and – *slop* – chugged it before Jess could think about whether or not she was doing it correctly. Burberry man coughed, tears brimming in his eyes, and Jess handed him her wine, which he threw back into his mouth. 'Delicious,' he rasped.

'I don't know if I like them or not,' said Jess. 'Actually, I do know. I don't like them.'

Richard laughed, scooping one into his own mouth. 'Let's do introductions so nobody feels left out. Everyone has to say who they are, why they're in this God-awful part of the world and who they most fancy at the table. Bryony – I already know you're a journo.' He turned to the rest of the table, leaning in to impart his dazzling gossip. 'She practically told the hostesses they'd be on the six o'clock news if they didn't seat her. Bryony, tell us everything.'

Bryony caught Jess's eye and with the merest twitch of a wink, she wowed her audience. 'I'm Bryony, and I'm a features writer for . . . *The Times*.'

There was an *Oooh* around the table and Bea piped up with, '*Hel*-lo, bet you've got tickets to everything then, and celeb interviews coming out of your arse.'

Bryony shrugged and lifted her glass to her lips, but Richard stopped her. 'And who do you fancy most here?'

'*You*, of course.'

Richard roared with laughter. 'That kind of talk and we'll be schtupping in the sand in no time. Well I'm Richard, I'm a stylist – not that you'd know it from this revolting neckerchief – I'm here to be of service to my glittering clientele on the red carpet, and I fancy myself the most, too.'

A stunning young woman with glittery, glowy skin like an underwear model spoke next. 'I'm Tara, and I'm here for the parties and the booze and the fabulous, fabulous people. And my heart belongs to Richard, of course.'

The introductions continued, an eclectic mix of showbiz and/or party-crowd professionals, each professing their love for Richard and often straying off into theatrical anecdotes. Jess lapped it all up, the vibe playing on her own happy mood and lifting her higher. She noted that there were probably more expensive watches and diamond earrings around the table than in an entire House of Fraser jewellery department, but nobody was overtly flashy, and when the introductions came around to her she found herself wanting to be just like them.

'I'm Jess, and I own a café in England.'

'A chain of cafés,' interjected Bryony, with another wink in her direction.

'Are you some kind of descendent of Marilyn Monroe, because you look just like her?' asked Richard.

'She told you to say that,' Jess laughed, pointing at Bryony.

'She did, it's true. But you do have a little Miss Monroe quality about you. They say she lit up a room, not because of her hair, or her name, or her body, but because she sparkled when she smiled. But she was tough, too. She didn't have it all easy. She knew how to stand up for herself.' Richard threw back some champagne and gave Jess a twinkly-eyed nod.

Jess faltered for a moment, then continued. 'Well, I too am both sparkly and tough. And I'm also just here for the parties and fabulous people!'

She raised her glass at Tara, who whooped and said, 'Now we get to hang out all fortnight while these losers slog it out at work. Where are you staying?'

Oh no. They couldn't mention the Hôtel du Bliss. But what if everyone here was staying at the Carlton and they dropped themselves right in it? Jess struggled to think of the name of another hotel, but was saved from answering by Bea's fingers suddenly twiddling the side of her spectacles, her boozy breath ghosting her face.

'I *love* your glasses – are they Prada?'

'Yes,' Jess said, attempting to edge away. She'd had them for several years and they were looking pretty tatty around the ages, the Prada logo well faded.

'Are they like, Spring-Summer '17? I don't recognise them at all. How did you get them? Do you know Miuccia?'

Jess didn't know if that was a person or a thing, but did know that her glasses were *so* many seasons old they were unrecognisable to current fashionistas.

'Stop being such a wine snob, let Jess and Bryony pick the next bottle.' Two hours, several courses and a lot of harmless bluffing about their own fabulous lifestyles later, Bea told off Burberry Man and handed the wine list to Jess, who had to try very hard not to spit out her wine when she saw the prices.

'Ooo,' she mumbled. 'What do you think, Bry?' She pulled the menu up over their faces.

'I think ... my expenses budget will cover about one glass of this stuff.'

'I am so sorry,' whispered Jess. 'I had no idea it was this pricey. Shall we just split the bill now and leave?'

'No, why?'

'The house white costs more than I'd usually spend on a meal for two. I feel awful, we can't afford this.'

'Can I see your NUS card for a moment?' Bryony asked.

'Pardon?'

'Well, I didn't realise you were still a student.'

'I'm not . . . '

'I thought you owned a successful café.'

'I do . . . '

'So you *can* afford this. Treat yourself, let your hair down. You're on holiday.'

'But you're not. Let me pick up the bill for both of us tonight.'

'Would you relax? Yes, it'll be an expensive night out. Consider it one of those Red Letter Days experiences and enjoy it for what it is: one night to live like the other half do. To be whoever you've always wanted to be.'

Jess mulled this over for a moment. 'I *am* on holiday.'

'Exactly.'

'And I can afford a bloody expensive bottle of wine once in a while.'

'So choose one, and I refuse to let it be the house white.'

Jess selected not even the first bottle up, but the *third* from the bottom, and once she'd chosen, the table erupted into another impromptu round of applause, which made Jess feel more like Taylor Swift at the Grammys than someone who'd picked a bottle of wine.

After she placed the order, a thought fluttered through Jess's mind: *I don't want this to end*. She liked these people, this place, this feeling of freedom and excitement, and she liked herself when she was here. She didn't want to go back to being boring old party-pooper her at the end.

Jess shook her head almost imperceptibly. She had two whole weeks here; there was no point in thinking about this now. Right now she was exactly where she wanted to be. Determinedly reaching for another oyster – why shouldn't she be the kind of person who liked oysters? – she tuned back in to Bea's story about the movie star and the matted pubic hair.

The hours ticked by, the sun dipped and eventually sank, and Jess had laughed more, had let off more steam, than she had in over a month. They'd meant to explore Cannes this evening, shimmying in and out of all the exclusive hotspots, showing the town who was boss, but Noix de Coco had provided the perfect evening. It could only have been better if that one new person in her life had shown up. She'd watched out for him all night, just in case. Even when Richard and the rest of the table had called it a night, exchanging numbers and promises of fun to come, Bryony and Jess had stayed put, staring out to sea.

Jess let out a happy sigh. 'Let's take the last of the wine and go and sit on the beach. Is that okay?' she asked the waiter, who was clearing the crumbs from their table.

'Yes, please,' he urged, gagging to seat a group of twenty-somethings in leather and lace. Who'd want to just be sitting down to eat now? Youth.

The two of them stumbled onto the strip of sand in front of the restaurant, which was still pulsing with partygoers, despite it being God-knows-what in the morning. Sitting down, Jess dragged cool sand over her bare feet while, beside her, Bryony had her head tipped back and was now licking the last drops of wine from the neck of the bottle.

She hadn't meant to drink this much. At sixty pounds a bottle she *really* hadn't meant to drink this much. But what a night; what a way to get out of her own head. A woozy tiredness washed over her like the dark waves that lapped a few feet away.

'Confession time,' she hiccupped and Bryony put

the bottle down into the sand. Maybe this wasn't a great way to end the night, but Jess's mouth was open and the words came tumbling out. 'You know last month when we were at the pub, and I drank all that wine and asked if I could come to Cannes?'

'Yeah. You were going for it. I haven't seen you drink that much since the sixth-form leavers' ball.'

'My head hurt a lot the next day. I wasn't quite myself.'

'You were being drunk, sad Jess, and we don't see her often. Drunk, happy Jess is basically normal Jess with even more giggles.'

'Yep.'

'I'm being drunk, messy Bryony now.' She shuffled closer to Jess, all the sand on the beach creeping up under her dress, and slung an arm over her shoulders. Drunk Bryony was notoriously chummy. 'I knew you weren't being yourself that night. I should have asked you what was wrong, but sometimes you don't like to talk about things.'

'I know. You always talk about everything with me and I can be kind of closed off.'

'No, you're not closed off. When you're happy you go on and on and on and on and on—'

'Okay.'

'But when you're sad you do your turn-it-off thing

51

and pretend it's not happening, or just go quiet. Why so quiet?'

Jess gulped and stared out at the black sea for a moment, at the immense yachts that sat stealthily, looking back at the Côte d'Azur as if they, too, were waiting for her to talk. She was scared to tell her friend, and for a moment felt very small. All those emotions she'd swept aside since it happened came back to her.

'I had a pregnancy scare.' She winced, the word 'scare' seeming too harsh to her and her not-real baby, even though she had been scared, very scared.

'Jess . . . '

'I thought I was pregnant. For about two weeks, I actually thought I was pregnant.' Her eyes welled up. 'But I wasn't, which was great, and I didn't want to be, probably, to be honest. But my head was confused because part of me got really excited. And another part of me just thought, *Oh no* – I'm being trapped, just like I trapped my mum and dad.'

Bryony pulled Jess's whole body in so close she was almost on her lap, as if she weighed nothing, and squeezed. 'You thought you were a pregnant lady and you didn't say anything? Didn't you feel alone?'

'Yep.'

'But I'm right here. Even when I'm in London you're

not alone: I can rock up at yours with some Impulse O2 and a copy of *Bliss* inside four hours, so there. Big Bryony is always watching you. Big, fat Bryony. Like a nosy hippo.'

Tears welled in Jess's eyes, silly half-sloshed tears. 'You're not a hippo, you're brilliant.'

'What happened? Are you definitely not pregnant?' She glanced at the empty wine bottle.

'I took a pregnancy test as soon as I thought I was, and it was positive.'

The blood drained from Bryony's face. 'Oh, no . . . '

'No, no, I didn't lose it, nothing like that, thank God. It was just a false positive, or whatever they call it. I made a doctor's appointment and bought a baby book, and watched *Kindergarten Cop* like eighty times, but I didn't want to say anything because although it was real in my head, if I said it out loud it would be really real. Like, make-some-decisions-and-change-your-life real, not make-believe be-a-mum real. I'm stupid.'

'You are not stupid. What happened at the doctor's?'

'She said I wasn't pregnant; I never had been. Which was good news, obviously, because I'm not ready to be a mum and I haven't done anything with my life yet and I haven't seen the world.'

'That doesn't have to stop if you become a parent, you know.'

'It stopped *my* parents. Not with Cameron, but with me. And I was so wrapped up in myself – my little village with my little café – that when Dr Yung said I wasn't up the duff I thought, *Yay!*' Jess covered her eyes and wept. 'I feel so guilty.'

'Shhh, don't feel guilty at all. This happened, and now you're moving on. And when the real thing happens, you'll feel differently. You can't beat yourself up if the dress rehearsal doesn't go as planned.'

Jess wiped some snot away, nodding.

'Whose was it, potentially?' asked Bryony.

'Nobody.'

'What?'

'Nothing.'

'Whose was it? Was it that old guy who didn't want you to run off with a "Frenchie"? You love a man in salmon trousers,' Bryony joked.

'Urgh, no!' Jess laughed.

'Was it my dad? You've always had a thing for my dad.'

'No I have not!'

'Good, because I don't want you having a baby with my dad. That would be gross, and I'd have to call you my new mum. So?'

Jess looked at Bryony and shrugged. 'Guess who.'

'I don't know why I even asked. Is he *that* good in bed?'

'No. He's just there, and makes me feel a bit special sometimes.'

Bryony threw a handful of sand at Jess's feet in frustration. 'But he's such a moron, and you're not even sure he knows what your name is.'

'He knows my name . . . ' Jess tailed off. She'd met Anthony at the café one day, a surfer who showed up in town whenever conditions were good. She'd known him for a couple of years now, and he'd never called her by her name, always 'love', 'hon' or 'chick'. She knew she was even under 'chickie' in his phone. It had got to the stage where it would be incredibly awkward to say, *'You know I'm called Jess, don't you?'*

'Do you want him to be more than, you know, what he is?' Bryony asked, dreading the answer.

'No, he's not that interesting and I don't think he'd make a very good boyfriend.'

'Good, neither do I.'

'He's quite funny, though.'

'So are you! Don't get knocked up just because of a few knock-knock jokes.'

'You're hilarious,' Jess said, cracking a smile.

'And so are a million others who would at least hang around for a cup of tea the morning after. Anthony leaves first thing, to go surfing, without even *a cup of tea.*'

'The surf is good first thing in the morning, who am I to stand in his way? I'm not his girlfriend, and most of the time I want him out of my house so I can eat my Coco Pops in peace, just as much as he wants to be gone. Why are you smiling?'

'I'm not. It's nothing.'

Jess peered at her. 'Are you still laughing at your "knocked up knock-knock joke" quip?'

'Well, me being funny doesn't happen very often. You're Little Miss Sunshine, remember; I'm just your big, bad bodyguard. Hey, remember when I had that pregnancy scare at uni and I made you come with me to get the morning-after pill?'

'You were so embarrassed; you made me say it was for me.'

'No, no, you volunteered. I think you said it would be good role-playing experience for your drama module.'

'That's right! And one of my lecturers was in the pharmacy queue—'

'And you started to explain to the pharmacist, really loudly, that you were using two types of birth control at the time – as you were still in the first seven days of a new pill and you'd used a condom as

56

a backup, but it split, so actually this was your third safety net.'

'My third safety net! I said it in such a superior voice, I remember, and I looked my lecturer straight in the eye as if *he* was the scoundrel who'd tried to knock me up!' Jess laughed heartily, wiping away the last of her tears as a weight she had been trying to pretend wasn't there lifted from her shoulders.

Bryony grinned and stared out at the yachts, allowing Jess time to calm down. 'I bet those yachts hold a lot of secrets. I bet the people that own them do too. I'm not just talking about people using them as shag-pads, some of the most powerful people in the world own superyachts. How did they get their money? Unless you invented Google or have a billion-dollar recording deal, people can't legitimately, legally, make enough money to afford one, can they?'

'Said the roving reporter . . . '

Bryony smiled. 'Imagine owning one of those.'

'I know.'

'I think if I owned one I'd use it to float about the world, incognito.'

'Trust me, you would not be incognito in one of those things. That's like rocking up in a cross-channel ferry and being like, "I'm not here, just ignore me."'

'Fair point. How are you feeling now, Meems?'

'I feel silly for feeling sad about something that never was and that I didn't want anyway. And I feel worried that life will zoom past and I'll miss it and never experience all the fun of the fair. And I feel confused about being so confused. And I feel like I wish I'd told you ages ago because you're lovely and everything's better now.'

Bryony's lips wobbled and a fat tear dropped down her own cheek, which only started Jess off again. Would this roller coaster ever end? Damn all the alcohol. 'I love you. I LOVE YOU. Not just because of all this wine.'

'I love you too, and I'm going to tell you everything from now on. Everything. Like it or not.'

'I wrote some *True Blood* fan fiction,' rasped Bryony.

'You did? Is it erotic?'

'Yes it is. But it's only on my laptop and it's staying there. I know it's not the same, and I don't want to steal your thunder, I just wanted you to know we all have secrets. You're not alone.'

'It's good to share,' Jess sobbed.

'It feels so good,' said Bryony, tears gushing down her face. 'And healthy.'

Jess nodded. 'When I'm on a diet I still eat chocolate and sweets, only in private so people don't think I'm not trying.'

'My CV says my A levels range from A-star to C. But I didn't get any A-stars.'

'That's okay. I didn't like *Breaking Bad*.'

'I don't like vegetables. Any of them!' said Bryony.

'I actually quite like getting my period, because it makes me feel womanly.'

'Sometimes I put a hairbrush between my legs and stand sideways in front of the mirror, so I can see what I'd look like with a penis.'

Jess took a breath. 'You what?'

'Because it sticks out. The handle. Straight outwards. You don't do that? You don't do that . . . '

'I don't do that.'

'Oh.'

'But I have put a roll-on deodorant in the front of my jeans before to see what the bulge looks like. Does that count?'

Bryony laughed. 'That counts! Oh, hooray. Shall we go back to the hotel?'

'Yes please, it's *late* and I think all these teenagers want the chaperones to do one.'

Bryony pulled Jess to her feet and the two women stumbled back across the sand like Little and Large, heels in hands, Jess having a final glance around for night-owl A-listers.

'Thanks, Bryan Adams,' she slurred, holding on to her best friend's hand.

'You're welcome, Jessica Rabbit.'

The following morning the sun was out, big and full, shining a perfect yellow warmth over the Côte d'Azur – just as the celebrities had ordered on their riders.

'Jess, wake up. *Jess*.'

'Mmmm, that's *my* Nutella.' Jess reached up and stuck a finger in Bryony's eye as she leant over her.

'Urgh, stop having a sex dream and wake up.'

Jess came to and sat up, rubbing her eyes and then her head, which thumped. Fancy wine doesn't stop a hangover then, she thought. 'Last night was fun,' she croaked. 'I love Cannes.'

'I know you do, but I'm about to make you love it, and me, even more. Get up.'

'Why?'

'I'll tell you on the way.'

Fifteen minutes later, after a lightning-quick shower, Jess was jogging behind Bryony as she marched down the street in the direction of the Palais des Festivals. Her flip-flops clacked as she tried to keep up, while at the same time throwing her hair up into a messy bun that she hoped made her look like an off-duty A-lister.

'Where are we going? Will there be food there?'

'You are so going to love me,' Bryony said smugly.

'Will there be celebrities?'

'Oh yes.'

'There will? *Who?*'

Bryony stopped. 'Last night you said you had the most perfect night, except for one thing.'

'The crying?'

'Okay, two things. Your little face when we finally left and you still hadn't seen a single star was heart-breaking. So today, you're coming to work with me.'

'To look for those people having an affair again?' Jess asked with excitement.

'Even better: we're going to a screening of one of this year's contenders, and then to a Q&A session with the director and the stars.'

'No way!'

'Yes way.'

'You're shitting all over me.'

'That's nice: you should be a writer with that mouth. What would Marilyn say?'

'I'm going to be in the same room as some *movie stars*?' Jess fanned herself. 'Asking them questions?'

'No – you can't ask them questions. Leave the questions to me and the two hundred other journalists who'll be there. You listen, okay? No talking.'

'No talking.' *OhmyGodohmyGod*.

Bryony started marching again.

'What's the movie? Who are the stars?' Jess asked, trotting alongside her, an extra-large spring in her step.

'The movie's called … hang on, let me check the ticket again … *Love and Shit*. It sounds pretty cheesy.'

'It sounds wonderful.'

'It stars Yasmine Yeates and Ryan Maxpower.'

'But Ryan Maxpower is so yum!'

'He's okay.'

'And Yasmine Yeates is beeeautiful. Oh, can you ask her what foundation she uses?' Jess stopped. 'I have to go back and change.'

'I don't think Ryan's going to spot you in the audience and fall in love with you. No offence.'

'Well, no, not looking like this.' Jess pondered herself for a moment, then pulled Bryony into a ginormous embrace. 'Why is my life not always this exciting? I'm having the best time with you!'

Bryony laughed and wriggled out of the hug, picking up the pace again and pulling a sheet of paper from her handbag. 'These are the questions Mitch wants me to ask.'

'He wrote your questions for you?'

'He says they're guidelines, but yes – I'm basically his minion. The only reason I'm here instead of him is because he's a slimy grease-head who looks like Penguin from *Batman*, and he'd probably get arrested for stalking before he got close enough to any of the celebs.'

Jess peered at the list. 'Why have some been crossed out with red lipliner?'

'Because they're either too offensive for me to ask, no matter what Mitch threatens me with, or they're forbidden questions. And because I couldn't find a biro this morning.'

'Forbidden questions . . . by whom?'

'The golden couple themselves, or their publicists. It's pretty standard to be told you can't ask a star about certain things, like how you're not supposed to ask One Direction who their celebrity crushes are.'

Jess nodded as if she was totally aware of this. *Now all I want to know is who One Direction's celebrity crushes are*, she thought.

Bryony stopped and looked up at the Palais des Festivals, today a flawless synchronicity of white walls and scarlet red carpet, a twinkle even in her cynical eye. 'Here we are: this is where it all begins. You ready?'

Jess came out of the movie . . . nonplussed. In all honesty, it was a bit indie for her, with a few too many moustaches and vinyl records, but that didn't stop her senses from being on red alert for the stars the moment she and Bryony entered the press conference.

The room was abuzz with murmurs, mic checks and air kisses as journalists from around the world greeted comrades and found their seats. Bryony led Jess down a row near the back to a couple of chairs with laminated '*Sleb*' magazine name cards on them. Jess sat and gazed about her, not believing her luck that she was about to see, up on stage, drinking out of those Evian bottles, some actual Hollywood actors, *in real life.*

'This is so exciting,' she whispered to Bryony, who chuckled.

'It is exciting; even grumpy old me can appreciate that.'

'Do you think they'll do a meet-and-greet afterwards?'

'Unlikely, I'm afraid.'

'That's okay, I'll just stare and stare, and then spend hours trawling through the press photos online in case any of them capture both the stars and me in the same shot.'

'Sounds like a plan.'

'Quiet, please.' A man in a sharp suit carrying a clipboard came out on the stage and the murmurs decreased to silence, while voice-recorder apps on over a hundred smartphones were activated. 'Ladies and gentlemen, esteemed members of our global media, I present to you our stars of *Love and Shit*, Ryan and Yasmine.'

Jess leant forward, spending the next hour listening intently, laughing as loud as she dared, grinning manically should either of the actors catch her eye, and generally soaking it all in; she might never get the chance to be at a press conference again.

She began to drift when a question about the environment in Bali, where much of the film was shot, caused Ryan to drone on and on to the point that even Yasmine was stifling a yawn. Jess wanted to stand up and say, 'Yes, but Ryan, what the world wants to know is: do you have a foot-long?'

Jess glanced over at Bryony, who was engrossed in her smartphone. 'What are you looking at?' she whispered.

'I've found my angle.'

'Isn't your angle whether the on-set chemistry is still fizzing? Don't you need to be watching them?'

'I'm not going to write about that. I'm going to focus on what he just sidestepped regarding the state of Bali's environment after filming finished, and exactly how the profits of the movie will be put back into it. Don't worry, I'll add something about how the stars looked lovingly into each other's eyes when discussing the future.'

Jess went back to listening, while Bryony went back to googling. She found herself staring at Yasmine and Ryan's faces. These people she'd seen on screen a hundred times were in front of her in the flesh, and it felt unreal.

Until it became real.

'Let's have another question,' said the moderator.

Jess raised her hand before she even had time to think it through, and Ryan's eyes locked onto hers. He smiled and she nearly passed out, then thought, *I can't wait to update my Facebook status about this.*

Only, she had no idea what to ask. She'd just known that, in the spirit of adventure, she didn't want to pass up the opportunity to have a conversation with two of the world's biggest movie stars. She stood up and Bryony gripped her hand.

'Meems ... *Jessica*! What are you doing, what are you doing, what are you doing?' she hissed.

'Hello,' Jess called out in her friendliest voice.

'Hi,' said Ryan.

'Hi, Ryan,' she replied, blushing like a brand new pot of blusher. 'Um, I'm Jess from *Sleb* magazine—'

'*Sleb*? I haven't heard of that. Are you a British publication?'

'Oh yes,' Jess tittered. 'The Queen regularly reads us.' *Twat.* 'Um, so, I was wondering ... ' She was wondering nothing. There was nothing in her brain at all to ask, nothing. Until one question, a lifeline, popped into her head. 'I was wondering, are you and your mum back on speaking terms?'

There was an audible gasp, and the eyes of two hundred journalists turned to her.

The temperature in the hot, stuffy room suddenly plummeted to frosty, and Ryan answered her with a sharp 'No' before the moderator flashed to another journalist, another question.

Jess sat down, her heart thumping, and turned to whisper to Bryony, who scowled at her. 'Should I not have said that? What did I do wrong?'

'It's the Forbidden Question.'

'Oh! That must be why I thought of it. I can see it now on your bit of paper, all highlighted in red.'

'Not highlighted, crossed out. It says on the press release that nobody is allowed to ask him about his mum.'

'Why?'

'Because it was she who sold his sex tape to the media a few years back. They haven't spoken since.'

Jess's heart plopped out of her chest and rolled away under the chairs, too embarrassed to be with her any more. She covered her face with her hands. 'OhmyGooooood, Bry, ohmyGoooooood, I totally forgot.'

'It's fine, calm down.'

'*Shitting shitting shitathon*, I can't believe I did that. In front of the world's press.' Hang on, was that actually kind of cool? No, no, it was definitely very bad. 'Do you think he'll sue me? I don't have any money. Will he take my café?'

'No, but shush.'

What an idiot. Ryan's face was fixed in the firm expression of someone trying to listen but inwardly thinking how they want to ruin the life of the person who just wronged them. And it was Jess who had wronged him, her first proper celeb encounter. 'Sorry, Bry.'

'It's my fault really: I should have properly briefed you before you started asking questions.'

'Sorry, I got a bit overexcited.' Jess cringed and went back to trying to listen to the rest of the Q&A. 'I should apologise,' she hissed, leaning back over to Bryony. 'Shall I put my hand up again?'

'*No.*' Bryony slammed her arm down on both of Jess's hands.

'Shall I go and see him afterwards?'

'Why?'

'I don't want him to be angry at me. I'll explain it was all just an accident. I think he'll like that, he seems like a nice enough man.'

'Just leave it. You won't get past his entourage anyway.'

'I can't just leave it: look at his jaw – it's all angry.'

'Seriously, leave it, it'll be fine.' Bryony rolled her eyes, and a smile erased the scowl. 'Everyone probably thinks you're an absolute legend for saying it, to be honest. But maybe you shouldn't come along to these with me for a few days. In case security is looking out for you.'

'Do you think they are? Am I going to prison?'

'No, I'm joking. Relax.'

This was *so* not going on Facebook.

Coming outside into still very bright early-afternoon sunshine brought Jess back to the present, and she switched her phone back on to find two voicemails awaiting.

''ello, buttercupsh,' came Richard's chirpy voice down the phone. 'Lashtnightwashfa-boo-lash.' There was the sound of spitting and a muffled 'Hang on, darling, back in a mo.' 'Sorry, had pins in my mouth and Cate Blanchett's marvellous, tulle-covered arse in my face. Anyway, last night was fab: let's do it all again tonight. Big bash at the casino, Paris Hilton DJ-ing, all the celebs partying their pretty little socks off – and you two are on Bea's guest list. We'll have none of that bollocks from last night, with those snobosaurus hostesses who couldn't recognise the glitterati when they slapped them in the face. Can't bloody wait, see you there! Cate, just look at your hips, you ravishing—' His voice cut out.

The second voicemail was Richard again. One line. 'Dress code: stonkingly fabulous.'

Jess hung up and turned to Bryony. 'Any more work today?'

'No, that'll do for now.'

'Well, we need to go shopping.' She looked down the road at a string of high-end designer shops. 'Is there a Topshop round here?'

Jess had probably been staring at Paris Hilton for a good thirty minutes now. If photography was going to be banned inside the casino, she was damned well going to imprint her face on her memory. The music was too loud to have any decent conversation anyway, and when she danced she looked like Joey in *Friends*, so instead Jess sipped her clementine Martini and gawped at the unabashedly beautiful people who filled the room with their good looks and nice clothes and general aura of wonderfulness.

'Everyone is just so stunning,' she shouted into Bryony's ear, not taking her eyes off Paris. 'It's hard to tell which ones are the celebrities because all of them seem to sparkle.'

'*What?*'

'I said—' Jess stopped and squeezed Bryony's hand as hard as she could.

'Oi, what are you doing?' she hollered over the music.

'Veronica Hay ish curming towardsh ush,' she said through a fixed grin and wide eyes.

'WHO? Oh!'

Veronica Hay, socialite, party animal and paparazzi dream had come to a flamboyant halt after striding, catwalk-style, across the dance floor to their table. She flicked her blonde locks behind her, into the eyes of one of her entourage, and beckoned for Bryony to follow.

'Holy crapoly,' said Jess. 'You have to get a photo with her. Get a photo of her with me in the background.'

Bryony rose and followed Veronica to a booth, where the music was quieter. She wasn't sure if she was about to be hit on, asked to do something or told she'd never work in this town again. She racked her brains to think of any incriminating thing she'd written about Veronica, but other than mentioning her hosting some Playboy event a few years back, she couldn't think of anything.

Unless this was something to do with Mitch. Hadn't *Sleb* run a story in the last few months about Veronica and Lindsay Lohan having a spat?

'Heeeeey,' Veronica said in a sickly Southern accent, with the distinct undertone of someone utterly bored by the other person's mere presence. 'Do you want a drink?'

'No, I'm fine, thanks. Do you?' Perhaps she'd mistaken Bryony for a cocktail waitress.

'Yeah. Can I get a daiquiri?' she asked her security guard, and the whole entourage scuttled off. Veronica turned back to face Bryony, and her voice dropped an octave, losing the little-girl twang. 'You're Bryony, right?'

'You know who I am?'

'Bea told me she'd met you. She's my make-up artist.'

Bryony's eyes flicked briefly to Veronica's eyebrows. Yep, makes sense.

Veronica went on: 'I trust Bea – she's a good chick and she said you're a good one, too: intelligent and a little fierce, which I like.'

'That's nice.' So being yelled at was probably out, but being hit on was still on the cards.

'You write for *The Times*, right? In London, England?'

Uh-oh. 'Yep ... Sure ...'

'I want to give you an interview while you're here in Cannes.'

'Really? With *The Times*?'

'Yeah. But only with you, because of Bea. I'm trying to break into acting, movies specifically. That's why I'm at the festival.'

'Weren't you in a movie a few years ago? The one about vampire shopping malls?'

Veronica rolled her eyes. 'Don't remind me, it sucked. Even I only watched the first twenty minutes. I need people to take me seriously now, and that's where you come in. I have some things about me that I want people to know. I'm not just a pretty girl.'

'Okay.'

'I'm saying, I need to open up about some things, but in a tasteful way, not in one of those gossip magazines where it'll be all sensationalised headlines and ugly photos.'

Mitch would l-o-v-e her if Bryony could dig a piece of exclusive dirt on Veronica that would warrant a sensationalised headline and some ugly photos; it would be *Sleb*'s biggest scoop in years. He'd probably give her anything she wanted, even a regular feature on a topic of her choice … And then she could pull *Sleb* out of the gutter, and the gnawing panic that she worked for the worst magazine ever published and was going precisely nowhere in her career would melt away. It was perfect. But … Didn't this type of double-crossing go against everything she wanted to be? Or did some short-term harm on a woman who has it all anyway, for some long-term gain, not really matter?

'So are you in?' Veronica asked, one eye on her phone.

Bryony nodded. Perhaps she could figure out some way they could help each other, if she just had some time to think. 'I'm in. Here's my number,' she pulled a pen out of her clutch bag and scribbled on an embossed napkin. 'Have your publicist call me and we'll set up the interview.'

When Bryony returned, Jess was mentally adding up how much she'd spent that day on a very plain and very expensive black dress, plus endless cocktails and table service here at the casino. Her poor debit card. Ah well, yolo, as the kids might still say. *C'est la vie*, in the words of the French.

'*C'est la vie!*' she shouted to Bryony as she sat back down beside her.

'I don't think Paris Hilton will play B*Witched, but I can ask if you want,' Bryony hollered back.

'No, it doesn't matter – tell me what happened with Veronica.'

At that point Richard leant over the table. 'I didn't know you were friends with Veronica Hay, you dark horse. She and I go way back. Actually, she fired me from a shoot once because I tried to put her in a turtleneck. In fairness to her I don't know what I was thinking. Anyway, who's ready for an after-party?' He shimmied his pecs at them.

Jess gulped. This lifestyle was an absolute ball, but she was going to have to come clean and admit that her bank balance couldn't keep up. 'Richard, I—'

'You *have* to come! Tara's friends have rented the most sublime superyacht for the Festival – a two-hundred-footer – so we're all going off to have a perv at it.'

'A superyacht?' Jess had never been on one of those, and surely you wouldn't have to fork out an entrance fee or twenty-seven euros for a bottle of water once on board. She met Bryony's eye, who was nodding enthusiastically, the journalist in her gagging to be allowed on board for a snoop.

'When we get there, I'm going to have to play it cool, okay, like this happens all the time. If I were a *Times* journalist I'd be at yacht parties every Festival.'

'But I don't have to play it cool?'

'They think we're from their world, but haven't necessarily done everything they have. They know you're along for the ride and Cannes itself is new to you. Besides, you're not a great actress: there's no hiding your excitement when you're all "*I've never had oysters before!*"'

Jess cemented Bryony's point by stopping short and gawping as she rounded the corner. 'Look at these boats ...' They trailed behind the others, taking their time to walk around the cobbled marina, gazing into every gleaming superyacht they passed. Each was magnificent, their spotless white, navy blue, maroon and even gold exteriors bulging upwards from the still harbour. Names like *Lap of Luxury*, *Lady Atlantis*, *Into the Blue* and *The Codfather* were emblazoned across their sterns, and soft lights and tinkling laughter glowed within each of them. 'Imagine if we suddenly saw Jennifer Lawrence just reclining on one of these sofas, watching *Real Housewives* on her giant plasma.'

'I think we're here.'

They stopped and looked up at a yacht four decks high, tall and immaculate: the nautical equivalent of Beyoncé. They stepped aboard, Jess having a quick, last glance down the marina just in case Leo – the real Leo; she'd all but forgotten about Mr DiCaprio – was about, but nothing. She probably wouldn't see him again, but she was just keeping an eye out wherever she went, just in case . . .

Jess felt like she was in a dream, or in the fanciest show home she'd ever seen. Polished wooden decks, gold railings and spotlights reflecting off crystal glassware. The stereo system was playing chilled club classics at low volume, but she could still feel the beat of the bass in her heart. There were at least fifty people on board already, and it looked like a large-scale photo shoot for *Vogue*.

Tara whizzed past them in a tiny red bikini, holding four champagne flutes. 'I'm off for a hot tub if anyone wants to join me. Don't you just love finishing a hard day with a Jacuzzi and some Cristal?'

'Totally,' Jess agreed, thinking there was no way she was about to strip down to her control pants and get in a hot tub with Tiny Tara.

Bryony leant in towards her. 'Fancy having a little explore?'

'You can't snoop, Bryony. Stop trying to find a story.'

'I'm not going to snoop, I'm just going to look around and, you know, see if there are five hundred bags of cocaine lying about in any of the public places.'

'I don't think Tara is a drug smuggler. But yes, I would like to explore.'

The two of them took a couple of champagne flutes from a sturdy-looking waiter and stepped through (one of) the doors into the yacht's interior.

'It's huge,' Jess marvelled. 'This is amazing; it's like a hotel suite.'

'It's like a whole hotel.'

Like a naughty child at a museum, Jess walked around the circumference of the main lounge touching every single thing. There was a lacquered walnut gleam to every piece of furniture, thick cream carpet and chairs that looked like they shouldn't be sat on but more leant against while puffing on a cigar and discussing maritime laws. A spiral staircase at one end led them up a deck, where they poked their heads out to see Tara holding the fort in a hot tub the width of the yacht. Back down they went, passing a cinema, a dining room and a cabin entirely dedicated to bean-bags, apparently, eventually reaching the bedrooms, but then Jess stopped.

'We can't go in the bedrooms,' she said, and then quickly pressed her face against the frosted porthole on the door of the master bedroom to try to get a glimpse of the inside.

'Not even a little look?'

'No.' Jess dragged her face away. 'I really, really, really want to as well – it would be like being in an episode of *Cribs* – but it would be rude. There are no breaking stories in there, and if there are, they'd be exactly the kind of story you're trying to get away from writing about. Come on.' They ascended the stairs back to the main deck, where huddles of people had begun to gather in the lounge.

'I don't think there's any scandal on this actual yacht, to be honest,' Bryony sighed. 'But I'm just going to look a little bit more. Will you be okay on your own?'

'Of course I will, but be careful, won't you?'

'I will, I promise. I just think I need to talk to some of these people, maybe someone, anyone, could point me in the direction of a story that's not about cellulite.'

Poor Bryony. 'Fine, go, but try and enjoy yourself as well, okay?' As she left she heard Bryony turn to a man helping himself to a bourbon.

'Why hello,' she said, adopting a Southern drawl. 'My name is Lola. I'm a showgirl.'

Jess made her way back outside and skirted through the revellers, eager to pause and have a moment to herself. She found a quiet spot at the stern and relaxed into the soft cream leather seats. In front of her the party crowd peppered the decks, dancing, laughing, flirting, clinking champagne flutes and shot glasses, glittering like fireworks. Their noise melted away as Jess took it all in. Behind them the ink-black sea merged with the night sky, and a soft Mediterranean breeze tickled at her face and tugged at her hair despite her hairspray.

She took in every detail, every spotlight, every outfit, every emotion, forcing herself to be completely present and aware that she was here, living and experiencing life. Experiencing something she might never have the chance to experience again. Marilyn had never actually come to Cannes, but Jess bet she would have loved it: she would have found the place captivating, magical, and all a little silly. She breathed it in and closed her eyes.

'Well hello, can I interest you in some Nutella?' A voice interrupted her thoughts, and she opened her eyes to see a jar of chocolate spread thrust under her nose by a hand reaching across the water from the deck of the neighbouring superyacht.

Stretching across the gap, looking as pleased as punch, was Leo, and among this huge crowd she realised his face was that something she'd been missing. 'Leo,' she sighed, smiling.

She took the Nutella, and he passed her a spoon. 'You have to have some after that line. I saw you sitting there and was like, *I've got the best ice-breaker ever.*' Leo sat down – his starboard to her port – on the seat next to her upon his own yacht, separated by the sliver of water.

'Well, hello yourself. It's nice to see you again.'

'And you! You look pretty, if you don't mind me saying.'

'I don't mind at all,' she beamed. 'You look pretty too.' Jess looked at him in the darkness, just hanging out on his yacht, relaxing. No parties or flashiness, just a man enjoying the evening. On a bloody great yacht.

He was as she'd remembered, though a little cleaner this time. Had it really only been yesterday that they met? She felt like he'd been wandering in her mind on and off ever since, like a hazy dream.

'Thank you. You bring out all the Nutella in me.' They passed the jar back and forth between them.

'How was the rest of your run?'

'Heavy. But those crêpes were completely worth it. How was the rest of your day?'

'Fun, thank you. My friend and I went to one of those seafront restaurants in the evening, Noix de Coco?'

'Wow, nice. Fancy.'

'It was, it was beautiful, but do you want to know a secret?'

'Always.'

She leaned closer, the water beneath her, his face and smile a foot away from hers, and for a moment she forgot what she was going to say, the glitz and glamour and crazy partying gone too, as she wanted to just look at him.

'Don't leave me hanging,' he urged quietly, and Jess was so close to swooping in for a smooch, which would have been his own fault for being so suggestive and yummy.

She regained her composure. Tumbling head first

down a gap between two yachts just for a quick snog with a boy she didn't even know anything about would not a happy rest of holiday make. 'The secret is … that restaurant had nothing on those crêpes.'

He laughed his joyous laugh and reached a big hand across to pat her arm. 'So how's your party?' he asked.

'It's good. Great. How could it not be? Look where we are, look at this boat and this scenery. I mean, *you* know.' She glanced at him.

He nodded and looked back into his own yacht. 'Yeah, definitely. So these are friends of yours?'

'New friends.'

'Well they have a very nice dinghy,' he grinned, running his eyes over the yacht and then settling on her face, a questioning look on his own.

'Thanks. You have a nice tugboat yourself.'

'Thank you.' He nodded, sucking on his spoonful of Nutella. 'I kind of think of it as my home.'

'Tell me: apart from eating Nutella, what are you doing here in Cannes? Are you part of the festival?' she asked.

'Sort of, I'm … here for business. I'm in the food industry.'

'Oh God, tell me you don't own Noix de Coco.'

'Yeah, I do, actually. It was my pride and joy, but

it's being shut down because everyone just wants to go to the crêpe kiosk instead. It's really heartbreaking; thanks for laughing.'

'I hope you're joking, otherwise my laughter is going to seem very awkward in about ten seconds.'

'I'm pleased to inform you that I am joking. What brings you to the French Riviera? The playground of the rich and famous? The place that puts the "Cannes" in *Cannes You Feel the Love Tonight*? Please stop me.'

'I'm pretty much here for this.' She waved her arm around her. 'It was about time for a holiday, so here I am.'

It had dawned on Jess that she and Leo were very different people, from different worlds, as much as she was enjoying pretending they weren't. They were like Romeo and Juliet, but less dramatic, probably. Or Rose and Jack – Kate and Leo – but the other way around, and the fact he was called Leo made her all the more want to strip off and ask him to paint her like his French girls.

Leo was rich, very rich, with a yacht the size of a house, while Jess was just a silly impostor trying to keep up with the Joneses. She didn't want to be that girl who fawned over him because he had cash. Would he think she was a gold digger if she admitted that she wasn't part of his world now? *But I like your company*, she wanted to tell his lovely face. *I like you*.

What if she just kept the playing field level?

A while later, the conversation was still flowing: easy, comfortable. Jess was learning about Leo, how he loved to be at sea and took his yacht around Europe and sometimes further afield for his business, and she loved thinking of him as a bit of a nomad, waking up to different sunrises and staying far away from the corporate rich-boy lifestyle. In turn, Jess told him about her, about her café and her village in Cornwall – which he thought he'd been to once, when he was little, on a family holiday. She was careful not to lie, but glossed over some details.

All of a sudden, Bryony flopped down near to her. An over-filled champagne flute full of Cristal was balanced delicately between her fingers and she air-kissed at Jess from two feet away before pulling her legs up onto the seat.

'Meems, this party is *crazy*. Can you believe these people?' she hissed, squiffy. 'I was thinking to myself, what do they do? How can they afford this? There's like, diamond curtains and diamond diamonds and . . . guess what? I have two words for you: *blood diamonds*.'

She sat back, nodding, an 'I know what they're up to' look on her face.

'Bryony,' said Jess, motioning to her left with her eyes. 'Meet Leo.'

Bryony squinted across the water. 'Bloody Leo DiCaprio! I'LL NEVER LET GO, I'LL NEVER LET GO!'

'No,' Leo laughed. 'Just Leo. Nice to meet you, though.'

'Oh now hang on to your nuts, you're *Nutella Leo*,' she snickered.

'Leo, introduce me to these ravishing young women,' purred a boy, barely out of his teens, who came up behind Leo and immediately locked eyes with Bryony. It was like a lion spotting its prey, but with all the pursed lips and eyebrow game going on it was hard to tell which of the two was the lion.

'Harvey, this is Bryony, and this is Jess – the girl I was telling you about.'

Jess's heart boinged. 'You were telling him about me?'

'You were telling *her* about *me*?' he countered, waving the Nutella jar.

Harvey flexed his muscles under his slim-fit T-shirt. 'Bryony, hmmm? Hey girl ...'

'Hey yourself. How was school today?' Bryony

flicked her hair behind her and adopted a goddess-like pose, arching her back, and Harvey lapped it up.

Jess and Leo exchanged bemused looks. When did they tune in to the Discovery Channel?

'All right, I get it, but I'm not too young to teach you a thing or two about men.'

'Is that so?'

'And maybe you could teach me something, too?'

'Harvey,' Leo interrupted, 'control the hormones. These are classy women.'

Bryony smiled, never taking her eyes off Harvey. 'So you're friends with Leo?'

Leo jumped in. 'Yep, we go way back. He's here with me on this trip, just living it up at the film festival.' Harvey dragged his gaze from Bryony to glance at Leo for the tiniest moment.

'How do I know Leo is good enough for my Jess?' Bryony asked Harvey.

'That's not awkward!' Jess cried.

'How do I know Jess is good enough for my Leo?'

'Because she's awesome and gorgeous and successful, and Leo would be the King of Luck if he even got one date with her.'

This was so embarrassing, but then Leo squeezed her arm and happiness pumped into her bloodstream. Bryony wasn't trying to be embarrassing; she was just doing her best Olivia Pope and cutting to the chase. It usually worked.

'How about we talk about it some more when I treat you to dinner tomorrow night, anywhere you like?' Harvey licked his lips and Bryony couldn't help but laugh.

'So, Bryony, do you live in Cornwall too?' Leo asked, not moving his hand from Jess's arm, which tingled with both pleasure and mild pins and needles, but she really didn't want to move it.

'No, work means I have to live up in London, but I'm from there originally – we grew up together.'

'What do you do?'

'She's a jo—'

'—jolly good fellow. Thanks, Jess, you don't have to sing that every time you introduce me. I'm a hand model for Naomi Campbell.'

Another undercover identity. Jess just knew Bryony was going to 'have' to spend the next two weeks 'researching' Harvey, digging for info on whatever this new theory was that she had about the underworld of the rich and famous.

But right now, if that meant more time with Leo, that was fine with her. He was the loveliest man she'd met in a long time, and she wanted to get to know him better. Even if it all had an expiry date.

Harvey was fawning over Bryony's model-like hands, and she was letting him, so Leo and Jess went back to quiet conversation, leaning in close to each other, his hand still warming her forearm.

'Match made in heaven,' Leo said.

'She does have a thing for younger men.'

'And he has a thing for older women.' His face drained. 'I didn't mean ... I'm not saying she's old – it's just that he's only twenty-two.'

'It's okay, I'm not in denial that we're thirty-two.'

'Me too! Twins. But not, actually. Luckily.'

'Your voice is very deep.'

'That is true.'

'You guys, let's take this boat for a spin, woooooooooohoooooooooooooooo!' Tara suddenly cried from the hot tub on the top deck, and the motor started up within moments.

'I guess we're going for a spin,' said Jess, reluctantly pulling her arm out from under Leo's. 'You two want to come along?'

Harvey shook his head. 'Nah, we've got to wait for—'

'Some people. Some people are meeting us here in a little bit.' Leo interrupted Harvey and met Jess's eyes.

Oh. Did that mean some women? Not that she had any right to feel snubbed. 'Okay.'

'Catch you later?'

Did he mean it? 'Sure.'

'Could I take your number?' The boat shuddered forward.

'It's zero-seven-eight—'

'I can't hear you,' he called as the engine roared and Jess edged away from him. 'Where are you staying? I'll come and find you tomorrow.'

'Uhhh, I'll come and find you.'

They waved, and the superyacht pulled out to sea, the twinkling harbour of Cannes left behind them, full of movie stars, socialites, and one very nice man whose touch still echoed on her skin.

The cold sea breeze sobered up Bryony and Jess and, huddling together under a ginormous fluffy blanket, they both became dozy.

'Tomorrow, no alcohol. I need to be sharp for the rest of my stay here. I think there's big work to be done.'

'You think?'

Bryony yawned and snuggled in closer. 'I do, I can feel it. I feel on the verge of . . . '

'Bry? Can you stay awake a little longer?'

At that moment, Richard collapsed onto the sofa

next to them, handing them each a mug of tea, which stirred Bryony.

'You look how I feel. Bit late, isn't it?' he yawned.

'Teeeea,' Bryony cried, sitting up a bit.

'I think we'll go back to our hotel once we've docked. No more after-after-parties for us,' yawned Jess.

'Besides, I have a breakfast interview with Clooney,' said Bryony, and for a millisecond Jess believed her.

'Did you tell me where you were staying?' Richard asked. 'I'll walk you back. Don't worry, not in sleaza-licious way.'

Bryony was now wide awake. 'Where are we staying, did you say?'

'Yeah. I'm in the Marriot – booked too late for the Carlton this year.'

'Yes, it's a busy time . . . well, we're in the Hôtel du Cap-Eden-Roc.'

'How grand,' Richard commented.

Jess rubbed her tired eyes. 'The wh—'

'It's lovely, isn't it, Jess?' Bryony interrupted her with a glare. 'Very rugged and beautiful out there on the cliff edge, and only half an hour from Cannes, but too far to escort us back to, thanks anyway.'

'Well you two are very lucky ladies indeed.'

'Yes,' Jess agreed, not really knowing what she should be saying. 'It's a very, very nice hotel.'

'Indeed it is, but guess what?' Richard grinned, putting down his mug of tea and standing up. 'You are going to love love love me.'

Jess and Bryony exchanged glances.

'Look!' He pointed over the handrail and into the darkness. 'Don't you know where we are?'

Bryony and Jess stared at the dark cliffs against the dark sky and the dark sea, just a few twinkling buildings and car headlights showing them where the three separated.

'Don't you recognise it from this angle?' Richard pressed.

'What are we looking at?' Jess asked through another huge yawn.

'That's your hotel, right there. Hang on!' He scampered off inside the boat.

'Oh it does look nice,' said Jess as the superyacht pulled in closer and cut the engines, and she spotted a large, glowing swimming pool carved into the cliff. 'Good choice for a fake hotel, Bryony. Very chic.'

A moment later Richard reappeared. 'Ladies, your wish is my command. The tender is on its way over now to take you straight to your luxurious beds for the night.'

'To take us to the Hôtel du Cap?' Bryony spluttered, tea dribbling down her dress.

'That's where your beds are, aren't they?'

'*Yes*,' said Jess. 'Obviously.'

'Fab-u-lous, because here they are already. No waiting around for valued Eden-Roc guests. You are so having me over for a nightcap sometime in the next two weeks – it's divine in there, isn't it?' Richard looked wistful.

'So divine,' agreed Jess, and she and Bryony omitted giant, fake yawns. 'Time for our beauty sleep now, though.'

As Jess and Bryony were helped into the sleek, private tender, Jess said under her breath, 'Once we get to the hotel, we'll walk straight out the other side and just hop into a taxi, okay?'

There was a chorus of 'goodbyes' and 'same time tomorrows', and then the tender zoomed across the could-have-walked-it-if-it-weren't-for-the-sea short distance from the yacht to the pier. At the end of the pier stood a man in a suit, blocking their way up from the boat.

'*Bonsoir*. I am Philippe, the General Manager here at the Hôtel du Cap-Eden-Roc.'

'*Bonsoir*, Philippe,' Jess and Bryony chorused, and Jess attempted to climb the steps but Philippe stepped closer, allowing them no way to come ashore.

'I'm afraid we have a problem.'

Jess gulped and stepped backwards, huddling closer to Bryony, the small tender swaying under their feet.

She suddenly felt very cold, and very exposed. 'What's the problem?'

'The problem is that this is a private pier, for our very private hotel, and I'm afraid I don't have any record of your names as our guests.' He folded his arms.

'Everything all right over there?' Richard's voice rang out across the water.

Jess turned and waved, forcing a grin, to see Richard, Tara, Bea and most other members of the party coming over to the side of the superyacht to see what was happening. 'Absolutely fine, thanks, Richard. Bye everyone! Our names are on the list,' she hissed to Philippe, lamely.

'No, I'm afraid they're not, *madame*.'

The bass thump of the music on board the yacht suddenly stopped, and the bay seemed very silent. *Not in front of our new friends.* It was like being sent to the front of the class when you'd been naughty. Jess turned to Bryony, guessing the fun was over. How humiliating; she didn't want it to end like this, so quickly, but what could they do? What could they tell Philippe, or the people on the yacht?

Bryony shrugged. 'Sorry, Meems,' she whispered.

Philippe edged closer. There was no way he was letting them up onto the pier. 'So, shall we send you back to your party boat?'

Part Two

'So shall we send you back to your party boat?' Philippe the manager asked, an obviously rhetorical question as he held his arms wide in a *don't you dare step onto this pier* fashion.

'No,' said Jess. *'Noooo . . .'*

'And why not?'

'We're here for . . . the party?' Bryony ventured.

The manager's expression changed instantly into one of panic and regret. *'Mademoiselles*, I am sorry – I was given the incorrect information that you were guests staying at the hotel and when I couldn't find your names . . .' He started to scan a piece of paper that he had pulled from his pocket.

'No problem,' Jess tittered, patting Philippe's arm and chuckling as she hastily climbed off the boat, gripping Bryony's hand. Bryony was goddamned *genius*.

'We'd better dash in there quick, we're a little late. Okay, bye.'

'One moment please. You are not on my list for the party either. May I ask of whom you are guests?'

'We are the daughters of . . . ' Jess racked her brains. 'I mean, isn't it obvious?'

The manager looked at their very different faces. 'I'm sorry, but no.'

'We're the daughters of . . . Dan . . . ny . . . DeVito. Danny DeVito. *Daddy* DeVito we call him.'

'You are both the daughters of Danny DeVito?'

'Yes,' Bryony set her chin. 'Racist.'

'Um, anyway, I know he's not here, but he wanted us to come and say hi to everyone on his behalf.' Jess fixed Philippe with a smile fit for a Stepford Wife.

'No.'

'No?'

'No, your father is here already, I will take you to him myself.'

'He's *here*? How . . . *fantastic*.' Jess had mixed emotions. Meeting Mr DeVito would be amazing, but meeting him while masquerading as his daughter – not so much.

'Please, follow me.' The manager turned and made his way along the pier toward the hotel.

'*Danny DeVito?*' Bryony hissed.

'He was the first older male celebrity who probably wouldn't be here that came to mind. Come on, you have to admit it was pretty obscure. I think I did well.'

'Well, *sis*, we have probably less than a minute to get out of this before we meet "Dad". Any suggestions?'

'No . . . who would you have said?'

'What?'

'Who would you have said was our dad?'

'Samuel L. Jackson.'

'Hmm . . . he just doesn't look like me—'

'Hel-*lo?*' Bryony pointed at herself as they entered the foyer. 'Anyway, let's talk about this later. We're nearly there.' They approached a ballroom in which they could hear a party was in full flow.

'Mr Manager? Um, *Monsieur Philippe?*' Jess said, and stopped short.

'Yes?'

'I would like to use the bathroom.'

'Certainly, *mademoiselle*, there is one just through the ballroom on the right.'

'No thank you.' She gave him another Stepford Wife smile.

'*Excusez-moi?*'

'I don't want to use that one very much. Thank you.'
See, Bryony, manners are everything.

'Would you care to use the one in the lobby?'

'Actually, I think we would both appreciate a little more privacy, to freshen up and whatnot.'

The manager nodded, glancing at his watch. 'Certainly, *mademoiselle*. I will ask our concierge, Audrey, to escort you to our ladies' cloakroom on the second floor, next to the cocktail lounge.' He motioned to a woman behind a desk, who scuttled over and they spoke in hushed voices.

As Audrey led them up the stairs, Jess gazed back at the ballroom, wondering what A-list treasures could be found inside. Once at the door of the ladies' bathroom, Audrey stepped to the side and clasped her hands together in front of her.

'*Merci beaucoup*, Audrey,' said Jess. 'We'll make our way back down to the party in a moment.'

'It is no problem; I will wait and escort you back down.'

'No, really, we might be a while. My friend . . . um, sister – my lovely, friendly sister has a funny stomach. *Les merdes*,' she whispered, winking at Audrey.

'Thank you, Jess,' Bryony said through gritted teeth.

'It is no problem; I will wait as long as you need,' Audrey repeated, not budging, and averting her eyes from Jess.

Bryony stuffed Jess into the bathroom, and while she made use of the facilities – 'Since we're here' – Jess pottered about seeing if there was anything worth nabbing. *Ooh, Egyptian cotton flannels?* And then she struck gold.

Not actual gold, but a way out of their situation.

Bryony exited the stall, stuffing her bra into her clutch bag. 'Ahh, escape from boob prison.'

'I am the best. Check it out.' Jess pointed at a lacquered walnut door at the far end of the bathroom. 'That ain't no cleaning cupboard.'

'Is it Narnia?'

Jess opened the door quietly and peeped through, then swung it wide for Bryony. 'It's a service corridor, so the attendants can get to and from the bathroom without wheeling mops and buckets through the cocktail lounge.'

'Well thank you, Meems, I think I now know what I'll write my hard-hitting, Pulitzer-prize-winning article about.'

'All right, Sarky Mark. *This* is how we get away from Audrey.'

At last, the penny dropped and Bryony said, 'That's the kind of sneaky detective work that reminds me why you and I are friends. Let's go!'

They slipped through the door and made their way down endless stark corridors as quickly and quietly as they could manage, slowing only once as they passed the kitchen, to breathe in the aroma of lamb cutlets and rosemary.

'There's a fire exit!' Jess cried, feeling very like a modern Butch Cassidy.

'Wait!' The Sundance Kid, aka Bryony, grabbed her arm and they screeched to a halt. 'First of all, *keep your voice down*! Second of all, what if it's alarmed? Opening that door could set off a huge fire alarm, evacuating the whole hotel and leaving a hundred megastars standing about shivering in the streets for everyone to see. Stop looking at me like that, it's a *bad thing*!'

They dawdled for a moment, unsure what to do.

'There you are,' came a stern voice from behind them. But when they turned it wasn't Audrey who faced them, but a polished-looking woman with a neat blonde bob and an earpiece. 'I found them.' She spoke at the air in a crisp, clipped English accent. 'What are you doing back here? You should have been in the ballroom ten minutes ago.'

'Erm, gosh, sorry, we were just—' Jess stammered. 'I had the squits and—'

She took them each by the arm and before they even had a chance to say *sacré bleu* they were being pushed through some double doors and – oh!

They were standing on a stage at the far end of one the most beautifully decorated ballrooms Jess had ever seen. From the crystal and white rose centrepieces to the silver-thread table runners to the vast flower garlands to the hanging tea lights, it was a Pinterester's dream. And seated in huddles around circular white tables were more famous faces than Jess would see in an issue of *Heat*. Her eyes flicked from the Oscar winner showing a lead singer something on his phone to the Kardashian leaning across the table to talk to the supermodel. She reached for her phone; she didn't care if she was onstage. Must. Take. Celeb-background selfie . . .

But the blonde woman thrust a microphone into her hand before she had got to her clutch bag, and handed a second to Bryony.

'What do we do with these?' Jess asked.

'You're the singers aren't you?' The woman sounded exasperated. 'Why don't you try singing? *Now*.'

'But—' Bryony started.

'*SHOULD auld acquaintance be forgot,*' Jess sang, loud and clear into the microphone, and the room hushed. She met Bryony's wide eyes and kept going, her voice and hand shaking, '*And never brought to mind?*'

Tonight, in Cannes, Hollywood would not be finding a new star in Jess. But she kept going because Marilyn would have, and, besides, how could she leave now? When would she ever again get the chance to sing badly in front of her favourite actors?

Seconds ticked by as if in slow motion. All eyes were on her and all she could think was, *what's the next line, what's the next line?* And then something wonderful happened: Bryony linked arms with her and joined the hell in. '*Should auld acquaintance be forgot, and auld lang syne?*'

At this point, Jess really believed Johnny Depp might have jumped up and linked arms with Kylie Minogue, Kanye with Reese, and the whole ballroom would have erupted into an impromptu singalong sway-fest. But as they were about to start belting out the chorus, their mics were switched off and, out of nowhere, a pianist slid onto the piano stool in front of the white baby grand and began a tinkling rendition of 'Auld Lang Syne' before merging seamlessly into the more appropriate 'Beyond the Sea', and lullabying the partygoers back into their conversations.

At the other end of the ballroom, the blonde woman fixed Jess and Bryony with a death stare, and as she muttered a curse into the air Philippe appeared at her side.

'Time to go,' said Jess, with one last look at her unenraptured audience.

They placed the microphones on the floor of the stage and backed out of the doors. The last face Jess saw was Philippe's as he skirted between the tables, making directly for them.

'Go, go, go!' Jess yelped as they ran back through the bright, artificially lit service corridor toward the fire exit and – *bam* – shoved their way through. Instinct caused them to freeze momentarily in the still, cool blackness, awaiting a shrill alarm, but when nothing happened they continued to run, holding each other by the hand and leaving the hotel grounds as fast as their high heels could carry them.

They rounded the corner onto the dark cliff road that wound back into Cannes and Jess's glasses suddenly made a suicidal leap, slipping from her face to beneath her foot. *Crunch.*

'Bugger,' she hissed into the night air, and ran into a wall. 'Bryony, wait, I'm about to die.'

'What happened?' She swung back toward Jess; *crunch, crunch.* 'Oops, what was that?'

'My glasses.' Jess bent down, flailing her hands about on the tarmac until they hit plastic – twisted, mangled plastic.

'There's a taxi coming. Shall I hail it?'

'Um ...'

'Are they broken?'

'Yes.'

'Badly?'

'Yes.'

'Would you like to go to prison and be blind?'

'Not really.'

'Then I think we should get in this taxi and get the hell out of here. I'll guide you.'

Bryony helped Jess into the cab and they pulled away from the soft lights of the Hôtel du Cap-Eden-Roc. Jess flopped back against the leather seat, tired, foggy-eyed, sore-footed and unable to keep the smile from her face.

'Listen to this: "The questions came to a brief but abrupt halt when one journalist asked the forbidden, the one thing we'd all been informed was off the table, about the relationship between Maxpower and his mother, and that which cannot be named: the sex tape. But like true professionals, the stars pasted Hollywood smiles on their faces and moved on."' Bryony put down her iPad. 'You're famous, Meems! Marilyn would have been proud of ya.'

Jess's hands covered her face and she groaned behind them. 'I'm so embarrassed. I'm so sorry. Do any of them mention *Sleb*? Am I going to get you in trouble?'

'No, don't be silly – we journos are a loyal bunch. If someone cocks up we'll publish the hell out of it, but we rarely name names. Anyway, if they did name the magazine Mitch would probably hire you in a second.'

Climbing out of the bed, Jess squinted at herself in the mirror. 'Do I look as bad as my blurry eyes tell me I do?'

'No, glitter eyeshadow smudged on the cheekbones is very *in* this season. As are beehives.'

Jess laughed and touched the hairsprayed mess of curls atop her head. 'Will you help me figure out which is the shampoo and which is the shower gel, and then come glasses shopping with me?'

'You're going to hate me.'

'Why?'

'I have three screenings today, and the first is at nine. I have to leave here soon after eight, which is around about now actually, so I'm not going to be around until later.'

'Okay, no problem: I'll just relax here. I could do with catching up on some sleep.'

'I feel like I'm leaving you without a guide dog. Won't you be bored?'

'Not at all. I can just watch weird French TV – oh, no I can't. Well, I could go and sunbathe on the roof terrace; that would be lovely.'

'Hey, why don't you call Richard? Maybe he could take you shopping. You should get a taxi to the Croisette rather than have him meet you here, though.'

'Or at the Hôtel du Cap . . . '

'Right,' Bryony snorted. 'Where are your sunglasses? They're prescription ones, aren't they? You could wear them for the time being.'

Jess looked at the fuzz around her and ran her hands over the table and her suitcase. 'I don't know, can you see them?'

'No,' said Bryony, flinging things all over the place. 'They must be here somewhere, the room's too small for them to be that lost. Gahh, I'm so sorry I have to leave you like this but I have to dash. Let me call Richard for you, and then I'd better shoot off. Here's the shampoo, and here's the shower gel.'

'Thanks. Oh, and Bry?'

'Yep?'

'Thanks for yesterday. What with the embarrassment, the trespassing, the stage fright and the escape, I had one of the best days of my life.'

'So are you blind as a bat, or just as a newborn baby kitten?' asked a tall blob blocking Jess's sunshine who she assumed was Richard.

'I'm somewhere in-between the two, but they're pretty bog-standard badly behaved eyes. If you could point me in the direction of an opticians' – or perhaps lead me there by hand – that would be great, and I'll just get any old pair made up with my prescription.'

'God no, we can do better than that. Follow me old dear, let me take you shopping.'

They crossed the street and meandered past the hotels and designer shops, Richard clinging to her as if she would get smacked by a passing Ferrari if he wasn't there to protect her.

'Such a shame those retro Prada ones broke, they looked so cute on you, and so *now*,' he said.

'I feel like you're smirking at me, Richard, and if I could see your face I'd have half a mind to slap it.'

'Right, first stop Gucci,' he said, squeezing her hand and reaching out for a big gold door handle with the other.

'Whoa, I don't know if . . . I'm not sure about Gucci.'

'Darling, Gucci have some fabulous designs this year. You know how all those celebs are jumping on the geek-chic bandwagon? Well, you don't want to look like them, so stick to Gucci, Givenchy or Versace: classic elegance with a modern edge.'

Classic elegance with a modern edge was exactly how Jess would describe herself when no one was around to disagree. 'Okay, let's take a look.'

Jess followed Richard into the shop, running her hand along the racks of clothes that probably cost more than every garment she'd ever owned in her life put together. Low lighting and chocolate brown décor made it still harder to see, suddenly her hand brushed against something warm and rounded and she jumped back.

'Veuillez m'excuser, mademoiselle.'

Jess squinted upwards to see a large security man, whose stomach she'd just caressed, gazing solemnly down at her. 'Oh! I'm so sorry. *Excusez-moi, madame,* I mean *monsieur.*' She patted his tummy as if putting it back how she found it, and thankfully Richard pulled her away.

'Please tell me you like these glasses, because we need to get you seeing again ASAP.' He stood her in front of an open glass cabinet and she put her face as close as possible to the glasses in order to read the tiny prescription labels, looking for the closest match to her vision.

Finding a pair of rimless specs with the gold Gucci logo on the arm, she slipped them on and sighed with relief. It *was* Richard who was with her. The prescription was still a way out, but at least she could now look around her at all the beautiful clothes, the soft-looking handbags, the rows of powerful-looking shoes and the rotund security guard. Finally she looked at herself in the mirror. 'Well, these look okay.'

Richard pulled her hair away from her face. 'You look a million bucks, but . . . '

'What?'

'I'm not sure about rimless on you. You look a bit . . . '

'A bit what?'

'A bit Tom Cruise.'

'I like Tom Cruise. You don't think these look chic and classy?'

'I like Tom Cruise, too, and I like the glasses; I just don't think *you* should look like Tom Cruise when you wear glasses.'

'Okay, fine.' Jess pulled another pair off the rack and at that point noticed the price tag, which nearly made her drop them. 'I'm just not sure I'm a Gucci kinda gal. Shall we move on?'

'You're the boss; I'm just the lowly stylist. Come on then.'

'Bye!' She waved at the security guard as they stepped back out into the sunshine. 'Richard, let's not worry about walking too far. I'm sure I could get some crappy ones from a pharmacy, just to tide me over.'

'I will not have you looking crappy on the red carpet.'

'I won't be going on the red carpet, so it's not really a problem.'

'Oh yes you are!' He grinned devilishly and strode off down the Croisette. Jess tottered after him, her arms flailing before her.

'Wait for me! What are you talking about? Bryony says I'm not allowed back in front of the media for a while.'

'We can't let Bryony have all the fun, can we?'

Jess's heart fluttered with excitement, she didn't

even mind when she walked into a bollard and then apologised to it.

'Here,' he said, stopping at last. 'I think this might be more your cup of tea.'

Jess looked up hoping to see an H&M, but was instead faced with the navy awnings of Ralph Lauren. Ah good, a cheapy shop.

Inside, a crisply dressed woman in such sharply contrasting pinstripes that even Jess could make them out led them to the eyewear section. 'Let me know if I can be of any help whatsoever, sir, ma'am,' she said in a French accent dusted with American.

'Do you have those tortoiseshell frames? The new ones: kind of rectangular but only just?' Richard asked.

'I know exactly the ones you mean, sir. Ma'am, what strength are we looking for?'

'Strong. Like proper British tea. But I can't usually buy them over the counter . . . ' She gave the lady her exact prescription.

'That's no problem, ma'am, if you find some frames you like we have an opticians' we use and can get those made up for you within an hour. All part of the service. Now, how about these?'

'Cannes is a fabulous place, isn't it, darling?' Richard purred into her ear.

She slipped a pair of frames onto Jess's face, and when Jess squinted into the mirror she couldn't quite believe the transformation. She looked like her but better, though it may have been the lighting and the leather-trimmed white blazer she'd found herself trying on as well.

'*So* Jennifer Aniston,' Richard said admiringly.

She *did* look like Jennifer Aniston ... The glasses were feather-light and the flecks of amber in the frames brought out colours in her eyes that she wasn't sure she'd ever spotted before. She felt very A-list, so in a way wouldn't they be both practical and the perfect souvenir of Cannes? 'Glasses are an investment,' she told Richard matter-of-factly.

'Yes they are. Do we have a winner?'

She looked at the price tag. Not quite as wee-inducing as the Gucci ones, so really it was as if she were saving a hundred pounds or so. And she did need glasses; it was just part of her existence. If she needed a new kidney she wouldn't be worrying about a few hundred pounds. 'You really like them?'

'Yes I do.'

'How about you?' she asked the saleswoman.

'I think you look phenomenal.' Wow. In that case ... 'Would you like me to have them made up right away?'

'Yes, I think that would be best. Can I wait here? It's a bit safer than out there when I'm like this.'

'Absolutely. Please, have a seat.'

An hour later, with her belly full of both laughs from Richard's stories as well as fancy Ralph Lauren tea, the saleswoman returned, like a fairy godmother, with Jess's new glasses.

Jess sashayed through the shop feeling like a right Richie Rich, glancing to the right and left like she'd seen the models do at the Victoria's Secret shows, convinced that anyone who saw her would fall flat on their backside through envy and lust. Unfortunately the only other shopper was a woman in a large floppy hat who was more interested in the cashmere ponchos than in Jess's new spectacles.

Nevertheless, Jess felt truly part of the film-festival elite by the time they were back on the Croisette. 'The world seems sharper, Richard, it's like I'm seeing in Technicolor for the first time. I'm like Dorothy in Oz, or Reese Witherspoon in *Pleasantville*. Remember that?'

'Nobody apart from you remembers that, honeybunch.'

'Well you should, it was brilliant.' Jess sighed a

happy sigh. She was beginning to like Cannes very much indeed.

'What are your plans for the rest of the day?'

'Hmm ...' Perhaps now would be a good time to skip down to the marina, find the hunky Leo and let him whisk her and her glasses off for a ride on his superyacht. They could smooch on the ocean like Marilyn and Tony Curtis in *Some Like It Hot* and she could press her body into his, then they could come back and she could buy everything else in Ralph Lauren and just never return to England and therefore never get into trouble for having credit-card debt. Although perhaps that wasn't how it worked.

'Well, if it was nothing more pressing than slipping into a daydream,' Richard said, 'I wondered if you wanted to come to work with me today.'

'Doing what?'

'What do you think celebrity stylists do with their days when they're at the Cannes Film Festival?'

Jess smoothed down the black Dior maxi dress as she stood in a crowd of entourages in a hot marquee next to the Palais des Festivals. 'Are you sure it's okay for me to wear this? Someone else might want to use it.'

'No offence, but none of the actresses would be caught dead in something so plain on the red carpet. Don't get me wrong – for a shop around Rodeo Drive it's fab, and for blending into the background among a sea of stunningly detailed gowns, it's fab. Even the stars who always wear black will be in something much more eye-catching.'

'Well I feel very classic movie star; I like it.'

'So do I, just not on *my* movie stars.'

'Tell me one more time what I do out there, I just want to be a hundred per cent clear on the rules.'

'You stay with me, you fluff out the train of the dresses if you see them slinking underneath themselves, you tell me if you see a bra strap or nipple poking out, and you smile, smile, smile.'

'Smiling I am very good at. I got voted "most smiley" at school, you know. Will I be in the photos?'

'No published photos, unless you're caught scowling behind Natalie Portman or something. So don't do that.'

Her phone tinkled. 'Do I have time to take this?' Richard nodded. 'Hello?'

'Heeeeey, whatcha doing?' came Cameron's gormless voice down the line.

'I am about to make my red carpet debut.'

'I bet you're watching French TV in your hotel room.'

'All right – wait there one moment.' She pulled the phone away from her ear and snapped a quick selfie in the door of the marquee, making sure that the red carpet and the crowd were in the background. She sent it to him, and when he received it he audibly groaned. 'Who's having the adventure of a lifetime now? HA!' *Sorry*, she mouthed to a group of darkly dressed event organisers nearby who looked up at her from their clipboards.

'Whatever. Mum says black isn't your colour anyway.'

'Is she there?'

'No, I just . . . I heard her say it once.'

'Sure she did. Listen, I have to go: I'm helping be Penélope Cruz's stylist today, so . . . '

'What? That's not fair. You tell her about me. Tell her I'm single, if she wants.'

'She's married!'

'I know, but she might not have met someone like me before.'

He was such a loser. 'What, a mummy's boy? Yeah, she's probably okay with Javier Bardem. Gotta go, bye.' She hung up and walked back to Richard. 'That was my brother; he wants me to set him up with—'

'I want to hear all about it over a cocktail, but now it's showtime.'

Being on the red carpet was like having an out-of-body experience, and Jess felt that at any moment someone would spot her standing there like a lemon, dangerously close to the celebrities, and call security. She'd been there for about half an hour, discreetly following Richard's clients, adjusting a dress if she felt like taking the heart-thumping plunge of being within inches of a star, and smiling like a Barbie doll. Jess was someone who smiled a lot, but red-carpet non-stop smiling took it to a whole new level and her cheeks were aching.

'Oh, hi, Veronica!' Jess called and dork-waved, recognising Veronica Hay and greeting her like an old friend before remembering that it was Bryony she knew, not her.

Veronica side-eyed her and offered a small, polite smile that didn't reach her cheekbones, let alone her eyes, before stopping in front of the bank of photographers and giving them megawatts. She preened and turned sideways, looking over her shoulder in such an alluring way that Jess thought she'd try it. So, smile still in place, she twisted her body and looked over her shoulder at the red carpet stretching away behind her until Richard poked her in the shin.

'Oi, focus! Stop gawping behind you like an owl,' he said as he re-pinned a hem on a too-short-for-couture model in record speed.

'It's all just really exciting.' Was Leo here? She'd like him to see her like this, all glamorous and on the red carpet, the light hitting her just right. She'd feel a little more on his level then, not that he knew any different.

'I know it is,' Richard grinned, momentarily forgetting his professional cool and slinging an arm around her shoulders. 'You're doing fab, keep up the smiling.'

'Can I come to work with you every day? I could be your assistant.'

'Not every day, love. You've got other things to do while you're here in Cannes.'

'What are you winking for?'

'Where'd you find that sexy beast on the boat next door?'

She blushed a little and they moved a few steps further down the carpet. 'Leo? I just met him down near the beach a couple of days ago.'

'Do you realise how many people flock in to the festival every year to just "meet" a billionaire down at the beach? Don't tell the tourists that's where they hang out, you might have a fight on your hands.'

She laughed along, but felt a stab of sadness. Richard didn't mean anything by it, but she was one of the tourists, even potentially bagging herself a billionaire. Was she just one huge Cannes cliché?

'It's been such a long day,' Bryony yawned, entering their room and collapsing into a heap by the door because, even at a distance of barely three feet away, reaching the bed or desk-chair seemed too taxing. 'Oh, there are your sunglasses.' She pointed to the back of the boxy TV.

Jess poured some warm Diet Coke into a plastic cup, grabbed the remainder of a bag of bolognese-flavoured crisps and took them to Bryony, sitting down next to her on the floor. 'Tell me all about it, wife.'

'Thanks, wife. I don't mean to be a big moaner, because I'm sure a lot of people would kill for my job, but by your third movie of the day, followed by an in-depth discussion about said movie, you just feel like you need to see a bit of daylight. Remember when we watched all four *Scream* movies in one weekend?'

'Yep, we were pretty grey by the end of it.'

'We even considered going for a run.'

'But we drank a smoothie instead, which is just as good, I think.'

'I feel a bit like that.' Bryony sighed.

'Can I get you a smoothie?' asked Jess.

'No, but any chance you want to stretch your legs?'

'You want to *run*?'

'No, but a walk to the sea might be nice. Unless you've been walking about all day?'

'Nope, that sounds good to me. Where do you want to eat tonight?'

'Um ... would you kill me if I said somewhere low-key?'

'I would kiss you all over if you said somewhere low-key,' Jess laughed. 'And so would Mr HSBC.'

'I'm just not in the mood to be all dressed up and alcoholy tonight.'

'Okay, we'll don some flip-flops and live like the Norma Jeans we really are.' She pulled Bryony to her feet and they both changed into shorts, baggy light-weight jumpers and wonderfully flat flip-flops.

'Hey, look at you! Nice glasses,' Bryony grinned, just noticing.

'Thanks, they're Ralph Lauren, you know. Do you think I look like Jennifer Aniston?'

'I thought that's who I'd been talking to all this time. They look ace. Were they pricey?'

'No, Richard took me to a discount store down on the promenade.'

'Really?'

'No. And yes, they were pricey. But worth it?'

'Definitely. Do you think I need to shave my legs before we go out?'

'No way, honeybunch, we're off duty tonight: be as spiky as you likey.'

'This is just what I needed,' Bryony said, sinking back into her little wicker chair. They were sitting at a tiny table outside a tiny restaurant, on a tiny steep road where the al-fresco seating was tiered down the hill alongside the restaurant. A tea light flickered in a pink jar between them, and most of the surface of the table was covered by menus, glasses and a bread bowl. It was cheap, colourful and perfect.

Jess sipped on her Coke – soft drinks only tonight – and watched the tourists, proper tourists who were here to see the stars rather than try to be among them, as they wandered up and down the cobbled hill, taking photos and pausing to read menus outside restaurants.

'I still can't believe you spent your day on the red carpet. Didn't I tell you to lie low for a couple of days?' Bryony teased. 'And by lie low, I did not mean lie down and fiddle with the hem of Ms Cruz's dress in front of the paparazzi.'

'It was such a fun day. It's all a bit crazy, you know? To think that this time of day I'd normally be sweeping up the café or wondering whether the Bakewell-tart leftovers are worth dropping off at Mum's or just putting in my mouth. That all seems a very long way away.'

'I bet. I'm glad you came with me.'

'I'm glad, too. I'm not going home. Nope, I'm staying here for ever.'

'Now I know you won't want me to pry, so I'm not asking for all the details, but ... you have to tell me every single thing about Leo, including everything he said to you and you said to him, how many times you've touched each other and what your innermost thoughts about him are,' Bryony said, sprinkling baguette crumbs all over the table.

'Oh, no problem – so just an overview then?'

'An overview will be fine, please just leave in the specifics. So how did Mr Nutella end up the-boy-next-boat?'

A smile formed on Jess's face as she remembered him appearing out of the darkness, all grins and chocolate spread and warm skin. 'I was just sitting there watching all the manic partying, wondering to myself if I'd now have to remember to call you Lola the Showgirl in front of certain people—'

'Oh yeah! He was an interesting one. Didn't buy the showgirl act, though; must be the lack of big balloons. Anyway, I'll get to him – go on.'

'And then, like a big, fat, brilliant scene from *Love Actually* or something, there he was, and he was so pleased with himself for having a jar of Nutella to hand to use as an opening line.' She sank her chin onto her hands. 'He's so lovely. Can we get married and live on his yacht?'

'Wow, that escalated quickly! I didn't even know you were looking for a boyfriend.'

'It's not that I want a boyfriend ... I mean, I'm not adverse to it, but it's not like I've been plotting: *I want a boyfriend – he'll do*. I want *him*. He's nice, and yummy, and ... I don't know. Everything about this place is a bit of a dreamland and he's part of it, adding to the sparkle. But it's just a bit of fun.'

'Tell me about him.'

'He has a nice smile and when he grins it crinkles his eyes up in a way that looks like I've really made him happy. Wow, that was cringey.'

'It's not cringey. Go on.'

'He's in the food industry; I'm not sure what but, by the size of his yacht, I'd say he probably owns a chain of Michelin-starred restaurants or something.'

'Well that's a good fit with you. Did you tell him about the café?'

'*Cafés.*'

'Ah. So he thinks you're also rolling in it.'

'He assumed, since I was at the yacht party, and I didn't correct him.'

'How come?'

'Because I'm in dreamland.' Jess smiled and shrugged. 'And I'm a teenager with a crush and I want to keep seeing him, and I don't want him to think it's because he has money, because it isn't. If we do go on any dates I'll pay my share.'

'You better hope he takes you to McDonald's, then.'

'I'm not *that* broke.'

'And he's definitely single?'

'I think so. If anything, he seems kind of lonely. He just hangs out on his boat, being all sea-salty and windswept and sexy, I guess.'

'Hey – he has Harvey.'

'Ah, Harvey. I wonder how they became friends. Now, there was definitely some very strange heat going on between you two last night.'

Bryony sniggered. 'He's one to watch.'

'As are you, *Naomi Campbell's hand model*. What was that about?'

'I don't need everyone knowing I'm a journalist.'

'Did you like him?'

'He could be fun ... and useful. Which reminds me, I know how I'm going to make my fortune.'

'Count me in.' Jess let the subject of Harvey drop – for now.

'You don't know what it is yet. What if I was about to say I'm going to move to Vegas and become a high-class sex worker?'

'Then I'd say, how about I do the admin side. I'm good at that. Besides, I'm loving faking it as part of the young hot Hollywood crowd and am not ready to go back to being Lady Boring of Boringshire just yet.'

'Okay ... You know last night I was prattling on about rich people and how the heck are some of them so rich and why are they here at the film festival anyway?'

'And blood diamonds, don't forget the blood diamonds.'

'Yes exactly. It was a good theory, no?'

'Um ...'

'I'm not saying Tara or any of those particular people on that particular yacht are up to mischief, but the whole scene got me thinking. I spoke to quite a few people on the yacht and only about half of them were at the film festival because they actually have something to do with films. Bourbon man was a banker, another guy was a swimming trunks designer; a woman was there because she thought it was Saint-Tropez, for crying out loud. It got me thinking, were they just there for the parties and the sunshine and the glamour, or were they there because of other reasons, like to do business or buy *stuff*?'

The waiter appeared in front of them, flourishing two starters of baked Camembert.

'I expect in most cases it's the first – the parties and glamour option. What makes you think there's something more to it? Mmm, I love food,' said Jess, sticking her knife into the warm, flavoursome cheese.

'In most cases, I'm sure it is just the parties, and that some rich people just go where the party goes, but there were little things people were saying, comments here and there about late-night trips to other yachts to restock, about whether deliveries would be in the hotels when they got back, and, as I was saying, it got me thinking. So today, during the press conferences, I spent a lot of time googling Cannes's history. Do you know how much scandal there's been here over the years?'

Jess pricked her eyes, and momentarily looked up from her cheesy puddle of delight. 'Go on.'

'Well, not much actually. But that got me thinking

even more. There are references to drugs, prostitution, people dropping serious cash like chewing-gum wrappers. There are sweeping mentions of the party people that descend on the clubs and mansions, but it's all very skimmed over. It's alluded to, but nobody digs too deep or gives too much away. It's like the Cannes Film Festival is still this billionaire's club, and what happens here stays here.'

Jess chewed and listened, chewed and listened.

'In the past seventy years of the festival's history, do you know what the biggest scandals have been?' Bryony went on.

'Nope.'

'An actress whipping off her bikini top on the beach in the fifties and being asked to leave the festival, which seems pretty ridiculous nowadays when visible nips are practically celebrated on the red carpet.'

Jess nodded. She couldn't imagine a skin-on-show starlet being turned away and asked not to return to the VMAs.

Bryony took a long slurp of her drink and then continued, 'There have been people fainting and walking out of a couple of gross films that were screened, films that have bombed and been publicly condemned, and a director a few years back who joked that he was a Nazi during a press conference. I get that these are scandals in their own right, that they're appalling or embarrassing things to have happened, and there have been other things, too, but none of them relate to the bigger picture. Where are the drug raids? Where's the money laundering? Where's the bribery?'

'Maybe that kind of thing just doesn't happen here? You're looking at seventy years of Hollywood history, but this event only runs for two weeks a year.'

'You're right, maybe nothing does happen. Maybe I can only find little passing mentions because there really is nothing more to it. But maybe not. Maybe there's a huge story there, if I can just infiltrate a little further . . . Did you know that during the festival there are call girls who earn up to twenty-five thousand pounds a night?'

'Hang on, how is that not a scandal?' interrupted Jess.

'Because it's all hush-hushed, that's part of my point.'

'Oh . . . I did not know that. Is that true? How do they even do it? I mean, not actually *do it*, but like . . . ' she lowered her voice, 'where are they?'

'They're in the hotels. Some of the big ones.'

'Do the hotels know?'

'Certain employees know who they are and help steer them in the direction of the guests – at least according to the *Daily Mail* website.' Jess raised her eyebrows at Bryony. Bryony's mouth banged shut as the waiter brought their main courses – tartiflette for Jess and fish for Bryony. She eyed him until she knew for sure he was out of earshot and then leaned in closer to Jess, lowering her voice. 'Anyway, the sex side's not really the direction I want to go in. My point is you never know who's involved with these people, who's struck a deal, who's doing their dirty work. Trust no one.'

Jess accidently sniggered. 'Okay, Inspector Clouseau. You think our waiter could be on the phone right now to the Drug Lord of Cannes, telling him – or her – to intercept us on our way back to the hotel and throw us off the marina?'

'He's probably not, but you're catching my drift.'

'And you got all of this from pretending to be a showgirl to some guy on a booze cruise?'

'Oh no, the only thing that guy did was make me think about broadening my thought process. I was focusing on how they got their money, and he made me think that another potential area to look at would be how they spend their money.'

Jess eyed her. What was she not saying?

'What?' Bryony asked, innocently.

'I can read you like the world's easiest book. You tell

me what happened or I will sing *Frozen* at you, right here and right now.'

'Noooo, I hate that film so much.'

'No you don't, you love it and you love my singing. *Let it g—*'

'Okay, fine. If you must drag the humiliation out of me by the teeth, he thought I was a prostitute.'

'Ha!'

'And the worst part? He thought I was such an unappealing prostitute that he sighed, checked his watch and said, "Come on then, let's get this over with," as if he was doing me a favour by letting me sleep with him.'

Peals of laughter burst from Jess, making her shake and, in turn, the table wobble and several tourists stop to look at her. Some even then entered the restaurant, thinking it must be a fun place to eat. 'Wait!' She pulled herself together all of a sudden. 'You didn't then sleep with him, did you?'

'*NO.*' Then even Bryony let out a chuckle. 'The things I do for my career.'

Jess held her belly, full to the brim with cheese and bread and potato, but perhaps with a tiny sliver of room available, as an idea formed. 'Do you fancy having dessert somewhere else?'

Bryony looked longingly at a trio of crème brûlées

that whizzed past with the waiter. 'What did you have in mind?'

'You'll see, but you won't be disappointed.'

'These are sooooo good.' Bryony licked her fingers and then licked them again lest she miss any Nutella. She shovelled the last of the crêpe into her mouth with gusto.

'Told you. I didn't think I could stuff any more in, but ... well I can't be right about everything.'

'No wonder you fell in love with a boy while eating that slab of heaven, Meems. I'd marry that lamp post if it asked me.'

They strolled along the Croisette, a billion lights shining out on land and sea against the darkened sky. Cannes was buzzing, perhaps even more so now the festival was fully under way, but Bryony and Jess just observed while all the energy fizzed around them.

They kept walking, past the Palais des Festivals and down to the marina, where – if it were possible – even more mega yachts had shoehorned their way in. Jess looked sideways at Bryony to see if she'd clocked where they were headed.

'I wonder if Tara's boat managed to find a mooring

again back here. Or maybe they have set spaces. Hang on.' Bryony stopped in her tracks and looked around. 'You sneaky thing, are you taking us to see your man?'

'What? No, you've been leading the way.'

'You're the worst liar. You might want to try that again without a huge grin on your face.'

'Well, shush, there he is. Hey you!' Jess waved at Leo who was crouched on the deck, adjusting something with a spanner. Her heart rose in her chest at the sight of him, but simultaneously she suddenly felt very schoolgirl-crush coming to find him here.

He straightened up and looked over to them, a smile shooting across his face and he dropped the spanner, pulled off his polo shirt to reveal that strong torso she had peeped at previously and used it to mop his brow. He then threw the shirt onto the deck, glancing back into the yacht, and hopped down onto the boardwalk.

'Whoa. Diet Coke break,' whispered Jess.

'Keep calm, you're salivating like a pervert,' Bryony murmured.

'Hi,' he said, bending in to hug both of them. 'Urgh, sorry, I wasn't thinking – I'm all disgusting and I might have just ruined your outfits.'

'Got a leak in your dinghy there, Captain?' asked

Jess in a broad, fisherman-style voice that she immediately regretted.

'Not really, I just like to hang out playing with a spanner so I look tough in case pretty women wander by.' He walked them a little way away from his yacht, glancing back at it again. 'So what brings you guys here? It's really nice to see you. Why aren't you looking at me?' He smiled at Jess, who was averting her eyes. 'Why are you laughing?'

'Because I can see your nipples.'

'Are they funny nipples?' He looked down and flexed as hard as he could.

'No, they're just fine.'

'Not too big?'

'No, they're actually very small. I can barely see them.'

'We're here to . . . see if you want a drink?' Bryony said, stepping in. 'Harvey too, if he's around, I guess. Whatever.'

He looked disappointed, and brushed his hand against Jess's as he spoke. 'I would love to, but I can't leave here right now. We're sort of in the middle of something.'

'Anything fun?' asked Jess.

'Just work stuff,' he shrugged, and she didn't want to pry any more. She didn't much want to talk about her work, so she couldn't exactly fault him for not being overly forthcoming about his. 'I'm free for a while tomorrow, if you fancy doing something?'

He gallantly asked them both, but with a smile Bryony ducked out, blaming her job. She nudged Jess.

'I'D LOVE TO. I mean, cool, okay. Do you have anything in mind?'

'This is your first time in Cannes, isn't it? Have you been up to the castle?' He pointed up the hill behind them.

'No, but that sounds fun.'

'Let's do it. You'll have a gorgeous view across the whole of Cannes; I really want you to see it. Shall we meet around eleven then I'll take you to lunch?'

'Okay,' Jess said, shyness washing over her. 'Here?'

'No. How about the crêpe kiosk? Then we can have a cheeky snack before we go – any excuse!'

'It's a da— a deal,' Jess stammered. Bryony rolled her eyes in the background.

'It's a *date*,' Leo confirmed. 'I better get back to it, but I'll see you tomorrow.' He pulled her in for another hug, slower than the first, as if they'd been partners for years and this felt completely natural to him. Her fingers lightly touched the silky skin on his back, afraid that if she pressed too hard she'd give herself away. Or seem like she was trying to give him a couples' massage.

It was nice to be hugged by someone who didn't know her. Not to be hugged through sympathy or habit, but hugged because one human in the world had found another that they liked and wanted to be close to them. She rested her head on his bare chest for a moment, his warmth being just the comfort blanket she needed.

He pulled back, just a little, and dipped his head down. Their faces were inches apart, and her eyes were now level with his mouth, with that grin. 'Have you been eating crêpes this evening?' he whispered.

'Yep,' she whispered back.

'Well that's a nice memory to leave me with.' He stood back, trailing his touch on her until the end, then with a wave and a 'See you soon' to Bryony and a 'See you tomorrow' to her, he jogged back to the yacht.

Jess turned and walked away, pulling Bryony with her. 'Okay, let's go.'

'Why so fast?'

'I don't want to watch him go. Well I do, but I'm a grown woman, not a teenager, so I don't *want to* want to watch him go.' They rounded the corner of the Palais des Festivals and Jess took off. She ran onto the public beach, kicking off her flip-flops, sliding past a group of partygoers daring one another to go skinny-dipping, and ending with a whoop and an attempt at the splits in the sand. 'I LIKE HIM,' she yelled at the silent superyachts lit up on the water.

Bryony caught up with her, carrying their flip-flops and laughing at her happy, silly friend, who seemed to be herself again.

'Sorry,' said Jess, pulling herself together. 'Why's he affecting me like this? I don't even know him.'

'Because you're a gold digger?'

'Ha, maybe that's it. Shall we go back to our beautiful hotel and watch some French TV? I don't think I can take any more excitement today.'

'Good idea. I'd like to get in a bit more research, too. Tomorrow is full-on again and I don't want to run out of time.'

They began the long walk back, following the length of the Croisette, with Jess feeling every bit the twinkling starlet, before they'd have to veer off and head far, far away from the sea.

As they passed Noix de Coco, the hostess with the braid – the one who'd been particularly dismissive of Jess and Bryony – was staggering up the steps with a huge tote bag branded with the restaurant logo and bulging with of cartons of takeaway food. The scowl on her face could have brought children to tears, and when she looked up and caught sight of who was coming towards her, it deepened still further.

The hostess stumbled on the last step and Jess leapt forward to catch her, instinct overriding the part of her that wouldn't have minded if she'd fallen on her face.

Jess grabbed the tote bag before it hit the floor, and steadied the hostess.

'*Merci beaucoup, mademoiselle*,' she said with such sarcasm that, for a moment, Jess didn't know what to say.

'That's ... okay?'

'No friends tonight?' the hostess sneered, straightening herself and trying to hide her blush.

'Um, not at the moment. Just the two of us. Two gals out on the town, hahaha ...' She trailed off, feeling silly.

'Well, we are full right now, there's a private event with lots of industry professionals, so you'll have to find somewhere else. No press allowed.'

'We weren't planning on coming in anyway,' said Jess, affronted, and then tried to shake it off, not wanting anything to ruin her evening and determined to hang on to her happy memory of being squished against Leo's chest.

Then Bryony, normally queen of cool, ruined it by becoming Journalist Bryony again. 'What kind or party?' She craned her neck. 'Are people like, *really partying*?'

'Hey, Bryony,' said Veronica Hay, appearing in a minidress with a shady-looking man on her arm, and pushing past the hostess and into Noix de Coco without a backward glance. 'I'll call you tomorrow about that piece.'

'Hi, Veronica,' Bryony replied, smirking at the hostess.

'Veronica Hay, huh?'

'Yes, I'm due to interview her while she's in Cannes. She sought me out, actually.'

'Really?' The hostess raised her eyebrows, a satisfied smile seeping over her face. 'As Bryony, journalist from *The Times*? Or as Bryony, journalist from *Sleb* magazine?'

'Okay, I don't think you should listen into your customers' conversations,' Bryony said, flustered. 'I'll have you know I write for both.'

'Come on,' said Jess, pulling at her arm, while the hostess nodded, her smile still in place.

'What's her problem? I will not be treated like that.' Bryony fumed as they strode back to the hotel.

'I'd guess embarrassment – she was made to look a bit stupid on that first night, then we saw her nearly fall over and that's always embarrassing ... and kind of funny.'

'It was funny. Next time, don't catch her.'

'I won't, I promise,' Jess said.

'Do you think she'll tell Veronica?'

'That you don't work for *The Times*? Maybe. She seems strangely vindictive. But it's highly possible she won't even get close enough to her to tattle.'

Bryony nodded.

'Would it be the end of the world if Veronica found out? I thought you didn't want to do a celebrity interview anyway?' Jess pressed.

'I know. It's just that this might be different.' She shrugged. 'It's nice that someone *wants* me to write about them for a change.'

'Then let's not let her ruin the mood, it's been a beeeeeautiful evening. Listen, shake her off.' Jess waggled Bryony's arms then took her twirling off down the street, singing 'Let It Go' at full volume.

Jess arrived at the crêpe kiosk far too early the following day, only to find Leo already there, sniffing the chocolate-scented air like nobody could see him. When he spotted her approaching, he spun around to put in an order at the kiosk.

She couldn't keep the smile from her face as she

looked at him standing there, probably just as yum in a teal linen shirt and dark shorts as he would be in a sharp suit on the red carpet.

He greeted her with an excited smile, a kiss on the cheek, a whiff of his aftershave and a crêpe. 'I didn't want to be late,' they both said at the same time.

Leo stood back and twirled for her. 'Guess what? I'm not sweaty today!'

'That's fantastic! I'm so impressed.'

'See, I know how to treat a lady on a date.'

So this was really a date then? Did that mean he actually might feel about her how she was beginning to feel about him? No, surely not ... she doubted he was doing the splits on the beach thinking about her.

'Okay, let's go.' He took her hand. Then dropped it again. Then picked it up again. 'Hmm. I want to hold your hand, but I don't know if you want me to, and I don't want to ask because I think if I say "*May I hold your hand*" it kind of takes the romance away, and you might think I'm a bit sappy. But if I don't ask, I'm kind of taking liberties. What would you do?'

'Would I hold my hand?' She tried to keep up, but the knowledge he wanted to hold her hand was a pretty big thing to wallop her with.

'If you were in my position. Here, let's walk, and I'm going to leave my hand dangling.' He started walking off, an exaggerated-casual walk, his open hand swinging by his side. Jess caught up with him and took his hand.

'How's that?'

'I like it.' He squeezed her hand in his big paw. 'And see, you were assertive: you didn't ask first.'

'I asked afterwards.'

'Maybe that's the way I should have gone.'

'Are we going to have this kind of debate when it comes to our first kiss?' she asked, blushing furiously even though she'd tried so hard to be cool. He looked down at her, eyes twinkling.

'Well, we'll see, won't we?'

'Yes, I guess we will.' She stared ahead and they began to walk up the hill. *So when was that going to happen, exactly?* she wondered.

They climbed slowly toward the grey-stone castle, threading their way through cobbled streets, past tall buildings painted in yellows and pinks with rosé-coloured roofs and peppermint-green window shutters. Pashminas of pink and purple bougainvillea swathed the houses, hugging the walls and spilling from window ledges, as sunshine poured through gaps in the leaves and left the pathways speckled in light and shade.

'How often do you frequent Cannes?' Jess asked Leo, not meaning to sound quite so stuffy.

'I've been to the festival for the last three years and sometimes I stop here at other times in the year, too.'

'For work?'

'Yep.'

'You don't seem too happy about it.'

'Oh, I love Cannes, outside of the festival, when it's a beautiful, calm seaside town. But during the festival, I don't know . . . ' He crinkled his nose at her, seeming shy. 'I don't feel like I fit in.'

'You don't? You're right: a hot, lovely man with a honking great superyacht definitely doesn't fit in here.'

He smiled. 'You think I'm lovely?'

'You're okay.'

'It's the party scene more than anything. In the business I'm in, it's par for the course, but I always feel like the dork in the corner just wishing it would all finish so I can go home and read a book with a cup of tea.'

'If you like a seaside town, maybe you should visit me someday. I live in the best one, and no party scene whatsoever, thank you very much.'

'That sounds like perfection. Maybe I will.'

Come and live in my house and eat in my café and kiss me in front of everyone, even Anthony, she found herself thinking. Oh! Anthony! She never replied to his email.

Oh well. 'Tell me more about your job. It's in the food industry, isn't it?'

'Indeed. You could say I cater to the whims of the hungry and the wealthy.'

'So do you have to attend a lot of parties to do that?'

'Not so much attend, just be involved in the creation of. It's really boring, to be honest.'

'But you're obviously good at it.'

'I think I'm okay.'

He looked a little uncomfortable so she changed the subject as they rounded another curve in the hill. 'So what kind of books do you wish you were at home reading while the party people enjoy the fruits of your labour?'

'*Fifty Shades of Grey* is a favourite, obviously,' he joked.

'Obviously.'

'Pretty much anything. I'd love to say I only read the classics and I'm very highbrow – actually I'd hate to say that, what kind of a pretentious snob would you think I was then?'

'A book is a book,' Jess agreed.

'And it's all just entertainment. So really I read whatever I find lying around. I read a Jackie Collins a few months ago,' he said proudly. 'And I finally read

Bill Bryson's new one, so now I've caught up with the rest of the world.'

'Okay, we're going to have to get married.'

'Right you are. You like Bill Bryson?'

'I love him, mostly his travel stuff, but anything he does really.'

'You like travelling?' Leo's eyes sparkled.

'I like the idea of travelling, but until now I've never really branched out. There's a big old world I need to see as soon as possible.'

'Where do you want to go?'

'America – Hollywood, specifically. I want to put my handprints in Marilyn Monroe's. And Greece. And Africa, I've wanted to see Botswana since reading *The No. 1 Ladies' Detective Agency* years ago. And Iceland, my parents went there with my brother when he was a baby and there are these great pictures of them all in a hot spring, my dad with a huge moustache and Lego hair, and my mum in a humongous seventies sunhat and a cigarette in a cigarette holder, and Cameron is just bawling his little eyes out and holding his willy.' Jess laughed at the memory; she loved that photo. She wished she'd been in it with them.

'I bet he loves that photo, and you telling people about it. So just a few places then. Let me know if you need a lift on my tugboat.'

They paused at a lookout point and Jess turned to him. 'Tell me truthfully,' she dared to ask. 'From a nomad to a total homebody, do you get sick of travelling? Or do you wish you could keep going for ever, until you've put your feet on every country and into every ocean?'

Leo took a moment to think this through, and she watched his handsome face, his eyes lost in thought gazing at the horizon behind her. His lips parted while he thought and she imagined kissing him. 'I don't think I'd ever get sick of seeing the world,' he said eventually, interrupting her daydreams. 'But having a base, a home to come back to, is essential. If you don't have that you'll never leave a footprint, no matter how many countries and seas you put your feet into.'

Jess turned back to the vista, thinking about her family and about herself, and about him. 'Those are some wise words, mister.'

'I am pretty wise. Like an owl.'

They continued up the hill finally reaching the crest and turned, Cannes pooling beneath them, a gentle valley covered in a blanket of buildings and a fringing of boats in the harbour. It really was perfection; the Côte d'Azur – from the people to the place – was every bit as lovely as she'd dreamed.

'So to read your books and grow so wise you must get some downtime in your job then?' asked Jess.

'Some – I can't complain. But then, if I don't do my work, plenty of other people will.'

She mulled over his words, thinking about her business back home. 'Do you know what? Sometimes I think I should tell myself the same thing.'

'With your chain of cafés?'

She winced, minutely, at the lie. 'Yeah. If I'm ever having a moan about how boring it is, I really should just think, *yeah but you chose this*, you know? I'm the boss, and I love having my cafés and making them exactly how I want them and not having to answer to anyone else. And giving people a little haven in which to read, or write, or natter, or even have a cry over a piece of cake if they want to. Sometimes I should shut up.'

'Sometimes I should shut up, too.'

'How about we both shut up and visit this castle you've been telling me all about?' And she took his hand again.

'You're very easy to talk to,' Leo said to Jess over lunch in what appeared to be the most exquisite restaurant in Cannes, high up on the hill with magnificent views, tablecloths as white as yachts and silverware so shiny it kept glinting the sun in her eyes.

'You started it,' she grinned.

'I mean it. I don't meet a lot of ladies in my job – don't raise your eyebrows, I'm not a girl-in-every-port kind of man.' That was nice to know. 'You don't seem to be like the usual crowd who come here for the parties.'

That's because she wasn't, she so wasn't. She was a big fakey faker invading his world. 'Well, I'm not so much here for the parties as here to get away from the real world.'

'This isn't the real world?'

'Not day-to-day,' she covered. 'Sometimes you just need to get away, you know? Just get away and be somewhere lovely and forget about it all.'

'Can I ask what you're trying to forget? You don't have to tell me.'

Jess sighed and stared out at the blue. 'Okay, so you know I said that sometimes I get a little bored at home and I've barely seen anything of the world?'

'Yep.'

'Well I guess I'm trying to forget what a big boring-head I've been.' She chose her words carefully. 'I have a lovely life, my café, *cafés*, are doing well, my family are close by, but I feel like I've been a bit wasteful.'

'In what way?'

'In that I *haven't* been making the most of what lies beyond my lovely little life. And suddenly I thought, what am I waiting for? Let's get out there and have some adventure.' She smiled.

'Cheers to that.' He raised his beer and clinked it with hers. 'What brought on this revelation?'

Jess chewed. Did she want to tell him? There was so much she felt she was already hiding from him, and it was tiring. Besides, she had nothing to be ashamed of, and if he reacted strangely maybe he wasn't as lovely as she hoped. 'I had a pregnancy scare about a month ago. And if I'd really been pregnant then great, that would still have been an amazing adventure. But when it turned out I wasn't, I realised that there were some things I wanted to experience before I get back to that place again. Does that make sense?'

Leo nodded, munching on a chip. 'It does. You know, I had a pregnancy scare once.'

Well that wasn't the response she expected.

'Yep, about five years ago now. Not me personally, I am not "with womanly parts". I was a . . . well . . . I was a twat about it. My girlfriend and I had been together for about a year, but I travelled a lot for work, even then, and she didn't like it very much. Then she got pregnant, told me the day before I was about to go away and I was horrible. I accused her of doing it to trap me, and off I went in a huff. Sorry, I've gone all red haven't I? It makes me so embarrassed thinking about it.' He gulped his beer, blushing, and Jess stayed quiet to let him continue, tiny strands of her heart connecting with his in unexpected ways. 'Anyway, so after a horrible goodbye I sat on my yacht, awake all night, and by the time the sun came up I couldn't believe what a lucky man I was. I wanted a little me who I could show the world to. I could picture him or her being a mini sea-dog and following me about on the deck, tiny feet slapping on the wood . . . '

Okay, he was making her ovaries ache.

'As soon as I had a signal I called her to apologise and tell her I'd stop my work and would come home, but she told me she'd got her period. That I didn't need to worry about it any more, but that at least my running away had shown her where my priorities lay. She was completely right to leave me, and I wasn't ready. I still felt – still feel – like the biggest knob ever, though.'

'Do you miss her?' Jess murmured.

'Oh no.' He shook his head. 'It was a long time ago now; I think she's married and has one if not two kids now. My point was just that I know what's it's like to think you should make the most of a second chance, even if you didn't necessarily want that second chance. And for us, that second chance was waiting a while before having babies.'

She nodded again, suddenly feeling very close to him.

'Did that freak you out a bit?' he asked, fiddling with his bottle. 'Do you think I'm a horrible person?'

'No. I think something that shifts the course of your life can mean people don't know how to act in the most perfect way. Did what I said freak you out?'

'Not at all. If anything, I was like, "Whatever, listen to *my* story".' He smiled. 'Sorry about that.'

They sat back, stomachs full, and Jess closed her eyes and let the sun's rays seep into her face. What an unforeseen amount of sharing. She liked how comfortable he was with her.

A kiss appeared on her lips, as warm as the Riviera air, his hot nose and forehead pressing softly against hers. She breathed in the beer on his breath and the salt in the air, listened to the sound of nothing, and after a few delicious seconds flickered her eyelids open behind the shield of her glasses, moments before his opened, just long enough to enjoy the ombré detail in his eyelashes and the tiny frown line between his brows.

Leo's eyes opened but he stayed close, his forehead

resting against hers, and they grinned at each other. 'Was it all right that I kissed you?'

'Yes, that was just fine,' she said, flustered. He nodded then sat back and picked up his beer again, but she could see the smile remain behind the rim of the bottle. *I think I like everything about you*, she thought.

'So you want some adventure, right?'

'Mmm-hmm.'

'Then why don't we turn one holiday into two. Fancy visiting another country while you're out here?'

'What do you mean?' She tried to drag her kissed mind back to the present.

'I'm free tomorrow, how about I take you to Monaco?'

Take me to Monaco? That was his idea of a second date? Being rich would be amazing. 'How would you just take me to Monaco? Is it nearby? Would we go on your yacht?'

'Let's not go on the yacht; let's take the train, just for something a bit different. It's a really nice journey and takes no more than an hour. Would that be okay?'

Little did he know that she'd spent eleven hours on a train getting to Cannes, but of course it was okay. 'Oh, do you know who would love Monaco? Bryony.' Bryony wouldn't love Monaco at all, but if she wanted a story about the richest of the rich it seemed only right that she visited.

'Bring her, too.'

'Would that be weird? It's not that I'm scared of being alone with you or that I think you'll kidnap me or anything.'

'No, it's fine. I'll bring Harvey. It'll be funny.'

'Monaco it is then. Though ...' She leant back towards him. 'If we have to spend tomorrow with other people, there are a few more things I insist we do today, mister.'

'What's that, missus?'

'I'm going to need to have some more kissing.'

'Did you ever see *To Catch a Thief*?' Jess asked early the following morning, tying a pink scarf around her neck and observing her reflection. Did she look like Grace Kelly? Not much. She took it off again.

'No, why?' Bryony said, applying mascara with one hand and tapping away on her laptop with the other. She was screenings-free today, so celeb scandals be damned, it was all about her personal project.

'Some of it was filmed in Monte Carlo.'

'I saw the film *Monte Carlo* with Selena Gomez once – don't even ask me why – but that was good.'

'Are you sure you don't mind coming along today? I feel a bit silly making you hold my hand.'

'I won't be holding your hand, I'll be squeezing information from Harvey – I think I can break him and get him to tell me all his secrets.'

Jess laughed. 'I have no doubt you will break him!'

'Not like that . . . much. I'll also be sleuthing my way around all the Ferraris and Bentleys. What car would you own if you were up to some illegal activity?'

Jess inspected her underarms for stray hairs. 'Ooh, a Ford V8 from the thirties.'

'Are you joking?'

'No – like Bonnie and Clyde drive. That would be the coolest thing, you know, if I were a crim.'

'Well I'd get myself a Rolls-Royce Phantom and ride about being like, *You just try and mess with me, losers, in my flippin' giant car.*'

'I guess it would depend what type of criminal you were. If you're going to be ripping people off selling fake Avon lippies door to door, you can't rock up in a Phantom.'

'And if you're about to perform a casino heist, you can't rock up in banged-up old Ford.'

'You know there's a casino in Monaco, right?' Jess's eyes twinkled.

'Yes, I'm aware. I take it we're going in?'

'How could we not?' If there was one thing Jess loved, it was practising her poker face.

An hour or so later, the foursome occupied a pod on the top level of the SNCF train from Cannes to Monaco. 'I can't believe we're going to Monte Carlo – this is the coolest thing. Cameron is going to be seething. *Monte Carlooooo*,' Jess sang, her hands in the air, despite the raised eyebrows of the other train passengers.

'Who's Cameron?' asked Harvey.

'Jess's brother,' Leo said.

'They have a very strange relationship,' Bryony explained in a mock whisper. 'Always determined to outdo the other, but they don't realise they're basically the same person.'

'I am not the same as him: he is stupid and a boy. No offence, boys.'

'None taken.' Leo watched her as she looked with infectious excitement out of the window.

'Besides, it's not a strange relationship, it's normal for siblings to argue.' She turned back to them. 'It's like the only person you're allowed to argue with without people thinking you're an arsehole. Ooh, look at that one!' Jess cried, pointing at a superyacht on the water. 'They just keep getting bigger the closer we get to Monaco. Leo, your boat don't impress me much any more,' she teased and Leo hooted. 'You guys are excited too, aren't you?'

'I'm well excited,' said Harvey, licking his lips at Bryony, who rolled her eyes and fluffed her hair.

'What are you most looking forward to seeing?' Leo asked Jess and Bryony.

'Place du Casino. I want to stand where the Formula One cars rocket by,' Jess replied, grinning.

'The Palace,' said Bryony.

'Ooh, I want to see the Palace, too,' Jess jumped in.

'Well we have all day, we can see whatever you like and maybe even split off from each other if some of us want to see things the others don't want to see.' Leo raised his eyebrows at Jess.

This was going to be a good day.

The walk from the station to Casino Square had Jess dragging her jaw along the ground. Every car and every yacht was super, and super-sized. The sole of every shoe was Louboutin. Every shop was exclusive. Everything was mesmerising.

At Place du Casino, where tourists leaned in as close

as they could get to the Bugattis without touching them, Jess stopped in the middle of the road for a moment. She closed her eyes and imagined with her whole body the asphalt shuddering under the power of the Grand Prix cars. She imagined the roar, and when she opened her eyes she looked around to see Leo standing protectively behind her, stopping a taxi in its tracks with his hand held up.

She grinned at him and moved to the pavement. 'Why thank you, sir.'

'My pleasure. What do you think?'

'So far . . . pretty wow. I think I prefer Cannes, but I'm willing to give Monte a fair chance to talk me around.'

Leo took her hand. 'I'm not even asking to hold your hand this time.'

'I'm not going to ask to kiss you,' Jess said, glancing around for Bryony and Harvey who'd melted into the crowd, and then kissed him on the lips, breathing in his aftershave and suntan lotion.

'Well fine, that told me,' he said.

'What do you guys want to do first?' Bryony asked, suddenly appearing with Harvey, who had a hazy look and a touch of Bryony's pink lipstick on his face. 'What is that? Is that my phone? Did you change my ringtone again?' She rifled in her handbag while

'Let It Go' shrilled out and Jess sniggered. 'Excuse me . . . Hello?'

'Bryony?' An unmistakable American voice purred down the phone.

'Is that Veronica?' Bryony mouthed, *'It's Veronica Hay'* at the others.

'Veronica Hay?' said Harvey. 'Nice. But I like my women a bit feistier.' He looked Bryony up and down who shooed him away, but with a minuscule smile while doing so.

'How are you?' she asked Veronica.

'Good thanks, just having some cupping.' She moaned and Bryony frowned at the phone.

'Do you want to call me back when you're . . . done?'

'No, it's – uuuuuhhhhhh – it's fine. Mmm, right there. I'm on the carpet later in a backless dress so it's now or never.'

'Okay.'

'Have you ever been cupped? Really hard?'

'I guess . . . ' Oh God, it was like being asked by someone you barely know about when you lost your virginity.

'It feels good but it's so boring, huh? After half an hour I'm just like, stop sucking on me.'

'Uh-huh.'

'But like I said, I'm on the carpet later on. All the serious actresses get cupping and then show it off: it makes you look more Hollywood Zen.'

'Oh! Cupping therapy! Blobs and pink marks – I'm with you.'

'What did you think I meant?'

'Honestly, I thought you were being groped.'

Veronica howled with laughter. 'I know I said I wanted to give you an exclusive, but not a damn sex audiotape! You don't work for the tabloids, sweetie!'

'Absolutely not.' She moved away from the group. 'Did you have a good time at Noix de Coco the other night?' In other words, did she speak to the hostess?

'No,' Veronica answered vaguely. 'So when shall we do this interview?'

Shit. Bryony didn't quite know what she was going to do about this yet. 'In a few days?' she stalled.

'Fine. I can't do this weekend, or Monday because I'm holing up in a spa to recover from the weekend. But we're going to do this interview, Bryony.'

'I'm looking forward to it.'

'I need you on board. This is going to be a big freaking deal, the biggest of my life. It won't have the same impact coming from anyone other than *The Times* – do you understand?'

'Yes.'

'Cool, later. Uhhhhhhh.' Veronica hung up and Bryony stood for a moment feeling nauseous. Then, to add to her queasy stomach, a text message appeared from Mitch, perpetuating Bryony's deep-rooted fear that he was somehow watching her with hidden cameras:

I need some dirt from you ASAP. It's disappointing that I have to keep chasing you for this. Make sure it's juicier than an orgy in a Tropicana factory. LOL.

Bryony sighed and walked back to the others, slapping on a smile.

'Pals with Veronica Hay, huh?' Leo said. 'You guys are so in the in-crowd.'

Bryony nodded. 'When you're a hand model you tend to meet a lot of celebs at photo shoots and things. Anyway, enough about me. Did we decide what stop one would be?'

'Does anyone want to go in the casino for a little while?' asked Jess, salivating a tiny bit.

'I'm not sure Harvey's old enough to get in,' Bryony teased.

'Hey now, if I was older you'd have no interest in my fit young body – don't pretend.'

'Please, I have my own fit young body. Why would I need yours?'

'You are *killing* me, girl.'

They entered through the guarded doors of the Casino de Monte Carlo into a world of polished marble and chandeliered opulence. Despite the setting, however, the soundtrack of tinkling slot machines, chatter, rolling dice and whoops of delight meant they could have been in any casino in the world.

Leo caught Jess's eye. 'Look how excited you are. You're always so happy; I like that a lot. Now, do you want to watch or do you want to play?'

She squeezed his hand, her eyes flittering from table to table, taking in the snapping of the cards and the pushing of chips. 'I'm going to play.'

'Take it easy, Jess,' Bryony warned quietly as she practically skipped on ahead. 'Don't get thrown out this time.'

'This time?' asked Leo.

'I won't.' She fixed Bryony with a completely blank look, like her hard drive had been wiped clean. It was a face she could only ever manage in this setting. It was her perfect poker face.

'Then let's do this. Blackjack okay, gents?'

'HIT ME!' Leo cried for the third time, pushing his eighteen over to a twenty-four. The croupier scooped up his chips and he grinned at Jess. 'Ah, beaten again. This is fun though, huh?'

'Are you sure you're enjoying it? You must be down quite a bit.' But he could afford it, she guessed.

'It's brilliant. You're a bit bloody good, though.'

She leant in to him, beaming, and gave him the smooch of someone feeling utterly pleased with themselves. *Yeah, I know I'm hot shiz right now*, she thought happily, *feel free to worship me for a while.* They played another hand, her coming out on top again with twenty. The croupier twitched and Jess caught him giving a small signal to someone behind them. *Uh-oh, time's up.*

'Shall we call it a day, darling?' Jess asked, turning to Leo. 'Time to go, I think. Thank you so much,' she said to the croupier, gathering her chips and leaving a couple for him as a tip. 'Leo, I'll just go and cash these in. Can you grab Bryony and Harvey?'

'Sure, do you know where they went?'

'They're snogging behind a sculpture to the left of the high-rollers' tables. They think we can't see them, but actually the whole casino can thanks to those massive mirrors.'

She was bursting with pride as she cashed in her

chips for five hundred and twelve euros. Not one loss. She should wager higher, she supposed, but nerves always took over.

The four of them stepped back out into the sunshine, Jess feeling a million – well, five hundred – bucks.

'So tell me,' Leo said, taking her hand like it was an old habit. 'Where did that come from?'

'I'm good at blackjack, what can I say? A girl has to have some hidden talents.' She took her wad of notes and fanned herself with it. *Not such a faker now, am I?*

Bryony snorted. 'She's not just good, she's banned-from-a-casino good. That's right, Little Miss Sunshine's a pretty hardcore high-roller.'

'What?' Leo laughed.

'It's not as bad as it sounds; it was all a misunderstanding. I'm just ... I'm good at maths and I'm good at remembering things, and I just *get* blackjack. Then this one casino we went to on a friend's hen night thought I was cheating.'

Harvey whooped. 'Mate! Are you saying you were caught counting cards?'

'No, shush,' Jess blushed, glancing back at the security guards on the casino doors. 'I wasn't intentionally card-counting; it's just that I keep an eye on what's going on. It's an effective strategy.'

'Criminal-you is very sexy.' Leo grinned down at

her, chuckling, and she felt all her bits do a mini cha-cha-cha. 'What now, ladies?'

Jess looked across the road at the busy, famous restaurant. 'Let's go to Café de Paris, people-watch and spend the hell out of my winnings!'

Four hours later they were still sitting at their al-fresco table, the hot Monaco sun beating down, and the last drops of champagne and crumbs of blinis finally hoovered up.

Leo's phone rang, and he untangled himself from Jess and stole a quick smooch before excusing himself for a moment. He walked a short distance away from the brasserie; Harvey sat up and watched him carefully, his face becoming serious.

'Well I think we should go and see the Palace before it's too late,' Jess said. She stretched, lazily, languidly, like she could happily stay there all day to be quite honest. 'This fizz and nibbles are on me.'

'No way, man. What kind of a gentleman would I be then?' said Harvey, one eye still on Leo.

'Is everything okay?' asked Jess, glancing at Leo who was waving a hand around in frustration as he spoke. 'Is it work?'

'Um, sort of, yeah. We've got a business thing coming up and it's kind of sensitive.'

'Sensitive?' asked Bryony.

Harvey sighed. 'Rich people, eh? No offence. But we're all demanding buggers at times, aren't we?'

'What do they want from you, these rich people?' Bryony probed further. 'Can you tell me a bit more about it?'

Harvey squirmed. 'It's not really something I should talk about. You wouldn't get it anyway, love.' He grinned, knowing that would get a rise out of her.

But Bryony wasn't distracted that easily. 'Do you two do a lot of business with rich people?'

'Of course they do, Bry,' Jess interrupted, laughing. 'Stop pestering him. Is there anything we can do to help?'

'No!' Harvey said quickly.

'Okay. Well, anyway – back to the bill. My winnings cover it, it's nothing.' It wasn't nothing, but you know what? A few hours ago she didn't have this money, so so what?

'Leo will never forgive me, man.'

'Well Leo bought me a very fancy lunch yesterday, and it's not the fifties, so if I want to pay I damn well will.'

'Are you sure, Meems?' Bryony whispered to her.

'Let me put what I can on expenses. Let Mitch treat us to at least half this bottle of champers.'

'Okay, but we'll sort it out back at the hotel,' Jess whispered back. 'Come on, let's go.'

She paid and they made their way out of the restaurant and over to Leo, who was standing, still on the phone, with his back to them.

He sounded agitated. 'No, I'm busy today; I'm out of the country . . . Can't you tell him? . . . And it has to be tonight? . . . Fine, fine, I'll drop it off tonight when it's ready, but don't call me again today, okay?' Leo hung up and turned around, the frown on his face clearing like drifting rainclouds at the sight of Jess, and he pulled her close. 'Stupid work. What are we doing now?'

'You okay?'

'I'm fine, just the demands of divas again. Shall we go up to the Palace, Princess Grace?'

'You read my mind.'

They strolled through the gold-paved (not really) streets of Monaco; Leo took Harvey off ahead, leaving Bryony and Jess together.

'Do you think he's a bit cagey about what he does for a living?' Bryony asked Jess when they were out of earshot.

'Harvey?'

'Leo. Well, both of them, I guess, but I assumed Harvey was Leo's pal along for the ride, or maybe his assistant.'

'I don't know. Maybe Leo is a bit secretive, but I'm being the same with him, I guess, so I can't exactly complain. I wonder if he doesn't like his job any more, whatever it is. You know when you're in a job you hate and then someone asks, "How's work? Tell me about your job!" and it's the last thing you want to talk about because it stirs up all the feelings of sadness and resentment? I think it's like that with him.'

'But he's the boss, surely? If he doesn't like it can't he do something about it?'

'Maybe it's not that easy. Most of the time he seems fine with it, whatever "it" is, but he's not really part of the schmoozy rich-list set. He doesn't seem to want to be at the festival, hanging out, being seen, so maybe he has to be here for business but doesn't really like this bit of what he does.'

'Yeah ... I want to know *what* he does, though.'

'Well you would, you're a journalist.'

'Don't you want to know?'

'Of course I want to know, but he's opened up to me about a lot of other, non-work stuff so I figure this will come too, when he's in the mood to chat about it. There's no rush.' Jess sighed with a happy drunkenness and they walked on in silence, enjoying the tranquillity of the pretty backstreets. But finally Jess couldn't wait any longer. 'So what do you think of Harvey, really? Because he's practically on heat for you.'

'I don't know about that – he keeps calling me "mate". He *is* funny, though. And I like his hair.'

'And he's a good smoochywoochywooer? Good at the old lip-flapping?'

'We haven't kissed!'

'You barely *stopped* kissing to come up for champagne!'

'Fine,' Bryony sighed. 'Yes, he's hot as hell and I'm like the Christian Grey to his Ana Steele, but without the bondage. But it's all for research, of course.' Bryony winked and squeezed Jess's hand.

'And how's that going?'

'Well, I think just a little more coaxing and he'll admit to everything.'

'God, you're like a torturist. *Torturist?*'

'Tortur*er*, and no I'm not, not really. I'm finding out a lot about what yacht parties are really like, though.'

'On Leo's boat?' That didn't sound very him.

'I'm not sure. Maybe, but I expect Harvey's been to a lot of others, too. Wow!'

They had rounded the corner into an enormous

square with a huge peach palace standing proudly at one end. They walked closer and Jess had to stop and stare.

'Shall we live here?' Leo asked, rejoining her. 'Shall we buy this place and come and live here?'

'Yes, let's.'

'And no more real world?'

'None at all, just you and me baby,' she said, winking. 'I love Grace Kelly. Have you seen her in *Rear Window*?'

'That's my favourite. You really like old movies, don't you?'

Jess nodded. 'And old movie stars, especially Marilyn. Classic Hollywood just fascinates me, and Marilyn Monroe was so iconic, this Norma Jean who changed who she was with a little hair and make-up and became the world's biggest star, living the most fascinating life.' She shrugged. 'There's something about that little scenario that intrigues me.'

Leo stroked her hair and it sent tingles down the back of her neck. 'You don't have to change anything to be a star, you know. And thank you – I'll accept my Oscar for best leading male with the cheesiest lines now.'

Chortling, Jess turned back to the Palace. 'I wonder if Grace Kelly ever wanted to escape this life. Or maybe this was the escape she needed.'

'Hmm, that's a thinker.'

They strolled around the Palace courtyards and the surrounding streets until the sun started to dip, Bryony even allowing Harvey the pleasure of carrying her handbag for her when they weren't snogging against a wall, or a lamp post, or a cannon. Eventually they found a lookout point that gave them a view of Monaco harbour and rested their weary feet.

The two couples sat a distance apart from each other, Bryony and Harvey mixing between arguing and kissing, and Jess and Leo leaning against each other watching the twilight roll in.

Leo entwined his arms around Jess and brought his warm face to her ear. 'I like you.'

She smiled. 'I like you, too.'

'You don't really have to leave at the end of the festival, do you?'

'Maybe you could sail around and dock that dinghy off Cornwall.'

'I could do that. I like having you around, you make me feel less grumpy.'

'You've never seemed grumpy to me.'

'Well I am. I'm like Grumpy Cat.' He pulled a big frown. 'But then you appeared, scoffing your crêpe and making fun of my nipples, and I thought, I like this girl.'

Jess glowed like a sunset in the incoming darkness. What lovely things to say. And then her heart was pierced by an ache despite his delicious lips on hers. Her Cinderella moment was steadily counting down to midnight.

They were almost asleep by the time the train rolled back into Cannes, the sunshine, the walking and the midday champers having tired them all out, and four weary explorers climbed off at the station.

'Well that was a good second date,' Jess said softly up to Leo.

Then came a voice from behind them. 'Leo? You *are* back in town!'

The four of them turned to see the mean braided hostess from Noix de Coco, her arms open wide and a *voulez-vous coucher avec moi ce soir* look in her eyes.

'Céline.' Leo greeted her, leaning in for a hug that made both Jess and Bryony's jaws drop. 'How are you?'

'Very well. How are you? I haven't seen you since last year, on your yacht.' Her words dripped with suggestion.

'Yeah, I've been keeping quiet. You remember Harvey, and this is Bryony and Jess.' He took Jess's hand, which nearly caused Jess to punch the air in a fit of bubbly smugness.

'Ah, *oui*. I know ... Bryon and Jen, is it? They hang around the restaurant, they are very popular.' Céline then turned to Jess and purred, 'Leo comes all the time.'

'I used to go occasionally,' he clarified.

'We miss you. I will come by the yacht sometime soon and maybe we can do a little business?' Céline said quietly.

'Well it was great seeing you again. Off home now?' Leo said.

'Oh, you don't live in Cannes?' asked Bryony, a sickly smile on her face.

'No, too many tourists, too many people pretending they're someone they're not. Remember how annoying we always found that, Leo?' He nodded. '*D'accord*. Bye-bye, baby.' She leant in for a kiss but Leo swerved away, giving her no more than another swift hug.

They left the train station and Leo said, 'So you know Céline', when they were out of earshot of Harvey and Bryony.

'Not really, she was just a little snooty when we went to the restaurant – didn't seem to think we should be there, as if we weren't important enough.'

'Well, if she'd known you were friends with the girls on the yacht next to mine she would have changed her tune.'

'How do *you* know Céline?' Jess asked, dreading the answer.

'She hangs out at the marina all through the festival, trying to get invited onto the party yachts. She's a big wannabe.' Jess felt a pang of shame – is that how he'd view her if he knew the truth? 'She's only nice to the people she thinks can get her things. Shall we walk you guys back to your hotel?'

'No, thank you, but we'll get a taxi. Don't want Harvey getting any ideas.'

'Okay.' Leo hailed a cab for them. 'Can I see you tomorrow?'

'Sure, give me a call when you're free. I had such a nice time today.'

'It was fun, wasn't it? I like your lip balm.'

'You do?' She grinned, knowing they were both remembering their kisses throughout the day . . . it was like being back on a school trip again. Jess reached up and wrapped her arms around Leo, sinking into another yummy smooch. This man . . .

No sooner had the taxi pulled away than Bryony cursed. 'Shit! I've left my bollocking phone in Harvey's pocket.'

'What was your phone doing in his pocket?' Jess laughed, yawning. She was beat.

'It was – we were – the camera on my phone's better . . . it doesn't matter. Anyway, I'd better go and get it. *Excusez-moi*, erm, stop *le taxi s'il vous plaît*?'

'Can you get it tomorrow?'

'Better not. You go on, and I'll see you back at the hotel.'

'No way.' Jess sat up and forced her eyes open wider as the taxi rolled to a stop. 'I'm not leaving you to walk back alone. I'll come with you.'

'Have you seen how busy these streets are? I couldn't be alone during the film festival even if I wanted to be. Seriously, go. I'll pop over to the marina, grab my phone and then be right behind you.'

'If you'll be that quick why don't we both swing over there?'

Bryony sighed and raised her eyebrows. 'Because, my innocent little Doris Day, maybe I *won't* be that quick . . . *capiche*?'

'Oh!' cried Jess. 'You and Harvey are *so* going to be up a tree, doing God knows what! Did you make up that stuff about your phone?'

Bryony gathered her bag and opened the cab door. 'No, I really did leave it in his pocket and I really do need it, but sometimes you don't know where things might lead. And frankly, I'm open to being led right now. Or leading him.' She winked and, with that, disappeared.

Jess settled back in the taxi and thought of Leo. She rolled around thoughts in her head about whether or not she should turn the taxi around, send it to the marina, and pay him a late-night visit. As if she hadn't seen enough of him today, delicious thoughts of the two of them filled her mind and warmed her body. But no ... not *quite* yet.

Bryony strode past crowds of partygoers mingling in front of the yachts. Kissing Harvey had been a lot of fun today; she was a sucker for a younger man, ever since the *Desperate Housewives* gardener storyline. Would she take things further? Maybe. Lips aside, he was fun, he was funny, and he made her smile. He reminded her not to take herself too seriously, a quality he shared with Jess, though she wasn't about to let on about that quite yet.

He was also proving to be a great source of information, telling her all sorts of anecdotes which, although were perhaps a little too libellous for what she was hoping to write, were certainly opening her eyes. He'd alluded to the enormity of the business deals and money that could shift hands when so many millionaires were concentrated in one place, but had closed off when she'd tried to probe further.

She neared their yacht and stopped and smiled when she saw Harvey standing outside, his T-shirt tucked into his back pocket, staring out to sea. Under the harbour lights the muscles in his back shone. She was about to call out when Leo emerged from the back of the boat, pushing a large trunk; instinct told her to duck into the shadows and watch.

'Mate, do you have to go tonight?' Harvey asked him.

'I'm just going to drop it off. They can divide it up and do the rest. There must be some pretty big cheeses coming to this after-party for them to whack on an extra order of this size. Oi!' He slapped Harvey on the back. 'This is a good thing. The more we get off the boat, the better. Less time with this lot means more time with Jess and Bryony, hey?'

'She is fine . . .' murmured Harvey, at which Bryony smiled to herself.

'I better go. You stay here and make sure no one else comes on the boat while I'm out, okay?'

'All right, mate. Take care.'

Leo hauled the box up onto his shoulder and struggled off down the marina.

Hmm ... Bryony stepped out and walked over to Harvey. 'Hi.'

'Bryony!' He jumped, then took her face between his palms and kissed her.

She stumbled back and laughed. 'Down, boy!'

'What are you doing back here? Couldn't keep away from my hot body, right?'

'Something like that. And I left my phone in your pocket.'

Harvey tapped the side of his jeans and his face dropped a touch. 'Mate, you're right. I've left it inside: I'll go and get it for you – hang on.'

'Why don't I come on in and see this fancy ship of yours?' Bryony held her breath as he locked eyes with her, a smile on his lips and his hot breath on her face. It was happening.

No it wasn't. He growled, 'Gaaahh, I want you to come inside so bad but now is just not a great time, man.'

'Not a great time? I just saw Leo leave. Where was he going, by the way?'

'He'll be back soon, and I can't let you on,' Harvey said, squirming.

'What was in the box?'

'Just … food. Wait here for one second.' Harvey dashed inside the boat and came out again carrying her phone in record speed. She snatched it off him, feeling a little snubbed, and also a bit embarrassed.

'Fine, I'll go then. But don't be surprised if I don't make this offer to you again, kid.' She gave him a parting kiss he wouldn't forget in a hurry, and marched away.

'Jess, wake up. Meems!'

Jess came to in the pitch dark, with Bryony prodding her face. 'Why do you keep waking me up, lady? This is not how a holiday's supposed to be.'

'I can't sleep.'

'Poor you. Have you tried counting the number of times you've woken me up? That might send you off to dreamland.' Jess yawned and rolled away from her bed-buddy.

'Jess, don't go back to sleep.'

'I was having such a nice dream. I won fifty million pounds in the casino and bought a yacht even bigger than Leo's and we connected them with a walkway.'

'You didn't live in the same yacht?'

'No, we both wanted our independence; we were being very Helena Bonham-Carter and Tim Burton. They lived in separate houses, you know, before the divorce, but next door to each other. Uhhh, I guess I'm awake now. What can I do for you, ma'am?' Jess rolled back to face Bryony and sat up. 'Why's your laptop on?'

'I've been doing some more research.'

'Find out anything good?'

'I don't want to talk about it,' Bryony demurred.

Jess rolled over again. 'Okay, night then.'

'Wait, I don't want to talk about it but I have to. I can't sleep, Jess, it's going round and round in my head.'

Jess sat up again, as Bryony sounded close to tears. 'What's up? Did you find out something bad?'

'I might have.'

'About Cannes?'

'Sort of.'

'Okay, Lassie, I can't guess all of this. How about you give me a ballpark?'

Bryony closed her laptop, plunging them into darkness. 'Right ... Right ... So you know I've been researching the illegal activity that goes on during the Cannes Film Festival?'

'Yep.' *Yawn.*

'But I don't want to be a trashy journalist – I'm not just trying to make up stories where there isn't anything.'

'I know.'

'And I'm not trying to sensationalise anything. I think the festival is great, and fun, and I don't for a second think the whole thing is based on some seedy underworld of corruption, I'm just finding that there are elements of the kind of things that happen all over the world when wealthy partygoers descend on a place.'

'Like the prostitutes?'

'And the drugs.'

Jess yawned again. 'Oh good, you got somewhere on the drug thing? That would make a good story . . . Bryony? Did you fall asleep?'

'Can I show you something?' She opened her laptop again, temporarily blinding Jess with white light from the screen. She quickly minimised the open web page in which Jess, in her half-asleep state, spotted something she vaguely recognised. 'Look,' Bryony said, opening a page on a news site. 'This is a story from a few years ago about drugs being smuggled into somewhere in the Caribbean using a superyacht. Millions of pounds' worth of cocaine was found on board. But it was all really shady; politicians got involved, the police officers investigating were suspended and there wasn't a lot of resolution.'

'What's this got to do with Cannes?'

'I think someone, probably several people, are supplying the rich and famous with drugs during the festival.'

'Well yeah, I expect they are. It's no secret that some people take drugs. Even small-town Norma Jean me knows that.'

'But I think it's a big business; I think it's brought in on the superyachts.'

'You think Tara and her party again?'

'No, I think it's going to be people that probably don't let other people on their boat very often, who stay away from the actual party scene as much as they can.'

'I guess that makes sense.'

'Jess?'

'Yes, Miss Marple?'

'Do you see what I'm saying?'

Jess fell silent. What was she supposed to be understanding here? She stretched, her brain still clinging desperately to the fading, fragmented memories of her lovely dream of living on dual superyachts with Leo. Leo ... 'No,' she laughed.

'I think—'

'No you don't,' Jess interrupted, throwing off the duvet. *'No you don't.'*

'It was after I was speaking to Harvey today. Some things just didn't quite add up.'

'He's twenty-two, nothing adds up. Like what?'

'Like ... they're both very secretive about their work, they obviously make an absolute fortune, they have zero interest in the film festival or the people, but tolerate it. Don't you wonder why?'

'Because of work. We all tolerate things because of work. I hate lemon cake – there, I've said it – but I sell it every flipping day because other people want it.'

'But what does he, what do *they*, do?'

'Catering. I don't know the specifics, but rich people like rich food. Maybe he's dealing caviar or something.'

Bryony changed tack. 'Okay, as you know I went to see Harvey tonight. When I got there Leo was about to make a pretty late-night delivery, and Harvey was ridiculously cagey about letting me on the boat. It all looked a bit ... I don't know ... secretive. And then when I got back here ... well, let me show you something.' Bryony opened the browser window she'd minimised and a familiar image filled the screen. 'That's Leo's boat, I think.'

Jess sat in silence, her arms folded. She stared at

the screen and, in the darkness, Bryony watched her face carefully. Did she understand? Should she not have said anything? Bryony had always trusted her journalist's instincts, but suddenly she wished she'd never opened her mouth.

'You know what, let's forget this. I'm just tired and clutching at straws. Go back to sleep.' Bryony went to close her laptop.

'What website is that?' Jess asked, her small hand reaching out to stop the screen from shutting.

'This is a website about superyachts on a registered watch-list.'

'Registered by who?'

'The police.' Bryony winced. *I love you, Meems, I'm sorry.*

Jess sighed. 'So you just googled his boat and found it there? Maybe all the superyachts are on there.'

'Jess—'

'No, he's not . . . ' she spat.

'Jess,' Bryony stood up and padded over to her friend. 'I'm sorry, but I think maybe, only maybe, that Leo – and Harvey – might be trafficking drugs.'

Part Three

'You think Leo is a drug smuggler? That's ridiculous.'
Jess raised her eyebrows at Bryony, though her heart
was beating fast. *Ridiculous*. It was time to turn this
conversation off and retire to dreamland again. She
slapped a smile onto her worried face. 'Okay, I'm going
to go back to sleep.'

Bryony put the laptop aside. 'I just wanted to—'

'You just wanted a story, I get it, but this is such a
non-story. Don't be that journalist, just making stuff
up.'

'I'm not being *that journalist*. I don't want to have
found this, or to make you sad, but I had to tell you.
And you're right, it's probably nothing.'

'Of course it's nothing.' Jess walked to the window
and looked out at Cannes in the darkness. She chewed
her lip. Leo was not a drug smuggler, or a drug dealer.

Drug dealers were shady and horrible and wore baggy clothes and gold jewellery; she'd watched *Breaking Bad*, she knew the type. But then, that was about an ageing chemistry teacher who seemed normal but dealt crystal meth ... And her life was so sheltered, how would she even know what 'the type' was, really? But *Leo*? He hated the whole party scene. It couldn't be true – he made her happy. 'No. It's not him.'

'Jess—'

'It's not HIM, he's my—' Jess stopped herself and slumped down onto the bed, her face in her hands. Eventually, she raised her head and looked into Bryony's eyes. 'He's my favourite thing about this year. Don't tell me he's not real.'

'Meems,' Bryony shuffled closer. She paused before speaking again, carefully. 'Jess, none of *this* is real.'

'I know.' Jess felt very small as she remembered everything Leo had told her, or not told her, about his job. And everything she'd embellished or left out about her own life. This wasn't the start of a relationship, it was an improv show.

'Look, I'm really not going to be *that journalist*. I'm not going to plough ahead and try to get Mitch to print a story just because of an internet watch-list and a few things adding up in my head. I wouldn't run anything without proper evidence, okay?'

'Do you have to keep looking into him?' Jess asked, soaked through with sadness.

'Would you really not want to know, and just hope?'

Jess lifted herself from the edge of the bed and climbed back under the covers. 'I think you're wrong, that it can all be explained. I know you want a story, but I'm sure this isn't it.'

'Maybe you're right.'

'I'll prove it.'

'You'll help me?'

'I'll help prove there's nothing dodgy about them. First thing tomorrow I'm going to ask him flat out what he does for a living.'

'And you let me know what he says, and if you believe him.' Bryony also climbed under the covers and, being such a small bed, their feet touched.

'Of course.'

'Jess?'

'Mmm-hmm?' She was beginning to drift now, a sad, lost sleep of someone who could no longer keep up with the world she was trying to live in.

'You have to let me know honestly.'

'About what?'

'About if you believe him, and about anything else you find.'

'I'll be honest.' But would she? Could she be part of the undoing of someone who'd already pulled up a little chair inside her heart? Or, if it came to it, would she cover it up and just drift away, pretending they'd never been there?

When Jess woke up again it was light, and the room was utterly silent. Bryony had gone – working, probably – and Jess lay in bed, staring up at the ceiling and not moving her body even a centimetre. Was Leo a drug smuggler?

She laughed out loud, the sound reverberating loudly on the four hushed walls. Of course he wasn't a drug smuggler; her life wasn't an episode of *24*.

Pulling her tired body out of bed, she opened the curtains to another glorious day in the South of France. 'It's the Cannes Film Festival,' she told the slightly grimy window. 'It's classy and it's fun, and it's definitely not full of drug dealers.'

As Jess showered she felt a little lighter. Why was it that things always seemed a much bigger deal in the night-time, and by the morning could seem so silly?

But try as she might, she couldn't shake the

unsettled feeling. 'Goddamn my stupid brain,' she muttered, picking up her phone and scrolling through her photos of Monaco from the day before. Photos of her and Bryony holding up her winnings outside the casino; the four of them at the Palace; one of Bryony looking in a shop window while Harvey checked out her behind; Leo's finger pointing at something, getting right in the way of her picture of the harbour. And one of Leo and Jess cheek to cheek, the view of Monte Carlo behind them. Jess looked flushed, with her teeth bared too much and her eyes too wide, but so happy, and Leo looked happy too, didn't he?

Yes. She put on a swingy, star-patterned dress and curled her hair slightly, then looked in the mirror. Leo was happy with her, of that she was sure, and she wouldn't let anyone take that away from her. But whether he was smuggling drugs in his superyacht? Well, she'd just have to ask him, wouldn't she?

'I wanted to ask you something.' Jess's voice wavered; she was nervous of what the end of the conversation might bring.

'Sure.' Leo smiled. 'Go ahead.'

Jess had hovered by the marina for a good fifteen minutes, the sun on the back of her neck as she watched him and Harvey sitting on deck, poring over paperwork, while she rehearsed what she was going to say. It was only when Tara had leaned over the side of her yacht to empty the remains of a bottle of bubbly into the sea and spotted Jess, yelling, 'AHOY, SAILOR, YOU WANT SOME CHAMPERS?' that Leo and Harvey had looked up and spotted her. Leo had hopped ashore and jogged over to her, and her time was up.

'Well . . . ' Jess fidgeted. 'Well, I just realised—'

'Wait,' Leo interrupted and pulled her in close to him. She put her hand on his chest to stop him – she shouldn't go any further until this was resolved – but became distracted by his yumminess and forgot to pull away, so suddenly his lips were kissing her in the bright, hot morning light. Tara whooped from the hot tub.

Let him go, let his lips go, no do NOT put your tongue in there, she scolded herself.

'You were saying, you lovely lady?' Leo pulled away and she took a moment to catch her breath and look at his face, fresh and perfect.

Focus, Jess. 'Yes, anyway. Thank you, by the way, for the kissing, it was nice and much appreciated.' She cleared her throat. 'So I just realised, and I've probably done exactly the same thing so I'm totally not blaming you, but we've chatted about so much and I was thinking, do you know what? I've never actually properly asked you this thing!' She tittered at the hilarity of the whole situation.

'It's fine, go ahead. Ask me,' he said quickly, seeming a little rushed.

Jess tried to remain light and breezy. She tried to ignore the fact that as soon as the words were out of her mouth it felt as if her heart had plopped out of her chest and thudded to the ground. 'Um, so what is it you actually do for a living?'

She wished she hadn't asked. She didn't want to know, and now the babbling was coming, she could feel the desperate *blah blah blah* rising to defuse the situation. 'Not that you need to earn a *living* per se: just look at your yacht. Not that money's everything. Maybe it's nice to work even if you're loaded, but I'm not asking you about your money, that would be so rude of me – could you imagine? I was just wondering what your job actually was, or is, or was. I mean, you're so successful ... ' she trailed off, out of things to say. Now it was Leo's turn.

He looked around to see if anyone was listening – that was a bit strange, wasn't it? What, did he work for MI6?

Maybe he worked for MI6. Maybe he was trying to *catch* the drug dealers at it!

Oh my God, James Bond has kissed me. SEVERAL times.

'I work in catering,' he said carefully, after an eternity. He was definitely still holding back, and she had to keep asking. It was now or never.

'But what does that mean? Do you own restaurants, or are you a chef?'

'Yep.'

'Which?'

'Oh, um . . . both. Well, I used to be a chef and now I own some restaurants.'

'Which ones?'

'Little fancy overpriced ones in a few corners of the world. It's kind of boring really.'

'Yeah, sounds mega-dull.' Jess watched his face. Was he telling the truth? 'Whereabouts in the world?'

'Fiji. And . . . Hawaii. And . . . Miami.'

'That's a lot of places ending in "i".'

'Oh yeah. Also in Barbados—' He snapped his fingers. 'That ends in "s".'

'Bryony's been to Barbados! What's it called? Maybe she went there.' She felt awful, trying to catch him out.

'She's been to Barbados?' he sighed.

'Well . . . maybe.'

'So anyway, lovely lady, do you want to do something tomorrow? Maybe—'

'Would you cook for me?' She intercepted his sneaky change of subject.

And then, for the first time during these awkward few minutes, Leo looked relieved, a happy expression washing over his face. 'Can I? Tomorrow?'

'You really don't have to.' She realised she'd been a bit forceful. If he had been a chef, maybe cooking was the last thing he'd want to do now. Like asking a hairdresser to hang out and practise Pinterest hairstyles with you.

'I want to,' he insisted, positively fidgeting with excitement. 'I'm really good.'

'Where would you cook for me?'

'On my boat. Yes, that would be perfect. Oh, perfect. Is tomorrow okay?'

She wanted proof, and here he was begging her to let him prove his profession. His profession of chef, not drug dealer. 'What kind of a chef are you?'

'A bloody good one. Please, let me show you tomorrow. Unless you want to eat out? I mean, you're on holiday – you were probably hoping to try all the best restaurants. I can take you out if you'd prefer.'

'No, staying in sounds great …' *And cheap.* Jess took a moment. She pushed aside the confusion, the intrigue, the potential story, and focused on the fact that this man – who she was falling for, like it or not – was essentially asking her over to his house so he could cook for her. It was the best kind of date, full of potential and sparkles. Had it really only been a week since they met? She already felt like she knew him so well.

With a jolt she realised that was precisely the problem: maybe she didn't.

'That sounds really nice, I'd love to,' she answered, ignoring the niggling voice in her head, and he beamed at her, pulling her into a warm hug and burying his nose in her hair.

'I like you, you know that.'

'I know.' Whether he liked her or not wasn't the problem, it was whether or not she would like the *real* him, and in turn if he would like the *real* her. She pressed her body closer to his, savouring him and what they knew of each other right now.

When Jess got back to the hotel she was surprised to find Bryony waiting for her, pacing.

'Are you okay?' Bryony asked the minute Jess stepped in the door, striding over and gripping her by the arms.

'Yeah, are you?' Jess laughed.

'Do you hate me?'

'Why would I hate you?'

'Because of last night. Because I accused your new boyfriend, who, by the way, I really, *really* like, of being a drug smuggler. Because I'm the worst friend in the world.'

A huge smile spread across Jess's face. 'So you don't think he is a drug smuggler any more?'

'Well . . .'

'Oh.' Wishful thinking.

Bryony trod carefully, relieved that Jess didn't seem to be taking it personally. 'I think Leo is great, a genuinely lovely person who obviously is besotted with you, and that's a good thing, a really good thing to see. I don't for a second think you should walk away from him yet. But I do still think something's up, and I don't want you to get hurt in the long run. It all still seems pretty bad to me, potentially.' She paused. 'But then that's just my opinion.'

'As a very talented journalist.' Jess knew Bryony's opinion couldn't just be ignored . . . annoyingly.

'But if you're angry, if you don't want me to do

anything about this, I'll just back off. I'll find another story. There's always Veronica.'

'Do you even know what her story is yet? Maybe *she's* a drug smuggler?' The thought pleased Jess a little too much and she tried to rein it in.

'No, it's going to be about someone or some people she's slept with, with a few juicy bits of gossip about some other high-profilers. She'll lay it on with a "poor me" twist, and whether it's printed in *The Times* or *Sleb*, or on the back of a box of cereal, it'll sell shedloads.'

'Selling your stories by the shedload is good.'

Bryony shrugged. 'So where have you been?'

'To see Leo.' It sucked that Leo had gone from being someone she wanted to bring up in every conversation to someone who she was cautious about talking to Bryony about.

'And? Can I ask? Did you speak to him about any of this?'

'I asked him flat out what his job is.'

Bryony leaned forwards, practically salivating.

Jess busied herself with cleaning her glasses. 'He said he used to be a chef, and now owns a chain of fancy restaurants.'

'A chef, huh?'

'Yep.'

'You don't seem convinced,' said Bryony.

'Well, you'll be pleased about this: he's invited me onto his yacht tomorrow evening to cook for me. To prove it. Not that he knows he's proving anything.'

Bryony whooped. 'You're going to go on his boat?'

'Yep.'

'Alone?'

'He's not going to hurt me. Even if – *even if* – he's involved in drug smuggling, which I still think is insane by the way, I'm not scared to be around him.'

'Oh, I don't think you need to be scared. You're feisty, remember? I think this is a great opportunity.'

'For what?'

'Um, sex and snooping, if you need me to spell it out.'

She didn't need Bryony to spell it out, but it was still funny to watch her try. 'Bryony! There will be none of that.'

'None of which one?' Bryony's phone started ringing. 'Damn, hold that thought.'

While Bryony was on the phone Jess made her way to the window and stared out at the view of the hotel opposite. There was just a pinprick of sea in the far distance, peeping out from between the buildings. Suddenly she was tired. It shouldn't be this hard.

'Mitch – *Mitch* – would you calm down? Don't speak to me like that,' Bryony was fuming into the phone and Jess turned. 'No I will not. Yes, very aware, thank you. No, don't come out here, I'm working on some great stories for you. Just have patience. *Mitch!*' Bryony pulled the phone away from her ear and stared at it. 'What a dick.'

'What's up?' Jess asked, forgetting her own dramas for a moment.

'I'm going to be fired.'

'What?'

'If I don't give him an amazing story, like yesterday, I'm going to be fired and will have to reimburse him for this trip.' Bryony sat down on the bed, staring blankly ahead. 'On the one hand, great – good riddance – but I want to leave on my terms. I don't want to be fired. What do I do?'

'Could we go and spy on some celebs, maybe find some people smooching people they shouldn't be smooching?'

'That's not going to cut it. Maybe if I had, like, ten of those, but … it needs to be more significant.' Bryony looked so sad. 'How did it come to this? Why am I always so unhappy? Was I always this miserable?'

'No, I wouldn't love you to pieces if you were always miserable. You're serious and driven and don't take any nonsense, and you need to keep being those things because you're brilliant at them. Don't let those qualities transform into misery instead. You're Olivia Pope. You're C.J. Cregg. The White House Press Secretary wouldn't let someone like Mitch the Grimy Weirdo bring her down.'

'By the end she was Chief of Staff.'

'Well, maybe you will be by the end, too.'

Bryony sniffed, nodding.

'You know what?' said Jess. 'I'm going to help you with this story.'

'Which story?'

'The drug story. I'll do whatever I can, and while digging up the truth with you I'll also prove that Leo and Harvey have nothing to do with that scene. But we'll get you a story, okay?'

Bryony looked at Jess closely. 'Are you sure? Don't do anything you don't want to do, especially not for Mitch.'

'It's not for Mitch, it's for you. Let me start by crossing Leo off the list tomorrow night. I'll find out what I can and I'll have a little snoop around the yacht. Then we can move forward. How does that sound?'

'That sounds great. You're so good to me, Meems.'

'I know. Maybe you could hop over to Ralph Lauren and buy me some sunglasses to match my specs as a thank you.'

'Okay, I can do that!'

'I'm kidding.' Jess took a breath and chuckled. 'You've brought me on a crazy holiday where I've sung in front of celebrities and taken up with a potential drug lord. You've already done so much.'

Bryony laughed. 'You wanted adventure, you wanted out of your comfort zone ...'

That comfort zone was certainly receding further and further into the distance, and Jess took a deep, silent sigh as she watched it go. Yes, she would help her friend no matter what, because that's what people did. What was the female equivalent of 'bros before hos'? But nevertheless, she really, *really* hoped Leo would turn out to be as squeaky clean as that superyacht he was sailing about in.

Later that day, as Jess wandered about the prom-enade munching (another) crêpe and waiting for Bryony's screening to finish, her phone jingled with another text message. She checked it, expecting it to be Bryony saying she'd be yet another five minutes; this film was way longer than anyone had anticipated.

'Anthony?' she said out loud before she could catch herself. What did he want, texting *and* emailing her within a week? That was very unlike him.

Hey chickie, been thinking about you

Huh? That was unexpected. He'd been thinking about her? Her heart fuzzed a little, like a peach. She thought about Anthony sometimes, of course, though she was surprised to realise she'd barely done so since she'd arrived in France. But she never imagined him sitting at home and thinking about her . . .

Though he was probably just prompting her, to find out if she was going to be around next week, nothing more than that. And, actually, that was okay. With a pang of fondness similar to how you feel at the end of a holiday that's created a lot of fun memories, she realised she was kind of over being his booty call. It was sad, but it was true.

'Hi Anthony,' she texted back. 'Sorry didn't reply to your email. Not around next week, am on hols in Cannes.'

Jess leant against the railings and contemplated how to round off the message. 'Maybe next time' didn't feel right, but leaving it as nothing more also seemed a little rude, a little too clipped. Was this essentially a 'break-up' message? Or was it just managing his expectations? Could it even be a break-up message if there was nothing to break up? She still liked Anthony, just not in the way she once did. She didn't tingle with anticipation when she heard from him any more.

'Take care,' she wrote, and stuck out her lower lip.

She hoped he would take care. He was a good guy with a big heart, and he'd never led her on or pretended that what they were was anything more than it was, which she respected. Which made the next text message rather surprising.

> Miss you, Jess. Been thinking about the future, and wondering if you and I should make a go of it? You're an awesome girl. Call me when you get back?

Where did that come from? Jess involuntarily put her hand on her stomach as the feelings she'd had when she thought she was pregnant came flooding back. Anthony wanted to be with her? Make a future with her?

She sighed and dropped her hand to her side. 'Bloody boys,' she muttered. How long, *how long*, had she waited to see if anything would come of her and Anthony? And now she was in demand it was like he knew and was realising that maybe she was worth it.

But ... they didn't really know each other. Or maybe they did. They'd been together, in a way, for over a year, and maybe they didn't go on dates or talk for hours, and maybe this was the first time he'd ever used her name, but she knew him more than she knew Leo. For crying out loud, Leo thought she was a wealthy socialite with a chain of cafés, and she thought he might be a drug smuggler. It wasn't going to last any longer than one more week without some truths coming out, and even if they did, even if he didn't think she was just after him for his money, even if he was no more a drug lord than she was, he couldn't exactly park his superyacht off her little Cornish village and live happily ever after with her.

Anthony made her smile, he was local-ish and she knew that if she did fall pregnant from him, when the timing was right, she'd feel happy about it.

But he wasn't Leo.

'What does one wear to dinner on a superyacht?' It was the hot, hot, hot middle of the following morning on the Côte d'Azur. Jess flicked through her small wardrobe of holiday clothes while Bryony sat cross-legged on the bed in a T-shirt and knickers, frowning at her notepad and some French newspapers. The window was wide open and outside they could hear beautiful vibrant French chatter as a group of film buffs had chosen the café opposite to hold an impromptu meeting about every single film at the festival.

Bryony threw a newspaper on the floor and looked up. 'That depends. Is it just dinner on a yacht? Is it dinner on a yacht plus a sail around the bay? Or, and this is the most important, is it dinner *and breakfast* on a yacht?'

'Bryony, no! I'm not going to sleep over.'

'Why, because your hotel is so glamorous and you can't keep away?'

'No, it's just . . . '

'Are you scared about all this criminal stuff? I'm so sorry if I've worried you, this really hasn't changed my opinion of Leo as a person; I don't think you're in any danger.'

'No, that's not it. I'm a big girl.'

'Okay, so is it because we tripped into the nineteen-fifties and ladies liking sex is shameful, you disgraceful, disgusting girl?'

'No, it's . . . I don't know.' Jess tried to form the words, but it was embarrassing. 'Anthony.'

Bryony's frown deepened. 'This is because of Anthony? The surf dude with one heck of an attitude?'

'He's nice, don't be so horrible about him.'

'Do you know you hold your belly every time you talk about him now?'

Yes, Jess knew that.

'He's not the father of your unborn child, Jess,' Bryony pressed, gently.

'Well, it doesn't feel as simple as that. He's been a substantial – on and off – part of my life, and I thought for a short while he was going to be the hugest part ever, so I can't just dismiss him.'

'Is this because of that text message?' sighed Bryony. 'Are you saying you want to be with him, like, officially?'

'No. For a fleeting moment I thought I did, but he just doesn't make me ... you know ... *glow*.'

'And Leo does?'

Jess nodded. She couldn't cover up how she felt about him, even though yesterday she'd tried hard to convince herself that she wasn't falling for him and that someone else would make her happy. But eventually it came down to one thing: whether it lasted or it didn't, she needed to be with someone who took her breath away, not who made her sigh.

'Do you feel like you're cheating on him with Leo?' Bryony pushed, an incredulous look on her face.

'No, absolutely not!'

'What is it then? Stop making me journo-probe you.'

'Anthony's the only person I've been with—'

'No he's not!' Bryony screeched. 'You can't pull that wool over my eyes!'

'I was going to say, the only person I've been with – *intimately* – over the past couple of years, but thanks.'

'Oh. Well, I don't think anything's changed much.'

Jess laughed. 'I'm sure it hasn't, but nonetheless, being with someone new is a little bit scary, okay?'

'Just scary?'

'And a little bit exciting.' She was glowing again, bright, bright pink, she could feel it.

'Look,' said Bryony. 'If you want to stay over and not do anything, that's fine, I expect he has some spare bedrooms. But if the mood takes you, and you're having fun, well – what if you never get the opportunity to spend the night with a hunk on a superyacht again? Isn't that what this trip is all about? Being the you you can never usually be?'

'Hmm.' Jess mulled this over and went back to thumbing through the wardrobe. The truth was that she did want to stay over, but she couldn't move past the fact she still didn't feel they were being one hundred per cent honest with each other. And for that reason, she decided not to decide yet; she'd just see where the evening took her. So she'd wear a pretty dress and some matching underwear. Just in case.

'You look lovely,' Leo told Jess as soon as she arrived at the marina. The sun was low but still warm, a deep Seville orange in a Monet-sunset sky.

'*You* look lovely,' she replied, falling for him all over again as the sun gilded his face and reflected in his eyes. 'You should never not be at sea because the outdoors would miss you.'

He pulled her to him and kissed her slowly, and she melted into him. He was wearing a white shirt, open at the neck, sleeves rolled up and a tea towel slung over his shoulder. From inside the boat wafted the scent of seafood, lemongrass and dark chocolate, and he tasted of spices and sweetness.

'Come on,' he said, pulling away. 'Fancy a glass of wine?'

'Yes! I brought some.' Jess handed him two bottles and waited for his reaction. She'd spent far too long loitering in the booze aisle of the supermarket, trying to pick a *vin* that was classy and expensive without being too classy and expensive. If she'd been at home a half-price Hardy's would have been her go-to, but she stood in front of all the ruby-shaded bottles and gradually talked herself further and further toward the pricier ones. *What if he knows a lot about wine? What if he takes one look at my twenty-euro bottle and realises what a big faker I am?* Eventually she chose one at a cringe-inducing thirty-two euros, got as far as the cashier, and then realised she didn't know what he was serving so had to run back and get an equivalent bottle of white as well. Ugh, being rich was hard.

Jess followed Leo inside the yacht, taking in the details and feeling relieved that there weren't obvious lines of white powder zig-zagging about on the floor. 'Wow, your yacht is pretty nice,' she observed as he handed her a glass of red.

'Thanks.' He shrugged.

'Can I have a tour?' *Let's get the snooping over with.*

'Sure.' Leo removed the tea towel and tossed it into the galley, then took her hand. He led her to the different decks, showing her opulence and style that were beyond the realms of anything she could imagine owning. It was like watching MTV *Cribs*; it didn't seem real.

Jess perched on the seat in front of the control panel in the helm and looked out to sea. Leo popped a captain's hat on her head. 'You know,' she said, 'I've always loved boats. My dad had a fishing boat for a while, and I used to go out on fishing trips with him and pretend we were on the *Pirates of the Caribbean* ride in Disneyland, or other big adventures. In my mind, it was like I was joining them on their travels. I could totally drive your boat.'

'You could?' Leo laughed. 'Well then, ahoy there, captain.'

She studied the buttons on the control panel. 'Yep, it all looks very familiar. Maybe a *few* more controls, but in an emergency I could get the hang of it. So what I'm saying is,' she spun back around to face him, 'treat me nicely tonight or I might just take you out into open water and dump you there, then keep your yacht.'

'Message received. I'll be very well behaved.'

She caught his eye and they smiled at each other before Leo leant down and kissed her again.

'Come on, we can't sit here kissing all night. I need to see if your yacht is as fabulous as all the other yachts I've frequented.' Jess jumped up and took Leo's hand, leading him back down the stairs.

'Well I'm very lucky that you graced my little tug-boat with your presence, ma'am.'

'Yes, you are.' She still cringed inside when she thought of how he didn't realise how far from the truth she was talking. But as she explored the yacht, and he pointed out the various lounges and bar areas, the cinema and the guest rooms, she tried not to gawp, instead expressing the more dignified admiration of someone who really has seen this kind of thing before. But when they entered the master bedroom she couldn't help herself.

'Holy shit!' she cried, staring at the vast room at the front of the yacht, with huge domed glass windows overlooking the water and a bed so enormous she was surprised it hadn't sunk the vessel when they brought it in. 'This is your bedroom?' It was bigger than her whole house.

'This is my bedroom.'

'Where's your stuff?'

'It's all in compartments. Look, in here's my clothes – oh no, sorry, that's the TV. The clothes are in . . . this one. And behind . . . *this* door is the *en suite*.'

'I like it,' said Jess, her heart fluttering as she rounded the bed, trailing her fingers on the cloud-soft covers and standing in front of the windows. 'Shall I move in?'

'Please do. Plenty of room. We could share this room and barely even see each other if we wanted.' He stood on the opposite side and waved. 'Hellooooo over there!'

Okay, whatever was going to happen this evening, it wasn't bedtime yet. She'd promised Bryony she'd have a good nose around, and she really, *really* wanted to clear Leo's name once and for all. So she strode back out of the room, taking his hand, and continued the tour, descending down to another level.

'So this is just mainly supply cupboards, the odd extra bedroom, nothing exciting.'

'What's this room?' she asked, reaching for a door handle.

'It's nothing.' Leo slipped between her and the door and looked down at her with faintly pleading eyes. 'Just a ... machine room.'

She nodded. *As if.* 'Sounds interesting. Can I see?'

'Well, not now. I think dinner is probably close to being ready.'

'What have you got back there, shipmate, ten thousand bags of cocaine? HAHAHAHAHA.' She held her breath but it washed right over him.

'No cocaine.' He smiled, and began to lead her back upstairs.

Jess glanced back at the door, none the wiser. In fact, she felt even more worried, because he was definitely hiding something.

Well, if he wasn't a chef now, she certainly believed that he used to be. Leo served up course after course of effortlessly delectable dishes, from fresh mussels to Mediterranean vegetables to thick, lemon-scented sea bass to Thai pineapple dipped in a Nutella fondue.

Please don't be a drug smuggler, she begged him

with her eyes throughout the meal, and the more she thought about it the more convinced she was he had nothing to do with it. His chef story was now absolutely believable, and so what if he had a room he didn't want her to go in? Maybe it was full of dirty laundry and S Club 7's back catalogue. If he was in her house she probably wouldn't want him snooping in the cupboard behind the sofa, where her six hundred fitness DVDs were kept, including striptease work-outs and Mr Motivator, and she guessed that when your house is a massive great yacht just for you, you use whole rooms instead of cupboards to store your embarrassing crap.

'So Monaco was cool,' she enthused as he cleared away the last of the fondue.

He beamed at her. 'You really liked it?'

'It was amazing. It's such a funny little cramped place, all those buildings squeezed in on that hill—'

'And then the palace at the top. It is a strange place. Still prefer Cannes?'

'I love Cannes.' She turned to gaze out at the harbour lights twinkling against the dark sky.

'I think Cannes loves you back.'

'What'll you do after the festival? Next week? Oh . . . ' Her face fell. 'Only a week left now. It's going too fast.'

'I guess I'll head back out to sea, to another port. Get back to business.' His eyes searched hers.

'Visiting your restaurants?'

He nodded. 'How about you? What will you do?'

'Go home, get back to business too, I suppose. I'll miss you.'

'I'm going to miss you, and miss this face.' He cupped her chin, sighed dramatically and kissed her. 'But we still have a whole week, so I'm not going to let myself think about it yet.'

'Yep. Let's turn the sadness off – gone.' She stood up, finishing off her wine, and took his hand. 'Come on, show me your stars here in Cannes. And not the celebrity variety.'

She led him up to the top deck, where the dark sky seeped into the dark sea, and stars glittered in a dome above them. When she looked up in Cornwall she saw the same stars, but here they seemed closer, as if she could almost be a star herself.

Jess pulled Leo's arms around her and kissed him hard. Cornwall Jess would never have imagined being atop a superyacht, kissing a near-stranger under the Mediterranean starlight. But here she was, and as their kissing grew more intense she appreciated how little Cornwall Jess had been living, and how much she would be congratulating Cannes Jess for creating this memory.

'This, tonight, is perfect,' whispered Jess, pulling away a fraction and allowing a cool breeze to trickle between their faces.

'You're perfect. You came out of nowhere, but there's nothing I'd change about you.' He touched her hair and grinned with unembarrassed affection.

Jess pushed away that tiny nagging voice that kept popping up to remind her she wasn't who he thought she was. And to remind her that he too was hiding something. She didn't want to shatter this, so she pressed her lips against him again and let her hands slide up his shirt, touching the warm skin of his torso, his silky back, and back down over his nipples, at which he giggled slightly, causing her to laugh too.

'Want to get out of the cold?' he whispered.

'Where to?'

'I don't know . . . I have a lovely blanket on my bed that I can show you if you want?'

Jess laughed again – how could this man be so funny and sexy at the same time? He led her downstairs, the two flights seeming to take for ever as they kept pausing to kiss, or run hands over each other. Eventually they made it to the bedroom, and she pushed him against the door, pulling down the straps of her dress, and leant into him for more lip service.

The sound of footsteps above stopped her dead,

and she moved a fraction of an inch away from Leo, their lips still touching. Another footstep creaked on the deck. 'Leo . . .'

Leo slid his hand down her arm, pulling the strap of her dress back up, his ear cocked to the deck above.

'No,' came a deep, gruff voice, muffled through the flooring. 'They're not on board.'

'Leo, is that Harvey?' Jess whispered.

'No,' he whispered in reply, and edged her to the back of the room, where he flicked off the light and plunged them into darkness.

'What's happening?' she asked, pressed between the wall and him, her heart thumping and her breath hitting his warm chest.

'I can't find it,' the voice said, presumably on the phone but closer to them now, coming down the steps. He sounded annoyed. He turned before entering the bedroom and walked past, down the corridor.

'Who's on your boat?' Jess asked in a barely audible voice. 'Shouldn't we confront them?'

'No,' Leo said, cracking open a closet door and stepping them both inside. 'I know who he is. I . . . work with him.'

'Like a client?'

'Yeah, like a client.'

'Why's he just boarded your boat? That's rude.'

'Yeah, he's a little rude. I don't want to see him right now, or let him ruin our night, so let's just lie low until he's gone, okay?' In the darkness, but with a touch of moonlight shining through the slats of the closet doors, she could see Leo smiling softly down at her, reassuring her. But what the hell was going on?

The bedroom door opened and both Leo and Jess held their breath. Leo circled his thumb on her back comfortingly, while she stared through the slats, unblinking, at the man who stepped in to the room and looked around. He was tall and broad. His hair was dark, and if you could describe a man as having resting bitch face, he certainly had it. He gazed around the room and, with a grumpy snarl, tossed a pillow off the bed, then took a swig from the glass he was holding and, putting the phone back up to his ear, left with a grunt.

Jess exhaled.

'I'm not doing this now,' the man said, his footsteps ascending the stairs. 'I'll find it in the morning.'

Jess was silent, her breath unsteady until she hadn't heard footsteps for a few minutes, and then Leo extracted himself and left the room to check the man had gone. Jess sank to the floor of the closet, close to tears. What was going on? She wanted to go home; she was in way over her head. But then the lights came on and Leo appeared above her, swooping down to pull her up into a safe, warm embrace, and the fright subsided just a touch.

'That was a *client*? Someone to do with your restaurants?' she exclaimed incredulously.

'Yeah . . .'

'People who work in the restaurant business don't break into other people's superyachts and skulk about in the dark looking for things.' *Who are you?*

'We've known each other for years. He often invites himself on board – he probably just left something here when he came over for a drink the other day. He's harmless.'

She left the bedroom and went to the deck to see for herself that no one was around.

Leo followed her. 'I've closed the gangway; I should have done it before. He won't be coming back on – nobody will.' He stuffed his hands in his pockets, his chest, partially exposed behind his half-unbuttoned shirt, was still bare and beginning to goose-pimple.

Jess stood in front of him, hands on hips. 'I don't like that he just came on board and we had to hide in the closet. I don't get it.'

'Oh God, I'm sorry – I know how bloody strange this looks now. He's one of those people who you can't get rid of once he's had a drink, he just talks and talks, and I just thought that if we hid he'd bugger off pretty quickly and we could, you know, get back to taking our clothes off.' He blushed sheepishly. 'Although now I know it makes me look like a cowardly weirdo, stuffing you in a closet in the dark rather than just asking someone to leave.' He made a sheepish face. 'My bad.'

Well ... that did actually all make sense, she supposed. The drug-smuggling thing was making her jumpy, and her imagination was running wild. Damn Bryony. 'I don't think you're a cowardly weirdo. I *do* think you only got me in that closet to squash up against me, though, like some kind of teenager playing seven minutes in heaven.'

'Ha! You found out my master plan! Seven minutes is all you need with me, baby.' He grinned and offered her some more wine.

She refused. 'I think I'll take a whisky instead, please, if you have any. Calm the nerves.'

'Sure.' He poured her a tumbler of Woodford Reserve. 'Would you feel better if we got off the boat? Went into town or something?'

She shook her head. 'I want to be alone with you.'

'Right then,' Leo said, gulping down some whisky of his own. 'Thank you. I want to be alone with you.' He strode over to her and lifted her up, taking her by surprise, and wrapping her legs around his waist. It was a good job she was in a roomy dress. Their lips pressed together and he bumped their way to the steps and back down toward his bedroom.

'You can put me down, you know,' snorting a laugh that pushed his lips away.

'Nope, I'm being very gentlemanly and carrying you over the threshold. Then I'm going to eat you like a crêpe.'

Jess gasped, and a moment later so did he, as he realised what he'd said.

'Christ, that sounded more romantic in my head! I meant ravish you, enjoy you, I really didn't mean to suddenly be explicit as hell.'

A chuckle escaped Jess. 'Let's just take it one thing at a time,' she said.

He donkey-kicked the bedroom door open and sat down on the edge of the bed, her on top of him, their bodies still entwined. He tasted good, and his lips felt good, and his hands felt good, and all the worry she'd had about not being with anyone other than Anthony for a long time just slipped out the door unnoticed, like a party guest who knew when to take their leave.

For just a moment she pulled away and looked into his face, his smile, those eyes, his sun-kissed skin and the wave in his hair, and he twinkled up at her, looking so open.

He pressed his nose against hers and locked eyes with her. 'You know you're safe with me, right? And I don't just mean tonight.'

'Yep, I know,' she said truthfully, because even without knowing the full picture she knew that.

Rrrrrrrrrrrrrrrrrrrrrrrr.

'Shit, bugger, bollocks!'

Jess opened her eyes to see bright sunshine pouring through the window as large electronic shutters whirred open extremely noisily, and Leo hopping about in just a pair of boxers, trying to stop them.

'Morning,' she croaked, sitting up and shielding her eyes.

'Jess, I'm so sorry,' he said, starfishing across the window in an attempt to block the light. 'I thought I'd wake you up gently and naturally, and forgot how incredibly loud these seem when you're in slumberland.'

'That's okay. I like the sunshine.'

'Then good morning, sunshine,' he said, coming back over and giving her a morning kiss. She struggled to fix her crazy hair and smudgy mascara, but he scooped her up, bed sheet and all, and carried her out of the room.

'Hey,' she laughed, grabbing her glasses from the bedside table as he strolled her past. 'Will you never let me walk in or out of this room?'

'Time for brekkie!'

Out on the deck, wrapped in the sheet, with a warm morning breeze tickling her naked skin through the fabric, Jess watched Leo.

'Juice?' he asked, pouring her some freshly squeezed oranges.

'Yes please.' She picked at a croissant.

'Coffee?'

'Tea, please.'

'Early morning bonk in the hot tub?'

Jess laughed and it carried away on the breeze. Last night had been amazing. Fun, sensual, every adventure she'd wanted rolled into one. And now, try as she might, she couldn't stop staring at Leo.

'You know,' she said, 'Marilyn once did a photo shoot eating breakfast wrapped in a white sheet.'

'The guy who made breakfast for her must have fallen in love on the spot, too.'

'You are just—'

'*Leo?*' shouted a voice from the marina below. '*Leo, put the gangway down, I need to come up.*'

Leo leaned over the side, and Jess peeked at his bottom.

'Morning, Harv. Can it wait?'

'Not really, mate.'

Leo turned back to Jess and gave her a tender kiss. 'I'll get rid of him as soon as I can. Don't eat all my toast.'

Jess reached over and took a slice of toast, then, fixing the sheet tightly round her, walked to the railing to watch the boys below.

Leo lowered the gangway and greeted Harvey with a huge smile, but Harvey rushed past him, straight onto the yacht.

'He's coming back. He called me last night in a right strop, so he's coming back this morning.'

Leo cursed, running his hand through his hair. 'Did he say when?'

'No, but I think we should be prepared, don't you? Let's clear up and get the whites out.'

'What's going on?' Jess called down. 'Hi Harvey!'

'All right, mate?' he called up, shielding his eyes from the sun. 'You look pretty in the morning.' He turned back to Leo, fidgeting with a strange nervousness. 'Come on, mate . . .'

Leo swooped up the steps to Jess. 'Sorry, Jess, I could have spent hours just hanging out with you looking like that, but something's come up.'

'Something?' She made her way back towards the bedroom and he followed, looking pained.

'Just work. Work, work, work. Maybe we should just forget it all and go to Monaco and live in that Palace.'

She smiled, but a sense of dread came over her as she wondered if this was all a game: getting her into bed, then the friend coming with an 'emergency' so she'd leave first thing, then she'd never hear from him again.

'Maybe we could meet up again later, or tomorrow?' he asked.

'Are you sure?'

He saw her worry and his face softened. 'Hey, of course I'm sure. I don't want you to go at all – ever, frankly – so don't for a second think I won't call you later. We could go out. Anywhere you like.'

Stop being so clingy, she scolded herself. 'Let me take you somewhere this time, you've done three in a row. I'll find something really nice.' So she guessed she was spending the next few hours racking her brain for cheap-date ideas in Cannes then. Nice one, Jess.

'I can't wait, seriously.' He watched her get dressed. 'I don't want you to go. Can you leave me your bra or something?'

She chortled and threw a sock at him. 'You want my body *and* my clothes? How selfish are you?'

'Fine. Then you can't have my boxers.'

'Fine.' She primped her hair in front of the mirror, had a final look around the most beautiful bedroom she'd ever graced with her body and then stepped back up and out into the sunshine.

'Bye, mate, sorry to wreck the pyjama party,' sniggered Harvey. 'Next time, bring Ms Bryony, all right?'

'Maybe I will. Bye, Harvey, and bye, you.' As Jess kissed Leo goodbye and returned to solid ground, she found herself feeling able – given what she'd seen (or not seen) – to tell Bryony this whole drug thing was definitely a misunderstanding. Sure there was a room he wouldn't let her into ... and a strange man came on board looking for something and they had to hide in a closet ... and now she'd had to get off the yacht as quickly as possible ... and if she looked back she could see Leo and Harvey with furrowed brows and mildly panicked faces ...

'Are you bullshitting me?' Bryony asked, wide-eyed. The two of them sat at the café outside their hotel enjoying some coffee while Jess freshened her make-up.

'What?'

'Now I'm even more suspicious! A creepy guy *breaks into* the yacht, looking for the *cocaine* that Leo's hidden in his secret "machine room", then says he'll be back in the morning, at which moment you're scooted off the boat like a Heidi Fleiss special?'

'Thank you.'

'How does that not seem ridiculously dodgy to you? Actually, I know why: it's because you're all clouded by sex and suchlike.'

'Bryony!' Jess cried, ducking behind her bronzer compact. 'I'm not clouded, I'm just happy.'

'I know you are. And I'm so happy you're happy, so hoping I'm wrong about all of this. But I don't feel good about you being alone with him until this has been resolved.'

Jess sighed and put down the compact. 'He *does* make me happy, which is silly because we don't know each other very well, but I feel like we could, one day. I'm not scared to be alone with him.'

'But that guy last night—'

'Is a red flag – I know.' Jess sank her head into

her hands, glumly. 'Remember that feeling when we started the holiday and anything was possible, and there was still so much time ahead of us, even though I didn't know everything that was going to happen or what to expect. Only now . . .'

'Only now?'

'Only now that time is half gone, I can't say for sure I'm going to like the ending. Now that I'm not there with him, wrapped in his sheet and being on the receiving end of his Leo-smooches, I'm not blinded. I can see something's up. I'm so torn, and because of that I'm not going to *not* be careful, but the idea of having to stay away from Leo because he may be a drug smuggler still just seems too far-fetched for me to truly worry.'

Bryony nodded, studying her friend. She'd known Jess long enough – comforted her during break-ups, sat with her in hospital when she sprained an ankle trying to skateboard (aged twenty-nine), watched her extreme emotional reactions to *Dawson's Creek* – to know she was going through some kind of fight with herself right now. 'Fair enough. But please keep your phone on and call me any time if anything seems *too* out of the comfort zone.'

'Agreed. The *real* problem, though, is that I have to take him on a big fancy date because I don't want him to think I'm a gold digger, but I wish I was because

I checked my account on the way over here and you don't want to know how much dosh I've got through during the first half of this trip.'

Bryony finished her coffee. 'We'll think of something fun to do that's not too pricey.'

'What are you doing today? Any screenings?' asked Jess, glad to move the conversation on.

'No. There's a big press lunch but I don't think I'm even on the list, so I'll make myself busy elsewhere. Maybe a bit of sunbathing. I want to go and speak to Harvey, though.'

'You do?' Jess scrunched her nose. Bryony wasn't about to let it drop, then.

'Remember that even if this Leo and Harvey thing is nothing, Harvey is still a really good source of information—' she said softly.

'And a good source of a snog.'

'Yes, that too, haha, so it's useful for me to be with him regardless.' Bryony's phone rang. 'Gaahh, it's Veronica again.'

'It must be *sooo* hard to have celebrities calling you all day, wanting to meet up,' Jess teased, envious as hell. She sat back in the sunshine, mulling over their conversation, assuring herself she was doing the right thing. *What are your secrets, Leo?*

Bryony smirked at her. 'Hi, Veronica.'

'Hey, dude,' Veronica replied. 'Can we do the interview today?'

'Today? Um, sure – I guess. What time?'

'How's four p.m.? I presume you're staying at the Carlton, right?'

'Sure,' Bryony lied. 'I'll come to your room.'

'I'm not at the Carlton any more. We'll do it in your room.'

Bryony caught Jess's eye and grimaced. 'Or in the lobby? Or the bar?'

'No way, it has to be your room. I want total privacy and an environment I feel comfortable in and that I trust. Okay? Text me the details. Laters.'

Veronica hung up before Bryony could say another word to her, so she said one to Jess instead. 'Shit.'

'Trouble with the star?'

The InterContinental Carlton. It was fully booked, it was impossibly expensive, it was exclusive as hell and it was never going to happen. Bryony sighed and took a gulp of Jess's cold, strong coffee dregs.

'I need to get a room at the Carlton.'

'What exactly is your plan here?' Jess asked, tottering along beside Bryony, her eyes peeled for celebrities as they entered the InterContinental Carlton.

'I don't know,' said Bryony, her chin up, staring straight ahead and with a look of determination on her face.

'Isn't the Carlton fully booked anyway?'

'I don't know.'

'Are you totally channelling C.J. walking through the White House corridors right now?'

'Yep. *Bonjour*,' she greeted the woman behind the reception desk.

'*Bonjour, madame*. Would you like me to speak English today?' asked the flawlessly attractive woman.

'Yes please, *merci beaucoup*. I was wondering if you had any rooms available.'

'For now?'

'Yes. For today.'

'Certainly, *madame*. You are in luck, we have one or two vacancies. Would you like a suite?'

'Ooo,' said Jess.

'No,' said Bryony. 'Just a simple room.'

'*D'accord*. One moment, *madame*. We have a lovely deluxe room with a sea view, it's the last one left.'

'Urgh, a sea view. How much would that cost?'

'For how many nights, *madame*?'

'Just one, please.'

'How much for more, though, just out of interest?' Jess piped up.

'For one night that would be three thousand, eight hundred euro. For, let us say, three nights that would be—'

'Whoa, not necessary, thank you,' Bryony interrupted. That was nearly three thousand pounds for one night. She took a deep breath and lowered her voice. 'Do you, perchance, rent rooms by the hour?'

The receptionist's smile lowered minutely. 'No, *madame*, I'm afraid the rate is for the full night.'

'Right, of course. I am ... the personal assistant of Veronica Hay.'

The receptionist's smile rose again, minutely. 'Ah, Ms Hay is a great friend of the Carlton. She checked out only yesterday to go to a spa for the rest of her visit.'

'Yes, yes, she so loves it here. She has an interview this afternoon with a very esteemed journalist and would appreciate the privacy of one of your guest rooms to conduct the interview.'

'I see. If the publication could be in touch with us directly, we can certainly arrange—'

'Well, actually we would prefer complete discretion in this matter. Ms Hay does not want any attention drawn, so if you and I could sort this out between us right now I'd really appreciate it.'

The receptionist nodded and tapped away at her computer while Jess gaped at Bryony. The girl was a master of disguise.

'I'm sure we can ensure the journalist in question writes a fantastic account of the hotel and the staff,' Bryony continued.

Eventually the receptionist caved and agreed to let Bryony occupy the room for a couple of hours that afternoon. To celebrate, Jess took her for an over-priced gin and tonic on the terrace.

Jess sipped slowly. 'I'm sure I recognise that man,' she said, gesturing with her eyes, which only made Bryony look in every direction but the right one. 'I think he's a director, or used to be an actor, or maybe he's that guy, you know that guy ... ' Suddenly she gasped. 'Bryony, it's him.'

'Who? Spit it out.'

'No, forget the director-actor man. Over there in the dark suit, impossibly tall: that's the man who was on the boat, the one we hid from.' There he was, sitting a few tables over, a glass of Scotch in one hand and a copy of a very serious-looking newspaper in the other.

Bryony whistled, her eyes shining with excitement. 'That's your Tony Montana.'

'My who?'

'Your Scarface, the top dog, the don.'

'Now you think *he's* running things? I thought you said Leo and Harvey were the drug lords.'

'I think Leo and Harvey are the drug traffickers, but this guy looks like he controls the whole operation. Or maybe a rival operation, and he wants Leo and Harvey out of the picture.'

'Reel it in, *CSI Miami*. Nobody wants Leo and Harvey "out of the picture".' Hopefully.

'I'm going to talk to him,' Bryony said, getting up.

'No, you are *not* going to go and talk to someone you just referred to as "Scarface",' Jess hissed, but Bryony had already picked up her G&T and sashayed off to the man's table. He offered her a seat with a big, charming white smile, which was a bit of a shame because Jess was hoping for a gold grille or something.

'Hi,' Bryony said, sitting down. Jess gently scraped her seat sideways and leant back as far as she could in order to eavesdrop.

'Hi,' he said.

'You look like a busy man.'

'At times.' His accent was vaguely Italian, but Jess couldn't quite be sure.

'May I ask what you do for a living?'

It was a probing question for Bryony to ask someone she hadn't even introduced herself to, but she asked it in such a way that she sounded like she was in awe of this powerful man, and genuinely interested in his business. Maybe she *should* be on *CSI Miami*.

The man chuckled, and with a flick of his fingers another round of drinks arrived. 'If I tell you that, baby, I might have to kill you.'

Bryony laughed a fake, tinkling laugh. 'You wouldn't do that; you seem like a pussycat. I'll bet you're ... the chief of police.'

This time he let out a huge, booming guffaw that turned heads on the terrace, so even Jess decided to turn around for a brief look. 'That, honey, I am not. Excuse me a minute, beautiful, I'll be right back.' He picked up his phone and walked away from the table.

Bryony gulped the rest of her gin and tonic, raising her eyebrows at Jess over the rim of her glass, and then the two of them skedaddled.

'I don't know, I just feel like all this is very circumstantial,' Jess was saying as they made their way back to the Hôtel du Bliss. *I'd make a great lawyer* ... 'Yes, there are a few strange things happening and yes, Leo and Harvey are hiding something, but I think them being drug smugglers and hotel dude being the Tony Montana, as you say, is a pretty big leap.'

'You could be right. But it's all I have to go on; I'm just hitting brick walls.'

'You know who'd be good to talk to?'

'Who?'

'Céline.' Even saying that horrible woman's name made Jess wince.

'The Noix de Coco hostess? She's not going to help me!'

'Leo said she's a wannabe, a hanger-on. At the moment you're trying to get info from the people you think are doing the crime anyway, so of course they're going to be vague and weird. And while Richard et al. could probably give you some good, gossipy stories, they'll also want to protect their clients and their jobs, so they'd never name names even if they knew something. But Céline might have a price. If you can get her into a party, or even do a piece about her in *Sleb* or something, she might just spill. I bet restaurant hosts know everyone and see everything.'

'Meems, you're a genius!' cried Bryony. '*And* she knows Leo, she even mentioned doing business with him.'

'I know,' Jess said through gritted teeth.

'I'll go and find her tomorrow. Brilliant idea, Jess. We're like *Sharky and George*. For now, I have a fake interview to prepare for. What are you going to do?'

Jess rolled her shoulders, feeling quite ready for a bit of holiday R&R. 'I'll go up to the roof terrace and sunbathe. And try not to think about Céline doing business with my man.'

'Well that sounds fun,' said Bryony. 'You're having a good holiday though, aren't you, Meems?'

'Of course I am! It's weird and wonderful.'

'And you'll come with me to meet Veronica? Not to stay for the whole thing, but just a meet-and-greet?'

Jess bounced with excitement and yelped 'Yes!' a little too loudly. If Leo was a billionaire and they married and he invited Beyoncé and Jay Z onto his yacht for dinner every Tuesday night she still would never get blasé about celebrities.

'Behave, though, okay?' Bryony said.

Well, Jess couldn't promise that ...

It was mid-afternoon and Jess had returned to the room with faintly bronzed skin and some wise words for Bryony. 'We need clothes, and shoes, and make-up and all that jazz.'

'Why?' Bryony asked, packing up her laptop.

'Because Veronica thinks she's coming to your room in the Carlton for the interview. It's not going to be very convincing if you claim only to use hotel toiletries and you have all your clothing laundered every single day.'

Bryony slapped herself on the forehead. 'You're right. You're right, what's wrong with me?'

'Saying that, I don't want to pack . . . '

'We can't march in with suitcases anyway: we're only supposed to be in there for an hour or two. We'll take some carefully chosen things in our handbags. We need a pair of heels to throw by the door.'

Jess grabbed her large pink tote bag and stuffed in some silver heels.

'And a few things to hang in the wardrobe in case she snoops. Pick thin things like that yellow floppy strapless thing.'

'Ooo, that wouldn't really go with the shoes I picked.'

'It doesn't matter.'

'If you want it to look authentic—'

'Fine, Meems, swap the shoes.'

Jess packed the yellow dress plus a couple of others, and switched the shoes for some shocking pink stilettos (of hers) that she thought went with everything. '"Give a girl the right shoes, and she can conquer the world" – that's what Marilyn said. Or maybe Bette Midler. But you get the point.'

Bryony picked up her own handbag and stuffed in hair straighteners, her make-up bag, a bra and a copy of *The Times*, 'to leave lying around'.

Jess shook her head. 'Not a good idea. Next thing you know, Veronica'll be thumbing through it, being all "which article did you write?"'

'You're right, again. Let's leave *The Times*. We better go – you ready?'

'Yes, are you?'

'I'm so ready. Let's just get it over with.'

The plan at the InterContinental Carlton was for Veronica to meet them at the room. Jess would pop down to the bar to get whatever drink Veronica desired and deliver it back to the room, and then sit on the beach until Bryony called to tell her it was done. Jess was quite happy playing PA when it meant being within drink-handing distance of a massive celeb, and then sitting in the sunshine looking out for other massive celebs.

The two of them marched straight up to the room and scattered their belongings about – it was like dressing a movie set. And then, surprisingly, there was a knock on the door. Right on time.

Bryony opened it and greeted Veronica, who was wearing a trilby, huge sunglasses, an oversized, billowing scarf and a T-shirt with *Team Hay* emblazoned on the back. She waltzed into the room, handed her accessories to Jess and ordered a French 75 with tequila chaser, which Jess raced off to get, ecstatic at having just touched a scarf faintly damp with celebrity neck sweat and wondering what the hell a French 75 was.

'Hey,' said Veronica, sitting cross-legged on the bed and removing her sunglasses to reveal a pretty, make-up-free face.

'Hi, how are you?' Bryony sat in a chair opposite, again noticing Veronica's lower-pitched voice, which was so different from the one she used in front of the cameras.

'I'm good, thanks. Detoxing now; I drank way too much last week.'

'I hear you.'

'You drink?'

'Well, moderately. I like a bottle of wine or two from time to time.'

'Are you drunk now?'

Bryony laughed. 'Of course not ... are you?'

'Mildly.' Veronica shrugged, then lapsed into silence, chewing the end of her hair like a confused toddler. 'Do you have anything to drink up here?'

Bryony looked around. 'Jess will be back soon with your cocktail, but I can get you something from the minibar if you like?'

'Yeah, that would be cool. Maybe just a whisky or something.'

Wow, Veronica Hay really does like to drink. Bryony wondered momentarily if she had a problem, but this seemed more like Dutch courage than an addiction. She handed Veronica a miniature Jack Daniel's and it was gone in seconds.

Veronica tossed the bottle into the bin and sat up straight, scrunched her hair, slumped down again, scratched her foot and finally leant forward. 'So, before we start, I need to tell you something. Because I can trust you, right?'

Shame gnawed at Bryony. 'Sure.'

'Sure?' Veronica's eyes drilled into Bryony, who nodded. 'Okay. In this piece you're going to write, I want to do something.'

'Do something?'

'Say something. Do something . . .'

Bryony waited patiently.

Veronica went back to chewing her hair, and then after a final, hard bite she spat it out. 'Come out. I want to come out.' She sat back and returned to chewing her hair, while side-eyeing Bryony for her reaction.

'Come out? Like *come out* come out?'

'Come waaaay out.'

'You're gay?' Bryony put down her notebook and pen. This she had not been expecting; it was hard to comprehend that she was sitting in a room with one of the most well-known faces on the planet, let alone that she was confessing her biggest secret.

'You got a problem with that?' asked Veronica defensively.

'Of course not, it's just a surprise. Not that you should have to declare it by any means, it's just you've been so—'

'Straight, right, and surrounded by boyfriends?'

'Well, yeah.'

'Yeah, that's basically my problem. At the start I just wanted to be famous, like Paris or Kim, but I noticed that if I went out for a night with a girl-friend people just thought I was with a *friend*. But if I started being seen with guys, and then famous guys, I got a lot more column inches.' Veronica paused as Jess returned with her drinks, curtsied and left. 'Trust me, I look back on myself then and realise how ridiculous it was, how ridiculous *I* was. But whatever, it happened, and then it snowballed. I was suddenly this party girl who was invited to everything and got whatever I wanted, and it all seemed so awesome because I thought I was the one getting the last laugh. My guy friends would sleep in the guest room and I'd be chilling in my own bed, thinking the press didn't know me as well as they thought. But after I grew up a little and wanted to have girlfriends, I started to struggle to keep them secret, and then it began to feel like the press owned me. Not just the press, that's not fair, the public too. It felt like I couldn't be me.'

'Did you ever think, I'm going to just come out?'

'I basically did come out. I took a girl to a club and kissed her in front of all the paps. Unfortunately, I hadn't realised Lindsay Lohan and Samantha Ronson had just got together, and I was accused of jumping on the bandwagon. And I chickened out of trying again.'

Veronica sighed and rubbed her eyes, and Bryony watched her. This was just a girl who was fed up of living a lie and wanted to be herself.

Bryony picked up her pen again. 'So what do you want this article to be? Like a "coming out" piece about you and your girlfriend, or ...?'

'God, no. First of all, I don't have a girlfriend right now. Do you?' Veronica asked with a wicked smile.

'No,' Bryony laughed. 'Are you flirting with me?' This was so surreal.

'Only a little bit. No, I want to come out in this article, but I don't want it to be a *coming out* article. The last thing I want is a bit picture of me looking forlorn with a headline about how I've lived in secret, blah, blah, blah. I want to do an article about the direction I want to take my career in, about me, about the things I'm actually interested in, which happens to include girls.'

'So you just want to slip it in there, gotcha.'

'Me being gay is no more newsworthy than Jennifer Lawrence being straight. I feel really strongly about that, Bryony. Homosexuality will never stop being "different" if it's reported as being some huge deal when a celebrity comes out. Just imagine how that makes kids in school who might be gay feel. I felt like I couldn't tell anyone at school because it was always assumed that girls liked boys.'

Bryony nodded. 'But even if we just mention it in passing in this article, you know other outlets will pick up on it and that's what they'll go with?'

'I know. But as long as it's not me saying, "Hey everyone, big huge announcement: I'm gay, isn't that *weird*?" I'll feel better about it all.'

'Coming out *is* brave though; good for you.'

'I don't want to be brave – I just want to be me.'

'Fair enough.' Bryony looked down at her list of questions – the usual *Sleb* fare: what's your favourite brand of underwear, best celeb snog, what do you think of Katie Hopkins' comments on so-and-so . . .

Just imagine those questions combined with the revelation of Veronica's sexuality, throw in a few easily dug up photos of her kissing that woman a few years back, and Bryony was sitting on Mitch's dream article. *Sleb* sales would skyrocket; Bryony would be the golden girl, her career saved. Perhaps she'd even be headhunted for one of the bigger-name gossip mags, the ones people actually liked. She'd be the reporter that global news outlets – be it magazines, websites, newspapers – would refer back to; *'Veronica Hay exclusively revealed her sexuality to Bryony Foster of Britain's* Sleb *magazine on Tuesday . . .'*

But at what cost?

Would it crush Veronica that she'd been duped? Was being quoted by someone you trusted, in exactly the worst way you had feared, something that would stay with that person for life? How was Bryony even considering this type of journalism?

It was hard to know what to do: she was on a seesaw that had got stuck midway. She scanned her questions one more time – underwear, snogs, celeb you'd most like to shag – and flipped the page over, feeling ashamed.

She started a fresh sheet. 'Okay, you want to talk about you, the real you, underneath all the bullshit – no offence. So let's start with your childhood. Tell me some memories from school, favourite subjects, where you grew up ...'

By the time the interview was over Bryony was exhausted, but in a good way. Her perceptions of Veronica had flipped completely; she was down-to-earth, funny, studious, intelligent and calm. The bad choices were behind her, and Bryony truly thought she deserved a chance at the acting career of her dreams. Bryony couldn't have been happier with the potential this article had, and couldn't be sadder about how she'd betrayed Veronica's trust.

Veronica left the room with a goodbye hug for Bryony, who sat on the bed for a while in the quiet, wondering what she could do to make it right. Could she write the piece anyway, exactly like this, and convince Mitch to print it? The only difference would be that it wasn't in *The Times* ... Maybe Veronica wouldn't even mind that much. *The Times* would possibly pick up the story anyway, afterwards, so the end result would be the same-ish.

Urgh, no matter how much she was trying to convince herself, of course it wouldn't be the same, and of course Veronica would mind, and of course she was an idiot for even starting this whole charade.

Tiredness lapped over Bryony, so she put the decision on what to do in a box, to think about tomorrow. She called Jess, to let her know it was time to come back up to the room, clear up and go home.

Jess walked through the door ten minutes later, cradling her phone against her ear.

'Yep, yep, oh that would be great, just hang on one mo ...' she covered the receiver. 'It's Richard, he wants to come over and hang out at our hotel. By the way, how'd it go?'

'It was really good. Can you just tell him we're out?'

'No, I've already told him we're in. He called and asked what we were doing, and I thought he might have something fun planned, so I said, "Oh nothing at all, just lazing about in the hotel, wishing we were invited to a glamorous party," and he goes, "Brilliant, I'm going to come and check out your pad."'

'Nice one, Meems.'

'*I know*. What shall I say?'

Bryony looked around at the strategically messy bedroom. 'Get him to the Carlton.'

'Here?'

'Yes, tell him we moved hotels and ask him to come and see us here. We'll meet him in the bar,' Bryony whispered.

'Okay. Richard?'

'Yes, love?'

'We actually moved hotels as we were a bit far from the action. We're at the Carlton now. Do you want to come here for a drink instead?'

'You bloody legends, I'll be right over. I'll bring some champers and we'll have a party in your room.'

'Oh, the room's dull, let's meet in the bar.'

'No bloody way. We're in the mood for a room party and we don't want to see any bloody celeb clients that we have to behave around. The lounge'll be crawling with them tonight.'

Well, that just made Jess want to go down to the bar even more. 'They want to come to the room,' she hissed to Bryony.

'Who's "they"?'

'Hmm ... Richard, who are you with?'

'Tara, Bea, the usual best blooming party crowd in Cannes, baby, and we're headed your way.'

'Great,' she tittered. 'It's all of them,' she told Bryony.

'Okay, we bring them up here, but just for one drink, then we'll insist we have to leave.'

'But Veronica's gone – we have to vacate the room.'

'The staff don't know that, we'll just pretend the interview's still happening.'

'Like *Weekend at Bernie's*?'

'She's not dead.'

'Hel-*lo*?' Richard's voice sang out of the phone.

'Okay, come on over, I'll meet you in the lobby. Byeee,' Jess sang down the phone and then hung up. 'We're so going to get banned from Cannes.'

'It'll be fine,' Bryony reassured her. 'So we keep the room for one more hour. Nobody'll even notice.'

Two and a half hours later, Richard was sitting on the bed doing impersonations of his celebrity clients and getting everybody to guess who he was. Nobody from management had come to check on the room, but Jess jumped at every noise from the corridor outside.

'Let's get room service,' said Tara, picking up the phone.

'No!' cried Jess and Bryony at the same time, leaping towards her.

'Does anyone else have a huge craving for sushi from that place down on the beach?' said Bryony hopefully.

This was met with a tipsy 'wooohoooo' and Jess breathed a sigh of relief as Bryony started rounding everyone up.

At that moment, her phone tinkled. It was a text from Leo, and she smiled before she even read it.

I just finished a long meeting, are you up for a date? I'm knackered, but it would be so good to curl up around you. Warning: might fall asleep prior to hanky-panky.

That sounded like perfection: she hadn't realised until he said it how tired she was. She texted back: 'That sounds nice, shall I meet you on board?' She looked up. 'Bryony, do you mind if—'

Bryony shook her head, smiling. 'Have a good time, Meems. Come *on* you lot, how long does it take to put on a pair of Louboutins?'

Several minutes of goodbyes, of 'Ooo I forgot my bag's, of 'Wait, wait, wait, I'll just down my Bloody Mary's and the door closed behind them. Jess's phone tinkled again in the luxurious silence.

Can I come to your hotel, instead? I actually have guests staying on the yacht tonight.

Balls. She yawned, a big, deep yawn, and looked around her. It was after ten and nobody had come to check on them. Would it really be a problem if she fell asleep on this big, beautiful, squashy bed? She could leave really early and they'd be none the wiser. She yawned again, her eyelids drooping. If there were any problems she'd sort them out tomorrow. Besides, a room at the Carlton was as good a way as any to keep up with the Joneses.

Sure, I'm in the Carlton, room 425. Come on by.

Ten minutes later, he did. And twenty minutes after that they were snoring softly in each other's arms.

A bang on the door woke Jess with such a start that her heart fell out through her throat and she yelped 'DRUGS!' before she could stop herself.

Leo lifted himself up onto an elbow and peered at the clock in the dark, which read 3:42 a.m. 'What?'

The banging came again and Jess remembered where she was: the InterContinental Carlton, having fallen asleep in a room she should have paid three grand for. And now someone had realised and sent the hotel police, who'd also recognise Leo and arrest him for smuggling drugs, and they'd be sent to prison, separately, and—

Bang, bang, bang.

Jess slipped out of bed onto the plush carpet, cherishing every strand of wool under her feet as soon she'd be walking on the concrete floor of a cell. She grabbed a bathrobe and opened the door, her hands shaking.

'Veronica?'

'Thank Christ I've finally got the right room. This is like the seventh door I've banged on. It's a good job people don't stay mad when they see who I am. I left my cell phone here earlier – I'm such a knucklehead, right?' She walked in and flicked the lights on. 'Well hello, you're not Bryony.' She smiled at Leo lying in bed shielding his eyes. 'You're hot, though.' She waltzed to the bathroom, grabbed her phone from the shelf above the bidet, and then strode out, winking at Jess as she walked past and saying quietly, 'But then, Bryony's pretty hot herself.'

Jess closed the door and padded back to the bed, letting the robe drop to the floor, and curled up against Leo's warm body again. She yawned into his chest. 'I'll explain why another time, but we have to be out of here at dawn.'

♥

As luck would have it, Jess received a call shortly before seven o'clock the following morning that made her get out of bed like lightning.

'Hello?' she said into her phone while Leo stretched his legs and started to make some tea.

'Sweetheart, *guess what*?' came her mother's voice down the line.

'WE'RE IN CANNES!' shouted Cameron's voice in the background.

'You're in *WHAT*?' Jess shouted back, then darted a look at Leo who turned to her, his eyebrows raised. 'You're in Cannes?'

'Cameron, get back ...' Patty muttered. 'Yes, honey, we decided—'

'I DECIDED,' Cameron shouted.

'Cameron *suggested* that since Cannes sounded so wonderful and sunny, and we'd otherwise have to wait another year to experience the festival in full swing, we should nip over for a few days, visit you, see some stars ...'

'So where are you right now?' Why did they have to be here? She loved her family, but this was her holiday. Her holiday, where she was pretty much faking everything about herself. Gaaah, it was like your parents turning

253

up at a freshers' week party at uni just after you'd made friends and told everyone you were really into dubstep when actually you just loved Britney Spears.

'We're in Nice, just getting on the train. Did you know you could fly from Bristol to Nice, sweetie? You don't need to get a sleeper train from London like you did.'

'I know, it was all just part of the adventure. Anyway, have you got somewhere to stay?'

'No, not yet, we'll sort it out when we get there.'

Cameron butted in again. 'It's actually really fulfilling to choose your accommodation when you arrive. You know, when we were in Nicaragua—'

'Cameron, put Mum back on.'

Patty returned. 'Where are you staying?'

Jess wriggled away from Leo, who had wandered over with a cuppa and was now trying to prise the covers from beneath her claws so he could have a bit too. He hopped about comically, pretending to be freezing, and she had to turn away, albeit with a smile. 'Um, I'll text you the details.'

'Would you mind popping down and seeing if they have any rooms?'

'I'm not actually there right now . . .' Cringe.

'Where are you?'

'Yeah, um, jogging.'

'Jessica . . . '

'Getting breakfast for Bryony.'

'Are you with a boy?' Patty hooted so loudly that Jess leapt up, leaving the duvet behind and ran naked into the bathroom.

'Mum, shut up.'

'Sweetheart, don't you dare be embarrassed. You needed a bit of love and sunshine in your life.'

'Ew,' Cameron said. She could hear her dad guffawing as well.

'Text me the details and we'll go to your hotel ourselves, then maybe meet you for brunch? Bring your man along if you like.'

'Okay.' *No.* 'I'll see if he's free.' *Not a chance.*

After Jess had hung up she grabbed a deliciously squidgy InterContinental robe and crept out of the bathroom to find Leo sitting up on the bed in a tight duvet cocoon that he refused to relinquish.

'What's going on? Was that your parents, are they here?'

'And my brother,' Jess said glumly.

'Brilliant, I love an awkward parental gatecrash. Can I meet them?'

'Sure, at some point. Let me get them settled in, though, and then we'll arrange something. Maybe for tomorrow or the next day, or never.'

Leo laughed and pulled her into his cocoon. 'Lucky

for you, I've got stuff to do today, but it would be nice if you didn't convince them to go straight back to Cornwall.'

Jess began to snuggle back into Leo then peeped at the clock. Seven-fifteen; maid service would start at any moment. With a groan she sat back up. 'Let's get out of here.'

Jess leant against the wall of the Hôtel du Bliss, wishing she smoked. She could really do with a cigarette, but this bottle of Orangina would have to do. She rubbed her eyes then looked at her watch again. She'd told her family to get a taxi from the station, but knowing her parents they'd have got chatting to the most eccentric person on the train and end up arriving via his tuk-tuk or horse and carriage or something.

Eventually they appeared, and even though she was still feeling aggravated that they'd gatecrashed her holiday, and even though she had no idea how she was going to prevent them meeting Leo, seeing their familiar faces light up at the sight of her made happiness wash over her.

'Hiiiii,' she said, rushing forward to meet them.

Patty threw her arms around her daughter. 'Honey,

you look beautiful.' She pulled back and looked at Jess. 'Doesn't she look beautiful? Cannes works for you, sweetheart, you're all bronzed and glowing and—' She gasped.

'What?' asked Jess, hugging her dad and Cameron in turn. 'Mum, what?'

'This boy has made you *very* happy, hasn't he?'

'Mum!'

'EW,' said Cameron.

'Don't be embarrassed, tell us about him.'

'I managed to get you a room here,' Jess said, changing the subject and leading them inside. 'It's not very glam, I'm afraid, but Cannes is chock-a-block at the moment.'

'That's all right, Jessie,' said her dad, waving at the receptionist. 'We've stayed in much shabbier places.'

'Yeah,' Cameron jumped in. 'Dad – remember when we stayed in that campsite in Alaska? Hey, is Bryony here?'

Cameron had always fancied Bryony, much to both Bryony's and Jess's disgust. Jess had called Bryony on the way back to her hotel to warn her of his impending arrival and she'd been only too happy to make an early start with work, for a change.

Jess rolled her eyes. 'No, she's working, I think she's at a couple of screenings today, probably hanging out with ridiculously good-looking actors. You know she interviewed Veronica Hay yesterday? Anyway, if you're all here, who's looking after the café?'

'Manpreet, of course,' Jeff said, hauling the bags into the lift, then leaving them to chug upwards while they all took the stairs.

'You left Manpreet in charge, on her own?'

'She's your manager, she knows what she's doing,' said Patty.

'I know, but she's only been with us for a year, and now she has no one to turn to if there's a problem.'

'She'll be fine. Besides, before your café she worked for years up in that cupcake place in *London*. You know how experienced she is. Ever heard of not sweating the small stuff?' To Jess's mum, if you worked in London you must be the crème de la crème, as if the queen had hand-picked you to work within the city walls.

Jess dragged the suitcases out of the lift. 'How long are you all here for, exactly?'

'Just until the end of the festival,' Patty replied. 'You don't mind us being here do you, sweetie? It's just that you made it all sound so fabulous.'

'No, Mum, I like you being here,' Jess answered truthfully. 'But I am going to be busy for some of the time, with Bryony.'

'Understood. We won't be getting in your way at all.'

'It'll be like we're not even here,' added Jeff.

'Can I go to some screenings with Bryony?' asked Cameron.

'No, they don't let weirdos and stalkers into the screenings.'

'Jessica,' her mum scolded. 'Cameron's not that bad.'

'Hey, not *that bad*?' Cameron protested.

They dumped their bags inside the triple room and took in their surroundings with a satisfied sigh. Her parents really were great, content with making a happy adventure out of anywhere they went.

'Before we get out of your way,' Patty said, squeezing her daughter's arm, 'would you happen to have a spare hour to show us your favourite bits of Cannes?'

As they walked along the Croisette, Jess's parents oohed and aahed with the best of them. Cameron tried to play it cool, of course, but his eyes were on stalks. Jess was sweating all over, convinced that Leo or Richard or Céline would spring out in front of them at any moment and blow everything.

'Well that's it!' she said, clapping her hands, as they reached the Palais des Festivals. 'This is where all the magic happens. Look at the red carpet, isn't it . . . red and long? Okay, who wants to go and sunbathe on our roof terrace? I'll buy the local rosé!'

'Oh, sweetie, let's just keep going a little further – I want to see the marina where all the mega yachts are kept.'

'Hahaha, NO. You don't even need to bother going all the way around there. Look at that one out at sea. And that one there, how big is that? Yachts, yachts, everywhere.'

'Come on, lazybones,' said her dad. 'Just a little bit further then we'll get you a glass of something. My treat.'

'Yeah, lazybones,' sneered Cameron as they began walking again, so she trod on his foot.

Her parents strolled leisurely past the yachts, stopping for a good ogle now and then, while Jess held back, straining to see whether Leo was pottering about on the deck of his yacht far in the distance. *Please don't be there, please don't be there.*

'Well, that's the lot of them,' she yelped a few boats before Leo's, and just at that moment he appeared on the gangway. 'Group hug!' she cried, pulling her parents and Cameron into a huddle. She peeped out and her heart caught in her throat to see the drug lord man standing behind Leo, smoking and looking like he was in a billboard for *Reservoir Dogs*. Leo was hauling a crate aboard the yacht when one of the boxes came loose and white powder puffed out of the corner. *No.*

But what happened next brought shocked tears to her eyes. The other man looked mad and berated Leo, loudly enough to turn heads. He then held up a large knife that glinted in the sun, and a desperate '*Leo!*' escaped Jess's mouth.

Leo and the man looked up, and then he scrambled over the boxes and crossed the marina to her.

'Hi,' he said, angling her away from the yacht. 'What brings you here? Are you Jess's family? It's great to meet you! Have you seen the beach? Let me show it to you.'

Jess searched his face, craning her neck to look behind him. 'Leo, he had a—'

'*Leo,*' called the man on the boat, his voice stern.

'I'll be one minute,' Leo called back through gritted teeth.

'Leo,' said Jeff, shaking his hand. 'Good to meet you, son.'

'Good to meet you, too. You have an amazing daughter.'

'Awww,' Patty melted.

Jess cringed, but still snuck a touch closer to Leo.

'So did you manage to get a room in the Carlton, too?' Leo asked politely.

'The Carlton? We wish,' Cameron spluttered. 'We're all the way across town in the—'

'Oh, *hi!*' Jess greeted the man as he stomped over to them.

Leo spun around and Jess noticed he took a protective step in front of her. She hated this intimidating bouncer of a man. 'Just need a moment, okay, Bruno?'

'We have work to do,' Bruno stated.

'Yep, I'll be right there.'

'Is that your boat, Leo?' Patty asked, taking a step forward.

'That's my boat.' Leo grinned, glancing at Bruno, who snarled at him.

Patty edged closer, skirting around Leo as he tried to block her path in the politest of ways. 'It's nice, isn't it, Jess?' said her mum. 'Bet you never thought you'd meet a man with a superyacht, did you?'

It was excruciating how quickly her mother was unintentionally undoing the past week and a half of trying *not* to look like a gold digger. 'Hahaha, oh *Mum*,' she said, through lack of anything else to say.

'It's lovely,' Patty continued. 'Bryony should write a story about this. Wouldn't that make a lovely story, Cameron?'

'Yeah, Bryony's really good at everything,' he said, beaming.

Jess gave a fake laugh. 'I suppose she might want

to write a lovely little short story about the boat, *haha*, "Once upon a time" et cetera.'

'No, for the magazine,' Patty corrected.

'Bryony's a journalist?' asked Leo.

'Yeah, sometimes, when she's not modelling ...' said Jess.

'Bryony's a model?' Cameron asked. 'What kind of modelling? Like, um, wedding dresses? Or underwear ...?'

'No, just a hand model.' *Shut up you bloody pervert*, she glared at Cameron, hoping he'd finally pick up on some sibling telepathy.

'For Naomi Campbell,' Leo added. 'Cool, huh?'

Bruno the Drug Lord stepped closer and glared at Jess. 'I know where I've seen you. On the terrace at the Carlton.'

Shit. Balls. Shitballs.

Patty gasped. 'Oh, you've been to the Carlton, honey? I'd love to go for a drink there. Eleven euros for an Earl Grey though ...'

'But what's eleven euros, hey?' tittered Jess again.

'Haven't you got into the holiday spirit?' said her dad.

Bruno was not smiling. 'You were with your friend, and she was asking me all kinds of questions.'

Jess's mouth felt dry. Bruno might just kill her. 'What? No. Not that many questions.'

'Bruno, you met Bryony?' said Leo, then turned to Jess quizzically.

'Well, I recognised him, and I told Bryony, and she just wanted to . . . I don't know . . . ' Jess murmured.

Bruno faced Leo again, cutting her off. 'So you're befriending journalists?'

'Actually, I didn't know Bryony was a journalist,' Leo sighed.

'He won't be pleased. You don't want to keep your job?'

Who wouldn't be pleased? There's a drug overlord?

'Are you a journalist?' Bruno turned to Jess, who backed away slightly.

'Oh no,' said Jess's mum, patting her on the back. 'Jessie owns a café.'

'*Chain*,' Jess coughed.

'What was that, darling?'

'Better get on,' Leo and Jess said at exactly the same time. *Yes, let's both put a lid on it.* Jess met his eye and they exchanged a *we'll talk later* look.

'Lovely to meet you,' Leo said to Jess's family.

'Oh and you, Leo. Maybe we could meet for a dinner while we're here,' said Patty.

No!

'I'd love that,' said Leo, backing away and blowing Jess a kiss.

'Lovely to meet you,' Jess said to Bruno, then cursed her good manners. He snarled a goodbye.

Jess turned and ushered her family away, confused as to whether her cover had just been blown, or Leo's.

Bryony burst in through the door of their bedroom where Jess was caught in the act of polishing off a bag of Bacon Goût. 'Harvey just called and told me I can't be seen around the yacht any more. He says it's safer if I stay away, and to tell you the same, too. What the hell?'

'I'll call Leo, this is ridiculous. Jess filled Bryony in on the highlights of the afternoon as she rummaged for her phone. It's Leo's yacht, we can go there if we want.' Jess started dialling, but Bryony snatched her phone away.

'I spoke to Céline today. Meems, she confirmed everything.'

'What?' No way, Jess refused to believe it could be true.

'I asked about drugs and how they come into Cannes, and if people like Leo and Harvey were involved and—'

'Whoa, whoa, whoa. You asked straight out about Leo and Harvey?'

Bryony paused for a moment and caught her breath, while Jess waited impatiently. 'She was having such a good time, telling me all these stories about things she'd seen, that I thought I'd stop skirting around the issue.'

'So what did she say, exactly?' Jess's heart thu-thumped. She already knew she didn't want to hear this, and when Bryony's gaze suddenly turned to pity-eyes she was close to covering her ears and singing '*Lalalalala*'.

Bryony spoke slowly. 'She said their boat comes in every year and Leo does all the business, that there's no party without them and that . . . '

'And that?'

'And that they always have girls hanging around them.'

Jess's heart broke in two, one half shattering for Leo, for what he was involved in and the waste of who he was, and one for her, for the fool she'd been. But she stared ahead, unflinching, refusing to cry again. This was her *holiday*.

Bryony stepped forward and reached a tentative arm around her friend. 'Jess, are you okay? I know it's hard to hear—'

Jess inhaled and cut Bryony off. 'Yes, I'm okay. Fancy a trip to the beach?' she said brusquely.

'The beach?'

'I need to speak to Céline, to hear this for myself. Do you think she'll tell Leo you were asking about all this?'

'She might do.' Bryony picked up her handbag and

they left the room, Jess marching and Bryony loping along beside her, watching her out of the corner of her eye.

They speed-walked in silence, Jess digesting what had happened, what she had learnt. So it was true. No, she still couldn't believe it. *Leo*?

After a while, Jess muttered, 'Bruno – the tall guy, Scarface – was pretty pissed off when he found out you were a journalist today.'

'He found out?' cried Bryony. 'So Leo knows, too? And Harvey?'

'My mum let it slip, said you could write a story about Leo's yacht. Sorry to blow your cover.'

'That's okay, your mum didn't know.' Bryony chewed her lip, a list of potential ramifications shuffling through her mind.

With every step all Jess heard in her mind was *Le-o*, *Le-o*, *Le-o*. How could he be a drug smuggler? She didn't know drug dealers; she was from Cornwall.

Okay, there probably were drug dealers in Cornwall, but she'd certainly never met any before, let alone slept in their beds and fallen in . . . whatever with them.

Noooo, her heart whined, pleading for it not to be true.

Finally they were at Noix de Coco, and Jess didn't hesitate to run down the steps, Bryony right behind.

Céline stood behind the counter and rolled her eyes, cursing in French when she saw who it was. 'Wow, the desperate journalist is back: *"Please help me with my story."* Well, you just missed your new friend.'

'I need you to tell me what you told Bryony.'

Céline scowled at her. 'I have a job to do, you know.'

'Wait, who?' asked Bryony, pushing past Jess's jutting elbows as she stood, hands on hips, giving Céline a thunderous look.

'Bruno. He is such a pussycat.' Céline smiled.

'Bruno was here?' Jess and Bryony asked in unison. Worry, more worry, trickled into Jess's conscious.

'Yes, he is here all the time. And when I found out we both knew Bryony, well, we had a good catch-up.'

Bryony snarled. 'Céline, what did you tell him?'

'I told him you were writing a story about drug smuggling on Leo's yacht, and that Leo's been helping you. Was that wrong?'

The worry stopped trickling and gushed forth like a burst pipe. 'Why would you do that to Leo?' Jess cried. 'I thought you were friends.'

Céline shrugged. 'I didn't know Leo wasn't supposed to talk to journalists.'

'But is Leo now in trouble?' Her voice wobbled.

'Well I don't think you'll be seeing him any more,' and she laughed wickedly at Jess.

Jess took off up the steps and Bryony raced after her. 'Meems, where are you going?'

'She said we just missed him. If he's going to harm Leo I have to . . . ' Jess paused on the promenade, all happy holidaymakers and sparkling seas, her panic a stark contrast to the idyllic scene.

'Have to what, Jess? This is over our heads.'

'I can't not do anything, it's Leo.'

'But Leo's a—'

'Don't say it,' she sobbed. 'I have to go.'

Jess ran down the Croisette as fast as she could, ignoring Bryony's calls. She had to get to Leo, whoever he was, because despite everything he was hers. As she neared the Palais des Festivals she spotted Bruno, tall and imposing, and leading a small group of people towards the marina.

Jess sprinted the other way around the festival hall, dodging tourists and red carpet barricades, ignoring her tiredness and focusing on her determination to get to Leo first.

'Leo,' she shouted as she neared his yacht. 'Leo!'

There was no answer, but she could see him in the galley, bopping along to some sounds on his headphones.

She called out again, darting a look back the way she came, but still he didn't hear her, so with a frustrated growl she grabbed at the thick rope and unravelled it from the mooring bollard as quickly as she could. Never had she been more grateful to her dad for teaching her the basics of boating on those fishing trips. And to her kettlebell teacher for giving her what were proving to be worthy triceps.

In no time, she'd flung the first rope up onto the deck and started on the second, and that's when Leo spotted her and stuck his head out of the galley, beaming.

'Well hello, lovely lady!'

Tears started to flow because she knew this would all be shattered at any moment, so lost for words she focused on unwinding.

'Hey, what's wrong? What are you doing?' he asked, running down to meet her, narrowly avoiding being hit in the face by the second mooring line, but she pushed him back on board and began struggling to lift the gangway.

'Help me bring this in,' she choked.

'Um, okay.'

'We need to leave.'

Leo turned her to face him and wiped away her tears as she searched his eyes. 'What's going on?' he asked.

'That's what's going on.' She pointed at Bruno, at

the head of a crowd of people, who had just rounded the corner and were marching along the marina.

Leo took them all in, the colour draining from his face, and then turned back to her. 'Jess, listen to me. I know this is new, and I know we're still getting to know each other, but I want you to know that whatever you find out about me, however it makes you feel, it's not going to change how I feel about you.'

'What does that mean?' It was like he was in her brain, saying the things she wanted to say to him, but it scared her because what he was hiding was so much worse than her silly little lies. If he really was involved in this, she would lose him, one day, one way or another: to prison, to death, or to the sea and the party crowd. This man whose eyes reflected the ocean shouldn't be locked away, so would that mean he'd always be travelling, moving on, escaping?

'It means I'm falling for you. So there. No one eats a crêpe like you do. No one reminds me of both brand-new sunrises and classic Hollywood stars at the same time like you do. I want to share a jar of Nutella with you for ever, just so you know.'

'I don't know if you will.'

'I will.'

'But you don't know me – oh God, he's coming.' She looked past Leo at Bruno, who'd picked up his pace as he neared the yacht, a bitter look upon his features. She turned and ran inside the boat.

'Jess, wait, I need to tell you something. *Jess*—' Leo followed her up the steps toward the helm, but his foot slipped on the final step and he came crashing down.

Jess spun around and gasped at Leo crouched on the ground, his hand to his head. He moaned, woozy and disorientated. Outside, Bruno shouted.

Jess ran to the control panel and made a snap decision. Whatever would happen later could be dealt with later. For now, he was hers, not this horrible man's, and she had to keep him safe, so with a holler of 'UP YOURS!' out the window, Jess powered up the engine and began to slide the boat out of the dock.

There were shouts from back on the marina, and no, in answer to them, she didn't know what she was doing. But luckily the superyacht faced open water, so she'd worry about that when she got out there. But the shouts were drowned out by Leo, who lifted his head, his eyes blurry, and just before passing out said, 'Jess, stop – this isn't my boat.'

Part Four

Thunk. Leo's head hit the deck and Jess stared at him in horror for a moment that stretched before her like a conveyor belt.

'*Stop – this isn't my boat,*' he'd said before going down. How could it not be his boat? She'd spent the night on here, with him. She'd talked to him across the water from Tara's boat. She'd seen him on here with Harvey and Bruno. And she was on here with him now, having just powered it up and pulled out of the harbour. In fact, it was currently motoring into open water.

If Leo wasn't the owner, whose superyacht had she just stolen?

And then suddenly she snapped to. 'Leo!' she cried, and with a glance out the window – nope, no impending traffic – she swooped down to him. 'Leo? Can you hear me?'

Tears stung her eyes when Leo didn't come round. He was breathing, thank God, but he'd had a cracking bump. Jess, shaking, covered her mouth with her hands; everything had gone so wrong and she didn't know what to do. She'd stolen a yacht and she had no idea how to return it, because yes, she'd been on fishing boats, and yes, she'd understood enough to pull the boat away from the marina and go dead ahead, but she couldn't bring it back in. She wouldn't be able to park a superyacht in between all the others like she was just driving her Toyota into Sainsbury's car park. She'd cause *millions* in damage. She was in over her head.

Not to mention the gang of drug dealers stamping about on the pier waiting to do who-knew-what to her, and to Leo. And Bryony! She'd left Bryony on her own with them. What a horrible friend she was.

Leo, the one person who might be able to help with at least part of the problem, the man she was falling for but who she didn't really know at all, was unconscious at her feet.

I want to go home, she thought. *I want to go home.* She'd had enough of this, enough of playing lifestyles of the rich and famous; she wanted to be back inside that comfort zone she'd been so desperate to escape, wrapped in a blanket, eating Mars bars and watching *Friends*.

She became aware of her phone ringing.

'Bryony . . . ' she wobbled down the receiver.

'Meems, can you ask Leo to bring the boat back as soon as possible,' Bryony said, her voice laced with anxiety.

'I can't, he's all . . . unconscious.' She looked at Leo lying there and her heart broke for the hundredth time.

'What? Are you serious?'

'He fell over and hit his head when I started the yacht—'

'*You* started the yacht?!'

'I just wanted to escape.' How true that was.

'Is Leo okay? Are you okay?'

'I don't know – I don't know what to do.' Jess, her mouth dry, tried to gulp away the lump in her throat and the nausea you get when you know you've seriously messed something up.

Bryony heard the panic in her voice. 'Is he breathing?' she asked carefully.

'Yes.'

'Is he bleeding?'

'No.'

There were muffled voices and then Bryony spoke again. 'That's good. Now, you have to come back.'

'I don't know how. As soon as Leo wakes up he can

bring us back. I'm sure he'll come to any minute, he has to.' She knelt beside him, searching every line in his face, every eyelash, for a sign of movement. *Please come to, please, please.*

More muffled voices at the end of the phone.

'*What the hell, Harvey? Jesus Christ!* Jess, Leo can't bring the boat in, he doesn't know how. It's not his boat, *apparently.* Here, Harvey wants to talk to you . . . *Tell her.*'

Harvey came on the line. 'Mate, is Leo okay?'

'Harvey, why is everyone saying this isn't Leo's boat?'

At that moment Leo stirred, making a low moan and fluttering his eyelids. Jess dropped the phone at her side and leant over him, relief and happiness overwhelming her to the point of causing her hands to tremble as she ran her fingers over his eyebrows and a tear to plop down onto his cheek. Look at him, he was so vulnerable. 'You woke for Harvey. You two are so sweet,' she murmured, smiling at him. She picked the phone up again. 'Harvey, he's okay, he's waking up. Now what's going on?'

'Um, yeah, so Leo doesn't exactly own the yacht.'

'So I've heard. It's the drug lord's, isn't it?'

'Eh?'

Jess sighed. 'Harvey, we know about you two. You

278

need to keep away from Bruno, he thinks . . . oh God, you're going to hate us. I'm sorry . . . he thinks you and Leo have been feeding Bryony information.'

'Wait . . . ' There was a pause before Harvey spoke to someone else, someone near him. *'Bruno, why would you not want us hanging out with the ladies?'*

'Is he there with you?' Jess panicked, a fresh wave of fear creeping up on her. 'Is Bryony safe? Put Bryony back on! BRYONY?'

'Jess, it's me,' said Bryony, coming back on the phone. 'Calm down, I'm here with Bruno—'

'Are you okay? What's happening?'

'I'm fine, he's not a drug lord. *Sorry – again – about that,*' Bryony spoke away from the mouthpiece.

'Who is he?'

'He's the security guard for the yacht and . . . um . . . he's called a police charter to come out and get you.'

'Oh, that's great,' breathed Jess. 'We're just outside the marina, pointing out to sea—'

'Yeah, we can see you. You're not exactly hiding. But, Jess, you don't understand, Bruno called the police before I got here. They're coming to *get you.*'

Jess didn't hear her, as at that moment Leo's eyes opened and he struggled up to a sitting position, holding his head.

'Hey, sailor,' Jess said to him with tenderness.

Leo blinked and looked around him with the confused gaze of someone woken from a weird dream. He made a noise that sounded a bit like a question.

'Are you okay? Leo, do you know where you are?' *If so, please enlighten me.*

He rubbed his head and the cloud lifted, and he smiled up at Jess.

'Guuuurl, you knock me out,' Leo joked weakly.

Jess turned back to the phone. 'Sorry, Bry, Leo's awake now. What were you saying?'

'Stop googly-eyeing Leo. I'm saying the police are coming to get you. The yacht does not belong to Leo and you just stole it from under the nose of the security guard and the owner. *Seriously*, Jess, do you get what I'm telling you?'

It felt like someone had just turned off a bright light. Bryony might physically tower over Jess but she never looked down on her. For Bryony to speak so bluntly, she must be really worried. Jess turned from Leo and spoke quietly to her best friend. 'Please tell me what's going on.'

Bryony took a deep breath. 'Okay. This is what Harvey told me. Leo is not the owner of the yacht, or of any yacht. He's the chef. Harvey is a deckhand, and Bruno is a security guard. And the rest of the crew were on leave because the yacht was due to just be docked at the festival for two weeks; the owner only needed security, someone to cater for on-board parties and someone to keep it shipshape.'

It took a few moments for what Bryony was saying to register, and Jess's first thought was, surprisingly: *good*. She was glad Leo wasn't a billionaire and, more to the point, glad he wasn't a drug smuggler. Never had normal seemed so comforting. But as Bryony's words sunk in, the momentary relief gave way to the realisation of how tangled up everything had become, with all its lies and implications.

'Leo's the chef?' Jess turned and looked at Leo, who peeped at her with heartbreak in his eyes.

'I'm sorry,' he whispered, his hand still rubbing his head.

She moved away from him. 'But, Bry, I spent the night here, in his room ... It wasn't his room, was it?'

Flashing blue lights lit up the windows from outside.

'I guess I'd better go,' Jess sighed to Bryony.

'I'll be right here on the pier waiting for you. Are you okay?'

'I don't know. I mean, this is obviously just a very bad dream, so I guess I'll be fine any moment now.'

'Meems—'

'See you soon.' She hung up and walked past Leo onto the deck, where the police greeted her with an unfriendly shout that she assumed meant 'put your hands up'.

'Do you want me to lower the steps for you?' she asked wearily. '*Escaliers dans le . . . sea?*' Whatever.

They ignored her and boarded the yacht as if by some kind of Spiderman magic, and she found herself looking up at the sky and laughing at the surrealness of it all as – *clip* – a handcuff was put on her, and then – *clip* – another.

But I'm just a tourist. I'm from Cornwall and I own a café. And I just fell in love with a boy who liked Nutella. Nothing to see here, officer.

The engine roared to life as one of the policemen, who she guessed was some kind of sea policeman who could drive anything, began to take them back into the marina. Another officer brought out Leo, who was blinking hard with the sudden motion of it all.

'Careful with him, he's hurt,' Jess sighed, because even through her confusion, and her early stages of irritation, he was still Leo. Whoever that was.

The officer pushed him down next to her, Leo wincing in pain, and then walked to the other side of the deck to make a phone call. Leo immediately turned to face Jess, asking, 'Are you okay? Are the cuffs hurting you?'

'I'm fine.'

'Jess—'

'So I hear you don't own this yacht,' she interrupted, her anger, fuelled by the adrenalin and panic of the last few minutes, finally bubbling up.

Leo shook his head. 'I'm sorry.'

'And I hear you're the chef.'

He nodded.

'So should I assume you also don't own a number of exclusive restaurants in exotic corners of the world?'

He finally looked down at his lap and she studied the back of his neck. It had all been lies; she felt so stupid. But . . . A tiny part of her, a tiny, nagging, irritating part of her, reminded her about her own lies, her own cover-ups. Jess pushed the thought away as Leo started to speak.

'The only things I own fit into a tiny cabin on the bottom deck, a little place I like to tell people is a machine room.'

Of course it was. 'So it's not full of cocaine then?'

'Cocaine?'

'I have to admit, despite you being a huge liar and a fake—' That nagging feeling fizzed in the depths of her stomach again, a warning not to be so ferocious. 'I'm glad you're not a drug dealer. Bryony was *this close* to writing a story about you for her magazine.' *And now she had nothing, and she'd be fired. Oh, Bryony.*

'I thought Bryony was a hand model.'

'She could be a hand model, she's got lovely hands. She's just . . . not. She's a journalist. Isn't today full of surprises?'

'Crap,' Leo muttered, then chewed his bottom lip. 'Are you a journalist?'

'No, I own a café.'

'*A* café?'

Busted. 'Yes, *a* café.' He raised his eyebrows at her and she looked away, blushing. 'Can we deal with one thing at a time, please? Why are you so anti-journalist if you're not doing something *illegal*?' She struggled against the handcuffs and hissed the last word as a police officer marched past.

'Because my boss, the real owner, is very private. He hates people snooping around his things.'

Jess let out a snort of disbelief. 'We spent the night in his bedroom! I was topless in his wardrobe!'

A snigger slipped out of Leo and Jess shot him a stern look.

As the superyacht glided back in towards the marina, Jess could see Bryony with Harvey, Bruno and a small gathered crowd, all watching from the shore.

'Why did you lie to me about everything?' Jess asked Leo. And yes, why had *she* lied to him about everything? This whole mess could have been avoided.

'I didn't, not about everything.'

'Jessica!' bellowed a voice from the marina, from a woman running around the side of the Palais des Festivals. *'Jessica, I will save you!'*

It was Patty, Jess's mum, followed by her dad and eventually Cameron, who was slow-jogging in that way you do when someone holds the door open for you at the end of quite a long corridor and the whole thing is awkward and embarrassing for everyone involved.

Leo nudged her with his knee to get her attention again. 'And I only lied because I like you, because I wanted to fit in with your lifestyle. If lying meant spending time with you, in my stupid brain that trumped telling the truth and risking you wanting to have nothing to do with me.'

'You think I only liked you because you had a superyacht?' asked Jess, gentler this time as the weight of her role in all this made itself very apparent.

'I'm not saying that's the only reason you liked me, but I know the circles you move in. Don't pretend you would have so much as given me the time of day if you knew I was only the ship's chef.'

Well now hang on a minute ... 'Wait, wait,

wait – that's presumptuous. How dare you say who I would have given my time to!'

'I'm not accusing you of acting better than me, but if you knew I had nothing, how could you not think I was after your money? Trust me, I've spent a long time on this scene and people like you don't fall in love with people like me. The dynamics just ... bump.'

'Oh boohoo!' Jess barked. 'People like me? I may have made friends with this crowd but *you're* the one who made the assumption that I was some kind of socialite.'

'*You* made an assumption about *me*; I just went along with it because I wanted to keep talking to you. So are you saying you lied, too?'

Jess huffed and puffed and eventually answered. 'I embellished. I didn't lie, much. You just assumed and I didn't correct you, because I didn't want you to think I was a gold digger.'

The boat slid back in beside Tara's yacht as if nothing had ever happened, and the policeman cut the engine.

Leo was pulled to his feet by one of the officers. 'So because you thought I owned a superyacht and had a room I wouldn't let you into, you and your journalist friend were going to expose Harvey and me as drug dealers? Which we're not,' he added to the policeman.

Jess was heaved up too. 'I was trying to prove you weren't, but you didn't make it easy for me.'

'Darling, are you okay?' Patty cried, running up to the back of the yacht.

Bryony was close behind. 'Meems, it's going to be all right. I'll help you explain everything.'

'Leo, mate, you hurt?' shouted Harvey, who was accompanied by a fuming Bruno, who blocked out the rest of his group with the enormous bulk of his body.

'Maybe you just need to check your facts a bit better next time,' said Leo to Jess, ignoring everyone else, and as they were led off the boat she narrowed her eyes at him.

'Well, maybe you shouldn't be working on a yacht that's on a police watch list, hmmm?'

He struggled to turn his head back to her, exasperated. 'It's on there for security reasons, it's an expensive boat! It's a watch list, like, "keep a watch out for it". Like Neighbourhood Watch.'

'Oh.' *Oh.*

'Jess, where are they taking you?' Patty asked. Jeff stepped forwards, fire in his face. Cameron leapt in with a gallant, 'Get off my sister, please, *s'il vous plaît.*'

The police ignored them, and Jess and Leo continued to ignore them as well, as they were too busy at each other's throats.

Jess blushed at her mistake about the watch list. 'Well . . . even so, don't you think it was just a *bit* shady letting me stay in your so-called bedroom with you?'

'Oh, I'm sorry I can't afford a room at the Carlton, Queen Jessica of Cannes.'

'Neither can I, we were there illegally. I broke the law for you. But not in a serious way,' she added to the policeman.

'So you're saying that even though you were letting your journalist friend write a story about all the drug dealing Bruno, Harvey and I were apparently involved in, you were the one actually breaking the law?'

'How else was I supposed to compete against a flippin' great superyacht?'

'It was never a competition!'

'But the stakes were still high. I wanted you to think we were equals, I wanted you to . . . to trust me.' It seemed really silly now.

'Jess, you should have trusted *me*,' implored Leo, coming to a standstill and facing Jess. The crowd of Jess's family, Bryony, Harvey, Bruno and whoever else was behind Leo stopped abruptly. 'I can't believe you thought I was a drug dealer. Did you just go back after our night together on the yacht and report it all to Bryony?'

'No! Only some of it.'

Leo sighed and let the policeman pull him back into a walk.

Jess trotted along beside him. 'I thought we were about to be *murdered* by Bruno the drug lord. I didn't know we were just hiding from your ship's security!'

'Will everyone stop calling me a drug lord in front of the police, please?' Bruno roared.

'Wait!' shouted Patty, and everyone came to a stop once again. 'I'm sure I've seen this boat before. Do you recognise it, darling?' she mused, turning to her husband.

Jess wriggled in the handcuffs. 'Mum—'

'I don't recognise it,' Cameron chipped in.

'No, I'm sure … I'm sure I've been on this yacht. In the sixties. I distinctly remember lying out on that deck trying to get an all-over tan—'

'Oh, now I remember!' cried Jeff.

'God, *Mum*, let's go.'

'Well, my eyes deceive me but my loins do not! If it isn't Party Patty and Gigolo Jeff. I knew I'd seen those wiggling hips strutting away from my boat before. And yours too, Patty, HA!' A short, sparkling grey-haired man dressed in crisp Dolce & Gabbana loungewear and a massive gold watch danced out from behind Bruno and struck a pose.

'Mr Nail,' Leo sighed. 'I'm so sorry about all of this.'

'Who's he?' Jess asked.

'He's the owner. He's the one you should have hooked up with.'

Fuming, she glared at Leo. 'Don't you dare—'

'*Eeeeee!*' shrieked Patty, slapping her hands on her thighs. 'Rusty?!'

'Rusty Nail? What kind of a name—' Bryony laughed, before clamping her hand over her mouth.

Rusty held his arms wide to embrace Jess's parents, much to the surprise of everybody else.

'Mum?' Jess called, struggling against the police.

'Oh, right. Rusty, this is my daughter Jess; Jess, this is my ex, um, friend, Rusty.'

'Is that what the avant-garde are calling it nowadays?' Rusty giggled wickedly. *Urgh*.

'Rusty was my best pal!' Jeff piped up with a proud grin. Evidently there was no animosity about the fact that his wife had been 'friends' with Rusty. What a strange time the sixties must have been.

'I remember,' Patty giggled. 'I remember cruising around on this bad boy – hahaha – when – hahaha—'

'WITH THE MARACAS!' finished Rusty, and all three of them fell about laughing. The police officers yanked Jess and Leo forwards.

'Oh, now, wait a minute, Mr Officers,' Rusty called. '*Excusez-moi, gendarmes*.' He turned to Patty and Jeff.

'This young lady who took my yacht for a joyride – she's of your DNA?'

'She is. She's our pride and joy,' nodded Patty, at which Cameron looked sulky. 'I'm sure she was just having a bit of fun. You aren't angry are you, groovy-boos?'

'Like mother like daughter, hey, doll?' purred Rusty. 'I'm not angry. Officers, release that young woman immediately!'

Bruno sidled over and spoke to the policemen in French.

'And Leo?' Patty asked. 'He seems like such a nice boy. You wouldn't fire him, would you?'

Rusty laughed and slapped Leo on the back. 'How could I fire someone who met the gal who reunited me with you two?'

'Mr Nail, thank you.' Leo rubbed his wrists when they were freed and, without thinking, took Jess's and rubbed them too. 'So you all knew each other back in the day? When you had those years of travelling before Jess came along?'

Jess tried to take her eyes off Leo and refocus on her parents, but his touch on her wrists, so gentle and relaxing despite all they'd just said to each other, left her brain befuddled.

'Oh yes,' her mother recalled with a happy sigh,

which snapped Jess back to attention with a reflexive eye roll she just couldn't control. 'We had an amazing summer here in the Med, going from island to island on this beauty—'

'Yeah, I remember it so clearly,' Cameron jumped in.

'No, honey, you weren't born then.'

He skulked back, pouting.

Suddenly, a sweep of tiredness nearly knocked Jess off her feet as she looked up at Leo. She could easily sink into his arms right now, but it didn't feel right any more. There was too much drama, too many lies – from both of them – and now she was confused about who he even was. She felt stripped naked. The problem with being someone you're not is that the real you will fight to the death to be heard. It was time to go back to being her.

'I'm going to go,' she murmured to Leo.

'Where?'

'My hotel. We're staying in a little lodge place over the other side of town.'

'That's where you've been sleeping?'

Jess nodded, the two feet between them feeling like five miles. She turned. 'Bry, Mum, Dad, Cam, are you ready to go?'

'Sure,' said Bryony, with a squeeze of Harvey's hand.

'Is this . . . ?' Leo searched her face.

'I don't know. I don't know anything right now.'

He stepped forwards, and although he didn't touch her he was so close she could feel his breath on her face. 'I'm angry at you. And you're angry at me. But I haven't changed, you know, not really. All you saw of me was *me*. Please don't leave my life before we've sorted this out.'

'How can I? How can we stay in each other's lives? It was never going to work really,' she choked.

He took a step backwards, wounded, and immediately she regretted what she had said.

'I guess if it was always going to have an expiration date, you're right, there's no point in carrying this on.'

'I just ... ' She was close to tears again. 'My brain hurts. I'm going to go.' She turned and walked away, and wouldn't look back because she didn't want to see how much she'd hurt him.

For a few moments she was alone, then Bryony and Cameron draped their arms over her shoulders and guided her back to the hotel.

'How are you feeling?' Jess and Bryony asked each other at the same time when Jess shut the door to their bedroom.

Jess sighed a heavy sigh, closed her eyes and tried to turn her feelings off. She'd thought all the way back. She'd wondered, remembered, rationalised and worn herself out even more on the route to doing so. So she slapped on a smile, shook out her hair, even sang the first line of 'Let It Go', but it wasn't happening. 'I feel blue,' she said eventually. 'But I don't want to talk about it right now because it's all weird and confusing. So tell me how you're doing instead. I'm sorry the drugs story didn't work out. I really am.'

'No you're not,' Bryony smiled, and began to remove her make-up. It was only early evening, but neither of them was in the mood for a big ol' party night out in Cannes.

'Well, I'm not sorry that Leo and Harvey weren't drug smugglers, but I am that you now don't have any leads. Or do you? Could you still publish something based on everything else you researched?'

'Not without any specifics – it'll be too vague and uninteresting. I got nothing.'

'I got nothing too. Let's have a moment to mope.'

They sat side by side on the bed and stared at the wall.

'I could just send over the Veronica story,' Bryony said after a while. Following the interview and before Richard et al. had shown up at the Carlton ready to paaaarty, Bryony had swiftly filled Jess in on the details, under strict instructions not to start blabbing to anyone about it.

Jess had been entranced. Even in hearing the shortened version she could see the delicacy with which Bryony planned to write the story. The angle she would take, the rawness and realism, the empowering messages – they were all there, glittering under the surface of the great journalist Bryony wanted to be. And it made celeb-mad Jess respect Veronica more, like her more, see her more as a real person. It would be nice if Bryony could be instrumental in helping the world see her that way too, rather than as just another scandal to be salivated over. 'Do you have to?' Jess asked finally. 'She seemed so nice.'

'I know, Meems, but should I just get fired? I mean, I deserve to be fired to be honest, but that doesn't mean I want to be.'

Jess went back to staring at the wall. 'No. Let's have one last try at getting you something else. Why don't we go out this evening and you can write about the parties and the people? We could get Richard, Tara and Bea together and you could interview them, tell them it's for a trashy magazine you're freelancing for and get them to tell you all their juicy stories.' Jess stood up and started hunting for something to wear.

This was the last thing she wanted to do, but if it would help . . .

'They'd never agree to it,' said Bryony. 'And I'm not going to lie to them and say it would be in *The Times* as well, even though they think that's where I work.'

'Don't you think it's worth trying?'

Bryony shrugged.

'Oh come on, Bryony, stop being a wet-wipe,' Jess scolded and Bryony looked up, surprised. *She* was the voice of reason in this friendship; it sounded odd to have Jess tell her off, standing there, hands on hips, like an angry little Doris Day. Bryony's mouth twitched.

'Don't you smirk at me.' Jess wagged her finger. She was not in the mood to be mocked, or to listen to anyone's whining, including her own.

'Okay, Calamity Jane,' said Bryony, and even Jess had to control a giggle from escaping.

'Shush. Listen to me: I'm the boss now. You're going to give it twenty-four more hours. It's the last day of the festival tomorrow, and if you haven't found a story by then, you send over the Veronica piece.'

Bryony thought about it. She hated – *hated* – the idea of betraying Veronica, so it was worth stretching that deadline just a day more. 'Deal. Twenty-four hours. But I don't want to go out again tonight – you're off the hook there. I'll just get my head down, maybe make some phone calls. And if I can't come up with anything else, that's it.'

'Fine.'

'Fine.'

'Do I really look like Calamity Jane when I'm telling someone off?'

'I only wish you'd had a cowboy hat on your head.'

Jess looked at herself in the mirror. 'Hmph. Well, whatever. I stole a superyacht today.'

Bryony stopped a snort escaping in the nick of time. 'You sure did.'

'What was I thinking? Like I'm some kind of Jack Sparrow, just seizing a boat and making off with it?' Jess caught Bryony's eye in the reflection and laughed a little.

'You were just trying to keep your man safe.'

'From the Drug Lord of Cannes.' Jess giggled some more, and Bryony joined in.

'Who turned out to be the security guard.'

'Not a very good one – I stole his boat.'

The absurdity of it all. What a crazy couple of weeks. This had definitely been a far, far from relaxing break, what with fleeing from supposed drug lords, gambling in Monte Carlo, seeing Paris Hilton DJ, meeting Veronica Hay in a hotel room they'd blagged at the Carlton, singing 'Auld Lang Syne' in front of the crème de la crème of Hollywood, causing a near-riot at a press conference and stumbling upon the best man she'd met in years.

Leo.

Jess wiped away the tears of laughter from her face and calmed down.

'You okay, Meems?' Bryony asked.

'Should I see Leo again before I go home?'

'Maybe. Do you want to?'

Maybe. 'The thought of never seeing him again hurts. And I think it hurts more than the fact we've been lying to each other for two weeks.'

'Then I think you need to see him, to be honest.'

'"Honest" is good right now.'

Bryony watched her friend, waiting to see if she would expand on her thoughts. Eventually she asked, 'Are you angry?'

'Yes, both with him and with myself. I'm angry that he duped me, and made me worry and panic while I was on this fabulous holiday, but I'm also really sorry that I made him feel less of a person, and that he had to pretend to be Mr Moneybags. And I'm so, *so* angry with myself. I just feel like I've ruined the holiday, and the ... whatever it was becoming with him, because if I hadn't been so desperate to be part of the in-crowd everything could have been avoided.'

'In the spirit of being honest, be honest with yourself here: would you really want everything that's happened these last two weeks to have been "avoided"?'

Jess was quiet as she thought this through. If she could go back in time and make none of this happen, would she? Really?

'Meems?' Bryony nudged her.

Jess snapped out of her thoughts. 'Yes, sorry. I don't know. I'll be okay though.'

'Sure?'

'Sure.' She stood up. 'Now you get to work, and I better go and see the family, convince them I'm not a criminally insane lunatic.'

Jess knocked on her parents' door. Cameron answered, holding a bag of Bacon Goût, which he offered to Jess. She took a handful, silently.

'Why aren't you all out sightseeing or getting dinner?' she eventually queried, hanging about inside the doorway.

'We were waiting for you, honey,' said Patty, putting

down a tattered copy of *Cannes Life* magazine and standing to hug her daughter.

'I don't want to go sightseeing,' Jess said quietly.

'We know. But we were waiting in case you needed us. In case you want to talk about anything.'

Cameron offered her the bag of Bacon Goût again, and then made her a cup of horrible Lipton tea. They must be worried about her if even Cameron was being his own brand of nice.

Jeff gave Jess a bear hug before sitting her down on the bed. 'Have you had a bit of a flopsy of a holiday, sweetheart?'

Jess shook her head. 'No. It's been kind of amazing, actually. Quite the adventure. It just . . . It turned into more of an adventure than I could handle.'

'Who says you can't handle any kind of adventure you want to?' asked Patty.

'I'm not like you, I guess. I thought I could be – you three seemed to have the time of your life when you were travelling – but I guess I'm too used to my comfort zone.'

Patty shook her head. 'It's never the wrong time to try and get out of your comfort zone. The world is there to be seen.'

'Do you wish you were still out there, seeing the world?'

'We're here now, aren't we?'

'But it ... it took me leaving ... ' Jess stared at the floor, feeling like a wimpy teenager.

'Spit it out, chicken,' said her dad gently.

'It took me leaving for you to go, "Finally, we can go on holiday again,"' Jess whispered, and there was a stony silence.

'We've been on plenty of holidays together as a family,' Patty eventually said. 'Do they not count? I thought you loved our weeks in the New Forest, and going up to Scotland?'

'I did. I mean going abroad.'

'Do you wish we'd taken you on more holidays abroad?'

'No, I loved our family holidays. I love our life, the village, you lot. I'm not worrying about *me*.' Jess avoided her mum's gaze, feeling awful for ever bringing this up. 'I mean for you – all of you. You three haven't been able to go abroad and do what you love since I was born. You put your lives on hold for me.' Jess looked up, guilt flowing through her, and her mum looked surprised, her dad confused. Cameron looked frankly disgusted. 'Um, I just feel like I ruined it all. You three were having so much fun before I came along. I can see it in your faces every time you talk about it.'

Cameron threw his bag of Bacon Goût onto the bed. 'You're so selfish! Let me ask you something. Do you know what it feels like to be the one who's always trying to get attention?'

Jess's mouth dropped open. 'What are you talking about? You're the favourite child.'

'*You're* the favourite child!'

'I'm the party pooper!'

'What in heaven's name—' Patty jumped in.

'Wait, love, let them thrash it out, the silly sausages.' Jeff folded his arms and sat back, a bemused look on his face. Patty parked herself next to him, furious at her two stupid children.

Cameron glared at Jess. 'I'm always in the background, blending in. When I was born Mum and Dad barely noticed, barely changed a thing – the travelling about just continued with me tagging along. And for six years it was brilliant and I didn't know any different, but then suddenly there you are and it was like they went, "We have a baby! Oh my gosh!" They obviously cared more about you, their little baby girl, because all of a sudden it was "Let's get a home, let's bring her up properly, no living out of a suitcase for precious little *Jessica*."'

Jess's head was spinning. This is what Cameron really thought? 'Oh my God, you are as delusional about this as you are about Bryony kissing you.'

'Bryony *did* kiss me! It was New Year's Eve 2007 and we had a moment by the fireplace—'

'You had a spark that popped out of the fire and landed on your goatee. She spat on her hand and tapped it out. A trace of her saliva getting on your mouth is *not* kissing.'

'She kissed her hand, she didn't spit on it.' He turned to his parents and said, 'She kissed her hand!'

'This is sooooo Cameron, you just don't see what's in front of your eyes. You think Mum and Dad wanted to stop travelling? You don't see it in their faces every time the past is brought up, that the happiest times of their lives were with you, going around the world before I came along and put a stop to it all?'

'Okay, young lady, young man, SIT DOWN,' Patty roared.

Jess and Cameron both looked away sheepishly and sat down on the edge of the bed.

Patty went on, 'Cameron, do you really think we didn't notice a new baby when you came along? You think we didn't change a lot of things about how we were travelling? We didn't just carry on exploring the world because we hadn't finished, we didn't think, to hell with you, we're carrying on. Your dad and I had you, saw your little face, and the most exciting thing we could imagine was having a new little person to show the world to. One of the best things about holidays is having someone to point things out to and to share the memories with. We wanted to point out the world to you, and now you have those memories.'

Cameron was staring at his hands, whispers of the little boy he once was showing through. 'Then why does everyone always try and shut me up? I do have those memories, and I want to talk about them.'

This sank straight into Jess's heart, and immediately she felt awful. She'd always thought of Cameron's constant comments about his 'travels' as just attention-seeking and intended as a dig at her. But he just wanted to be involved in the family in the best way he knew how, and she always shut him down.

Jess opened her mouth to say something to Cameron, but Patty continued, fixing Jess with a stern look.

'And Jessica, "Princess Jessica", comes along and controls the lives of everyone around her, making all their decisions for them. We did not decide to settle down because we were being dictated to by you, missy, we settled down because we wanted that to be the next adventure. We decided we wanted to grow up a little, cut down on the expensive travelling and put that money into a house for the family and the children's education. I'm sorry for not running that by you first, but, love. . . ' Patty softened and knelt in front of her daughter. 'We were, and have always been, thrilled to have you in the family. It wouldn't be a family without you. Or you, before you roll your eyes, mister,' Patty said in an aside to Cameron before turning back to Jess. 'Yes, we look back at our time before you came along with immense fondness. I look back at my childhood with fondness. I look back at our wedding day with fondness. And I look at the last thirty-odd years in Cornwall with fondness. Surely you can't say you don't see the same happiness in me when we talk about memories of Christmas, or your school plays, or that time we all went swimming at Newquay in January and Dad's willy nearly froze off?'

Jess crinkled her nose but smiled at her mum, who was right as usual. How could Jess have been so blind as to not see all of that? And now the blackout curtains had been opened and she got it. Her dad was right; she really had been a silly sausage.

'Hug your brother,' said Jeff. 'Cameron, hug your sister.'

They turned to him with a chorus of 'Why?' and 'Do I have to?'

'Hug it out and then, as punishment for being such knuckleheads, Jess, you have to listen to Cameron tell you his five favourite memories, and Cameron, you have to give Jess the rest of those Frazzle-Wotsits of yours. And after that, you have to let us do something for you.'

'What?' Jess asked.

'I'm not telling you, you'll just have to trust us.'

Jess turned to Cameron. 'All right. Can you tell me about the time you were in that toddler rodeo in Houston?'

Cameron's whole face lit up; this was one of his favourites. 'So we were on sheep, not horses, and it was a hot day in Texas, sun blazing . . . '

And that's how Jess ended up falling into a deep, peaceful sleep, curled up next to her mum on the double bed, while Jeff took the fold-out bed and Cameron ended up squeezing onto the end of the double like a Labrador. A family adventure.

Jess came to shortly after six a.m., crumpled, hot and with her family sleeping like logs around her. She quietly slipped out of bed and straightened yesterday's clothes, then crept into the corridor. She stood for a moment, facing a large framed photo of Sophia Loren, her mind already on Leo.

'What would you do, Sophia?' she whispered. 'Would you give him another chance? Would you ask him to give you another chance?'

Looking down the deserted corridor, Jess realised a little bit of peace and quiet was exactly what she needed to think, so, grabbing a plastic cup of (revolting, but complimentary) coffee from the machine on the way past, up to the roof terrace she went.

It was beginning to feel pretty up here, like home. Not perfect, not shipshape, not gleaming like a fancy superyacht, but like a little space she knew her way around, where she could look over the rooftops and see the Mediterranean in the distance. The weather knew it was the last day of the festival, and was forlorn. Clouds had rolled in, low, puffy white clouds, as if Cannes was having a duvet day.

Jess sipped her coffee and leant on the wall, looking at the view, and allowed her mind to wander wherever it needed to in order to straighten itself out.

So her parents didn't resent her; this was a good thing. She could almost laugh at what a wally she'd been all these years.

The truth was out between her and Leo, so her credit card could stop cowering in fear at the back of her wallet. This was also a good thing.

But Leo himself – this was where it got complicated.

Her hair was ruffled by a cool breeze, unexpected following the heat of the last two weeks, but a refreshing change that made Jess imagine she was getting a breath of air from home.

I think I know what I have to do.

Jess returned to her room, opening the door carefully so as not to disturb a sleeping Bryony, only to find her already cross-legged on the bed in front of her laptop, her hands over her mouth.

'Oh God. Oh godding godding god-heads. Oh, Meems, helphelphelp.'

'What's wrong?' Jess said, coming inside.

'I've had an email from Mitch. Oh *fuck*. It says, "Blah blah blah, great notes on Veronica, that dirty little madam. Knew you'd pull it out the bag. Get it written and over to me by midday and it'll go in this week's issue. I'll get sourcing pictures."' She looked up at Jess, defeat in her usually steely eyes. 'My notes – they were in my folder on the server. I'm so stupid.'

'He read your notes on Veronica Hay? Even though they're on your laptop?'

'They're on the shared server. I should have saved

them to my desktop, but we always keep everything on the server rather than on our own computers in case of a laptop failure. It's just habit. I can't believe he went scrounging through my folders.' Bryony reread the email, just in case she'd misunderstood something, just in case it was all going to be okay after all. Eventually she looked back up at Jess. 'What am I going to do?'

Jess walked the now-familiar route from the hotel towards the sea, leaving Bryony to her thoughts. Jess had calmed her down, convinced her to get dressed and had taken her for a walk around the roof terrace to burn off some anxiety. Stalling: that was the only answer they'd come up with as to how to deal with Mitch. Bryony had asked him for a couple more hours to 'make the article perfect', and what she needed now was to be alone, to use her analytical mind to break down the problem and figure out how to solve it. She'd get there, scrambling over the obstacle, guns blazing, and Jess was only a phone call away if she needed anything at all.

Being the last day of the festival, Jess had expected Cannes to have pulled the stops out, with a party on every street and the sound of champagne flutes being clinked coming from every open window. But for many places it was the end, no more screenings, no more events, no more parties. The big end-of-festival celebrations would be happening that night at the Palais des Festivals and in the hotels, but for everywhere else it was clearing-up time: banners being taken down, doors closed, red carpets rolled away. Even the yachts in the harbour seemed fewer.

The town that had buzzed with excitement and glamour for nearly two weeks was ready for some beauty sleep, and Jess felt an odd mixture of emptiness and calm. As she walked in the cool air she thought back over everything that had happened on this exciting holiday of hers. She thought of Leo finding her on the seafront, tucking into her first Nutella crêpe. She thought of Noix de Coco, with funny Richard and crazy Tara, and Bea with the drawn-on eyebrows. And Céline! Goddamn Céline! Jess shook her head, a small laugh escaping.

That yacht party, where Leo had leaned over with his tub of Nutella, so pleased with himself, and where they'd both made assumptions that had snowballed into what it had become.

Karaoke at the Hôtel du Cap, shopping on millionaires' row for a new pair of specs, nearly being booted out of a press conference but still walking the red carpet the following day, and her lovely day strolling around the castle with Leo under the Mediterranean sun.

She went to Monaco. Little small-town Jess swanned off to Monaco and gambled her arse off and kissed a boy outside Grace Kelly's palace. Then that boy gave her a night on his superyacht, where he cooked for her and kissed her and whispered to her in the dark.

It all came back to Leo. He was the one who'd held her hand while she took a flying leap out of her comfort zone. And even if it had all been smoke and mirrors, it had been two amazing weeks that she wouldn't change for the world. She wasn't going to close the door on this adventure yet.

'Nice tugboat,' Jess called up to Leo, trembling at the unknown of how he'd react. He looked down at her from the deck of the superyacht, a smile spreading over his face, and she smiled back, relieved. He hopped ashore, for once not pulling off his polo shirt and throwing it back onto the boat. Jess noticed a crew emblem embroidered on the chest and understood now why he'd always been so keen to show off his pecs.

'Thanks,' he said, shyness and uncertainty written all over him. 'It's mine, you know. I'm totally a billionaire. You came back.'

Jess smiled, but all words and thoughts appeared to have walked the plank so she was left standing, fidgeting and stealing glances up at Leo, drifting back in love whether it was a smart move or not. She hadn't really ever left.

Finally Leo re-broke the ice. 'So I thought of a great analogy for us.'

'Um, you did?'

'Yep. It's really good.'

'Okay . . . '

Leo folded his arms across his chest, his eyes twinkling. 'We're like jeans.'

'Jeans?'

'Yes, your favourite pair of lovely, comfy jeans that you *love*. You never want them to fall apart or to lose them because they're perfect as they are. But then someone came along and, thinking you'd really like it, they bedazzled the hell out of your jeans. This person didn't mean any harm; they just thought that's what you wanted. But actually, you have to pick all the sparkly bits off. But that's okay, they're still your jeans underneath, nothing's changed or ruined.'

She was trying to follow, she really was. He'd

obviously thought about this a lot. 'So are you saying I'm the jeans and you're the bedazzler?'

'I'm saying we're each other's jeans. Like a great pair of jeans, to me you're perfect. You don't need to bedazzle my jeans, but I know you only did it because you thought it would make me like you – the jeans – more.'

'Bedazzling being embellishing the facts?'

'Yes, all those little lies and exaggerations, all those added bits of glitz. And I did the same – I bedazzled your jeans, but I think it would have been better if I'd left them alone.'

'If you'd stayed being just you and hadn't embellished?'

'Yep.' He fell quiet, watching her to see if she thought he was mental.

'That's the weirdest analogy I've ever heard,' she chuckled. 'But in the spirit of it, fancy, um, picking the sparkles off together and showing off how great our jeans are?'

'What are you on about, woman?' Leo teased.

'Fancy getting to know each other a little?'

His face turned serious, hopeful. 'That would be brilliant – really?'

'Really.' She smiled up at him, reflecting his shyness. It was strange how new this felt.

Leo led them to the edge of the pier and they sat, legs dangling over the water. 'Okay, so here's some stuff about me: I'm the chef, as you know, and I don't own a lot of stuff, but I do like the sea and I do like you. Everything I told you about my feelings, my personality, they were all true. Here's what I ... bedazzled: not my boat, don't run any restaurants, though I'd love to one day, and the room we stayed in was Rusty's. He owns the boat but was away for the night at some event in Saint-Tropez. Every time I couldn't hang out with you, or pulled you away from the yacht when you came to see me, it was because I was working and didn't want you to find out.'

Jess nodded. 'Thank you. Well everything I told you about *me* was true as well, personality-wise, my likes and dislikes, where I live, my feelings.' She caught his eye, briefly. 'Bedazzled: I own one café in Cornwall, not a whole chain. I'm not really part of the elite party crowd, though I have enjoyed myself these past two weeks. I'm staying in a crap hotel and, before Tara's, I've never been on any other superyachts aside from yours. Well, Rusty's.'

'And are you really that good at blackjack?'

'Haha, yes, I really am, and yes, I'm banned from a casino in England.'

Leo looked pleased as punch. 'You are *so* more criminal than me.'

They looked out to sea and an uncontrollable giggle burst from Jess. 'I can't believe I just drove your yacht out there,' she said, pointing out to the blue.

'It's actually pretty flattering. You went all *Hunger Games* just to save me.'

'What can I say? I'm a very good girlfriend.'

'Are you my girlfriend?'

Whoa. Now that was an awkward question, and Jess didn't know how to answer, so she clamped her mouth shut for a few moments. 'I don't know. It's our last day together. What do *you* think?'

'I think there's something I need to know about you before we go any further.'

'Okay . . . '

'It's important, and you can't lie about it.'

'You can't lie either.'

'I won't.' He turned to her, bringing his legs up onto the pier and crossing them under him. She did the same, their knees touched and there was her Leo, in front of her again. She would be honest with him, whether it was for just one more day or for longer than she could imagine.

'So I need to know,' he said. 'Is it true? That you really do like Nutella? Is it true?'

Jess propelled herself forward and kissed him. To hell with distance, with mistaken identities, with the end of the festival. 'Yes,' she said, sitting back. 'I love Nutella. I wouldn't lie about that.'

'I'm so glad, because I can't afford another fancy lunch out. It's Nutella crêpes all the way if you stay with me, baby.'

'That sounds perfect; my credit card has had it. I have . . . ' She pulled her purse from the pocket of her dress. 'Fifteen euros and about thirty-five cents left.'

'Wow, then consider *me* the gold digger.' Leo pulled her back close to him and they locked eyes. 'I am sorry for lying; it was a little embellishment that got out of control because I didn't want to lose you. I should have come clean earlier, I just didn't realise that my lying was so crap you were about to finger me in the Cannes drug scandal of the century.'

'I'm sorry, too. Also for the lying, but mainly for going along with the theory that you were involved in all that. And please tell Bruno I'm sorry. And Harvey. Oh, and Mr Nail.'

'Bruno doesn't care, it's the most excitement he's had for a long time. And Harvey definitely doesn't mind – Bryony can use him for anything she wants. And as for old Rusty Nail—'

'Is his name really Rusty Nail?'

'He's really Jimmy Nail, but he didn't want everyone always thinking he was *the* Jimmy Nail, so wanted to go a bit more incognito.'

'With "Rusty Nail"?'

'He does have a sense of a humour, you can't deny that about him. I can't believe your parents know him.'

Jess snuggled in closer on Leo's lap, touching the familiar wave of his salty hair. It was good to be back here. 'I don't know if I want the dirty details though.'

'They called here, only about fifteen minutes ago, and flat-out asked Mr Nail to hold a party on the yacht tonight. Lucky for them, he always does, and *he* was planning to invite all of *you* anyway. It's his annual end-of-festival party. The crew will all be arriving back today, and the captain will sail the yacht out into the harbour so we can watch the fireworks. Unless you wanted to sail it for him?'

Jess smirked. 'Funny. Do you want us all there?'

'Absolutely, I just didn't know if *you'd* want to be there, after my royal cock-up.'

'I want to be there. Will you be leaving tomorrow?'

Leo nodded, and Jess's heart sank again. He leant in close and smiled at her. 'Can we not think about it for a while? Let's have tonight, and worry about that in the morning.'

Jess agreed, but with a sudden sadness ribboning around her. Tomorrow: if only it *wasn't* a day away. Goodbye was coming way too soon.

Bryony hesitated before knocking on the door of the little lime-green bungalow hidden within the gardens of the Riviera Spa Retreat. The Carlton was beautiful – everywhere in Cannes was beautiful – but, looking around her, Bryony could quite understand the draw of spending a few days on a stunning clifftop on the outskirts of town, away from the bustle and the spotlights.

She was going to tell Veronica. She'd been back and forth and turned it over and changed her mind a million times since early that morning, after Jess had lifted her spirits and calmed her down. Eventually she'd decided that, if the article was going to be in *Sleb* and not *The Times*, the least she could do was to try to hold on to a modicum of morality and fess up beforehand. Then she'd write the article, publish it and hate herself for a good long time.

Should she call Jess again, just for some reassurance? Her skin felt hot and sticky despite the unshifting clouds as she paused, waiting for the answer to come to her. More than once she considered darting in behind the huge jade palm leaves and pretending she had never come.

But then the door was flung open and there stood Veronica, pink-eyed and puffy-cheeked, holding a can of Coke and a crumpled TV guide, which she seemed to be using to mop her tear-stained face.

'Bryony!' she cried, welcoming her in. 'I'm so glad it's you. I thought it was going to be my shithead manager again, hovering about telling me to show my face on the red carpet. I *just don't want to*.'

'What's wrong?' Bryony asked, stepping into the bungalow and mentally photographing the stunning interior for the Pinterest board inside her head.

'What's wrong is that I've run out of tissues and toilet roll and I don't want to call anyone because I don't want them to see me like this.' She scratched another page of the TV guide across her face. 'What's wrong is that I'm weak and I'm drinking Coke even though it's forbidden at this spa, but I just fucking want it. And what's wrong is that nobody loves me.' Fresh tears swam the freestyle down her cheeks and Bryony fought the urge to cry herself, due to the awful timing of it all.

She led Veronica to the pastel-painted dining table and sat her down. 'Tell me what's happened.'

Veronica snorted unattractively, but it just made Bryony like her more. 'I said I didn't have a girlfriend and it was true, but there was – is – someone I like so much. I've liked her for a long time, and I thought she liked me too but she doesn't – *Snooort* – urgh, it's all just so shit right now.'

Bryony didn't know what to say, because she was afraid that if she said what she came here to say it would only make things worse.

'What makes it even shittier is that it's my fault,' Veronica continued.

I know exactly how you feel. 'Do you want to start from the beginning?' Bryony asked.

'Really, you want to hear this?' Veronica suddenly fixed Bryony with a guarded look. 'I don't want this in the article.'

'I won't even be making notes,' Bryony said truthfully, guilt stabbing at her. 'It won't leave this room.'

'All right. It would be good to talk it out with someone, if you're sure you don't mind?'

'It's the least I can do.'

'Do you want a Coke? Or some of this wheatgrass bullshit they've packed my fridge with?'

Bryony shook her head, worried she'd throw up if she took even a sip of anything right now.

'Okay, well, you asked for this.' Veronica leant her

chin on her hand and stared just past Bryony and out of the window. 'I met Angela at college. I did a year of law school – surprising, huh? – before dropping out to become an actress or whatever.' She raised an eyebrow, lost in thought. 'She was cool and funny, and we were like best buds who became more than that. But I didn't take it very seriously; I was pretty young and she was my first girlfriend, if you'd even call her that, and when I left college it fizzled out. But we stayed in touch; there was no anger or resentment. Over the years she's always been there as a friend, even when I drunkenly call her and tell her I love her, maybe once a month. Even when I flirt with her so hard I could kick myself for sounding like such a desperate teenager. And even when I get shitty with her for not wanting me, so send her photos of myself all over guys just to try and get under her skin.'

'This is all very familiar behaviour,' Bryony said and smiled. 'So what changed, what led to this A-list star sitting in a lime bungalow atop a Mediterranean cliff, wiping her tears with the TV guide?'

'You're what changed.'

'Me?'

'Your article, specifically. When I came out of that interview I felt so much lighter, so much more *me* than I'd felt in years, and I wanted to tell Angela all about it. So I called her and I told her that I was finally growing up, and that the world would soon know who I was. I asked her if it was too late to ask her to be my girlfriend again.'

Veronica blinked back more tears, vulnerable and lonely, then went on, 'And she said it was too late. She said I should have come out years ago rather than trying to hide away any trace of her, and that she couldn't trust that this wasn't just an attempt to bring in some publicity. She said she loved me, as a friend, but that she's now with someone she wants to marry, and I needed to find someone new to call.'

Bryony's heart broke for Veronica as fresh sobs rolled out. 'You didn't know she was with someone else?'

'I never asked; I never wanted to know. All I ever say when I call her is about me – how much I've missed her, that I love her, and she couldn't see how this call was any different.'

Veronica lapsed into silence.

'I always just thought she'd be there, you know?' she said eventually. 'Like we were just coasting until we were both ready, and then we'd get back together. I'm so used to people organising their lives around me, and waiting until I'm ready for everything, that stupid, delusional me forgot that she was there before all that,

that she doesn't have to be at my beck and call. I am *such* a dick.'

'You're not a dick,' Bryony soothed. 'You're human. And we all cock up on the fields of love at least once.'

'Have you ever done this?'

'Have I ever tried to get my university sweetheart to go out with me again, ten years later?'

Veronica chuckled. 'Or something like that.'

Shifting in her seat, Bryony wasn't sure what to say. She wasn't someone who had boyfriends, or long-lost loves, or ones that got away. She had Harveys. People who made her smile and gave her fun and happiness when she most needed it, but faded away when she wanted to get back to business. And that was exactly what she wanted at this point in her life. But yes, she knew what it was like to want something that could never be. She knew that very well, so she nodded and fetched Veronica another Coke.

Veronica chucked back the drink as if it were a shot of tequila, and sighed a weighty sigh. 'This article – I'm not going to try and win her back with it. I respect that she's moved on, I suppose, and she probably made the right choice, *I suppose*, but I'll send her a copy, and I hope she can see that it's an apology to her, in a way. A truth I've been too gutless to share, but now I'm going to own.'

'About the article . . . ' Bryony's voice trembled. She was about to crush this girl even more, and she hated herself for it more than she'd ever hated herself before.

'What?'

Veronica didn't deserve this, nobody did. Her life, her feelings, didn't mean any less just because she was a celebrity. It didn't mean that Bryony, as a member of the press, could play with them like a puppet master. Bryony had dug herself into this; it was her, not Veronica, who should pay the price of her lies.

Bryony slapped on a smile. 'I just need to make some little changes, and then I'm going to send it off.'

'Do you know when it'll come out in *The Times*?'

'No idea . . . ' Could she pull this off? 'But I'll get back to you.'

When Jess had returned to the hotel later that morning, Bryony was hunched over her laptop, a huge frown on her face, earplugs in. She didn't seem to notice when Jess walked into the room.

Jess hovered for a moment or two until Bryony looked up, her face wrought but determined. 'I think I have a plan,' she said, still typing. Nothing could stop Bryony when she was in this mood.

'You do?' Jess felt a flutter of excitement.

'Yes, maybe. I think I might be mad. Do you think I'm mad?'

'Urm, a bit. What are you planning to do?'

Bryony faced the laptop again. 'I'm going to fight back. I'm going to C.J. Cregg all over this mutha.'

'Right then . . . Well, that sounds like a bloody good move.' Jess raised her eyebrows.

'Really?'

'Really. Go for it. Show 'em who runs the world. Do you want to talk about it?'

'Not right now, if that's okay – I'm in the zone. But thanks for the pep talk. I'll fill you in when I've taken the plunge.' She looked at Jess again, even stopped typing. 'Oh my God, what happened with Leo?'

Jess allowed herself a small shimmy on the spot. 'We're okay! I think we're going to be okay.'

Bryony cheered.

'But I'll fill you in on that later, too. You look like you need to go back to planning some kind of war, not listen to me bleat on about luuurve and boyfriends.'

'Promise me you'll bleat later, though?' Bryony was already sneaking her eyes back to her screen.

Jess agreed, and then backed out of the room. Hmm, what to do?

Leo, to avoid being stowed away in the galley kitchen all night, was having to spend the afternoon prepping an exhaustive list of canapés and cocktails for the party. It was refreshing to actually know what he was doing and not to second-guess him.

So Leo was occupied, Bryony was occupied and her parents and Cameron were out sightseeing. What was a girl to do for her last tango in Cannes?

She stood by Sophia Loren in the corridor and took out her phone. After a few rings, someone answered.

'Hi, Richard! Fancy some lunch? ... Actually, there's somewhere I have in mind.'

Jess waited for Richard outside Noix de Coco, nervousness fluttering about in her tummy trying to edge past the steely determination.

'Noix de Coco at lunchtime, darling?' Richard said, appearing by her side, all white teeth and aviators. 'You are such a grown-up little star.'

'I'm going to be completely honest with you,' Jess said, taking his arm to walk down the steps. 'I chose here to rub someone's nose in it one last time.'

'Hmm, let me guess, Queen Bitch at twelve o'clock?'

Céline was standing behind the front desk, and her smile dropped when she saw Jess. '*Bonjour*, again,' she said.

'*Bonjour*, Céline,' smiled Jess. 'I was wondering if you wanted to come to a party tonight?'

'What?'

'*What?*' shrieked Richard. 'What party? I'm not invited but she is? No offence, love,' he added to Céline.

'Of course you're invited, as are Tara, Bea et cetera – that goes without saying.' Jess faced Céline again. 'It's on Leo's yacht. To celebrate the end of the festival, and all the fun of the fair it's brought with it.'

'It's on Leo's yacht?' Céline could not comprehend what she was hearing and Jess *loved* it.

'Yep, there'll be lots of people there, and we're going to be sailing out into the harbour to watch the fireworks.'

'You and Leo are still together?' Céline spat.

'Very much. He's just preparing the menu for tonight, otherwise we'd be together right now.'

Céline bristled and tossed her braid back over her shoulder. She leant on the counter and faced Jess head on. 'Let's stop these games. So you know he's a chef – well done you, bravo.'

Jess held her hands up. 'I'm not here for games, I'm

just here for sushi. And to invite you tonight. It's your call whether you come or not.'

Céline shuffled about behind the counter, grabbing menus and looking generally confused. Then she led Jess and Richard to a gorgeous table overlooking the sea, and with a suspicious side-eye left them to it.

When she was out of earshot, Richard leaned across the table and cupped Jess's chin. 'You sneaky little devil! I see what you did there.'

'What?' Jess asked, innocent as a smoothie.

'You were all *push-you-off-a-cliff* "I'm still with Leo, you bitch," and then *I've-still got-your-hand-and-won't-let-go* "Come to my party because I'm the bigger woman," with a sexy little sprinkling of *But-I-won't-pull-you-back-up-quite-yet* "It's up to you if you come, but I'm the queen of the castle and you're the dirty rascal."'

'Will you come to my party? Not that it's actually my party, I'm just tagging along.'

'Because you're schtupping the head chef.'

Jess flushed. 'Richard, I need to confess something—'

'That you're less Hermès, more H&M? More "The Girl Next Door" than "Diamonds are a Girl's Best Friend"? Less Marilyn Monroe, more Marilyn who works in the newsagent's?'

Jess covered her pink face with her hands. 'You must think I am such an idiot. A big fakey fake-face. I'm so embarrassed.'

'Don't be. Holidays are for having fun and for being whoever you want to be. If you're not going to explore different parts of yourself when you're abroad and no one's around who knows you, you might as well have a staycation in your own village.'

Jess laughed. 'Sorry for misleading you, though, I just got a bit caught up in it all.'

'You didn't mislead me for a second, darling, I saw right through you.'

Cringe. 'Even when we went shopping for my glasses?'

'That was *hilaire*. I would never have let you fork out for Guccis. I wasn't going to let you fork out for Ralph Laurens either, but you fell so in love with them, and you're a grown woman – if you were actually skint I presumed you'd just fob me off.'

'Does everyone else know?'

'No, of course not – the rest of them are completely focused on themselves. It's our little secret, darling.'

A platter of sushi arrived in front of them, and a bottle of pale-gold white wine, despite them having not ordered anything yet. Jess looked over at the hostess counter in surprise, just in time to see Céline quickly look away, busying herself with a stack of business cards.

'Now,' said Richard, tucking into the sushi, 'so I can use the same trick, tell me how you blagged that delicious room at the Carlton for the night.'

'*Call the police! She's coming to take my boat*,' Rusty Nail yelped dramatically – and loudly – from the top deck of the yacht as Jess and her family walked down the marina in the late-afternoon sunshine.

Jess rolled her eyes good-naturedly as Rusty, and everyone nearby, laughed, and then Tara, dressed in a bikini and a snorkelling mask, popped her head out of the hot tub on her own yacht. 'Jess, you bloody *legend*, you're the talk of the town. Well, of the marina. I'll be over later before you set sail – or the captain does, eh? Haaaaa! – and you can tell me all about it. Gotta go for now, chick, I've dropped a diamond earring.' Tara took a swig from a bottle of champagne and dived back under.

Leo appeared on the deck in a black tux, wiping his hands on an apron. He smiled and waved at Jess, and all women within a radius of two hundred metres swooned back.

'Oh, darling, he is just *dishy*,' said Patty.

'Mum, what if he becomes your son-in-law? You can't say that.'

'Might he become my son-in-law? Well this is a turn of events!'

Jess chuckled and flicked her eyes back to Leo. She stopped in her tracks and just admired him for a moment. He might not own a superyacht, but he looked no less at home on one than he had on the night of Tara's party. He stood there, tall and handsome and toe-tinglingly sexy in that suit, strands of his light, wavy hair being picked up by the breeze, and his smile as warm as the low sunshine.

'Welcome aboard,' Leo called out.

'Excuse me, mister,' Rusty said, sidling up to Leo. 'Let's not forget it's *my* yacht to welcome *my* guests on to.'

'Why don't we share it, Mr Nail? It's nice to share things.'

'Well that's true – what's mine is yours, son!'

Thank God he was joking around, happy as Larry. Jess had been nervous about showing her face tonight, well aware of the substantial damage she could have caused just yesterday. She boarded, with a helping hand from Leo.

'How are you doing?' he asked her quietly.

She stood close to him and he tucked her into his arms. He smelt of limes and cocoa powder. 'I'm good. Really, really good actually – very glad your boss doesn't hate me.'

'He's always in a good mood when he sees old friends. Hates new people, generally, thinks most of them are just out to spend his money, so he's been bouncing off the walls since your parents stood in front of him demanding the release of their daughter.' Then Leo dropped his arms and stood back, smiling at Jess. *'Ain't you a sight for sore eyes* . . . Sorry, my Humphrey Bogart voice needs a bit of work.'

Jess laughed. She did feel good tonight, wearing her favourite jade beaded maxidress – from H&M, thank you very much – which made her hair shine and her eyes twinkle.

'Tonight, Marilyn would have wanted to be you, looking like that,' Leo said.

'Oh, you,' Jess laughed, embarrassed.

More guests were arriving, people Jess didn't know, and so they moved away from the gangway.

'So, I just want to check something,' Leo said, taking her hand and leading her inside the boat. 'Just to make one hundred per cent sure we're on the same page.'

'Go on.'

'You know I'm just a lowly crew member, yes?'

'I know you're the chef on a superyacht, so in my eyes you're far from lowly.'

'Okay, fair point, and thank you. And I'm right that you, although a very classy, lovely, intelligent and independent woman, are not what society would class a wealthy socialite?'

'Correct. Or a gold digger.'

'Yes. But you still like me, despite all that. Am I reading this correctly?'

'You certainly are. I like you very much.' Jess struggled against the sadness that trickled in at the thought of him not being around after tomorrow.

'Then I have something to ask you: do you want to see my room? My *actual* room?'

Jess laughed and simultaneously scolded her lady bits for jumping to attention. 'Are you coming on to me, chef?'

Leo looked sheepish and even blushed a little. 'Maybe a little bit. Later, if you fancy it—'

'I fancy it . . .'

'BRILLIANT. For now, I wanted to just show you my room, show you a bit of the real me, and prove to you it's not full of cocaine.'

Leo guided Jess down the steps and paused outside the door of the 'machine room'. 'Ready? I warn you, it's a smidge less impressive than the room a deck above.'

He opened the door and Jess was faced with a sweet little cabin decorated in white and navy, with a single bed, a shelf full of paperbacks and a wall covered in photographs.

'Wow.' Jess stared at an amazing picture of a teenage Leo grinning at the camera with a friend, both had hair that was spiked and Sun-In'd to death. 'I didn't know you were in *NSYNC.'

'Funny. See, not wanting to bring you in here was for two reasons. One, because if you didn't know this was my room you'd think one of the crew had a seriously obsessive crush on me, and two, because I was afraid if you saw that picture you wouldn't be interested in seeing me naked.'

'Ah, cunning. So you went with naked first.'

'Well, you know . . . ' Leo mock-flexed. 'Once you'd seen me in my birthday suit I knew you wouldn't be changing your mind.'

'Who is this guy? He's in, what, half your photos?' Jess moved along the wall, and kept spotting the same face, at different ages, next to Leo's.

'That's Will, he's my best mate – my BFF,' Leo chuckled. 'He's my best friend from school and my best friend now, though I only see him about once a year. Look, this was the last time.' He pointed to a selfie of the two of them gurning at each other, the London Eye in the background.

'Why don't you see each other more often?'

'Because I live on the sea and he has a crippling fear of boats, basically. It sucks; I miss him. I should make more of an effort to visit him when I'm on leave. He has a son now, and his middle name's Leo,' he said with pride.

'I thought Harvey was your BFF.'

'He's my work BFF. Seriously, though, Harvey acts like a horny teenager but he's a good guy, very moralistic. I don't know what Bryony's thinking, but if she wants him, Harvey would treat her well.'

'With Bryony, your guess is as good as mine. She doesn't give a lot away.'

'All right, well we'll leave them to it. Anyway, look at this one – recognise this?'

Jess peered at the photo. 'Is that Sennen Beach in Cornwall? That's not far from where I live!'

'I know,' he said, and beamed. 'That was the only photo on my laptop from when I was last in Cornwall. I printed it out the other day and stuck it up because it made me think of you. In a round-about kind of way.'

She smiled at the photo and then at him. 'Leo . . .'

'Shush, you're about to say something sad,' he quietened her with a light kiss. 'Not tonight. For me – not tonight.'

Jess nodded and held it in, turned the sad feelings off.

The motor started, causing the yacht to come alive in a soft rumble around them. 'What's the plan tonight?' she asked Leo.

'It sounds like everyone must have arrived, so now we set sail.'

Back on deck, Jess was surprised at how quickly the yacht had filled up. Richard, Tara, Bea and their crowd were all aboard, cackling away and generally making everyone around them fall in love. Jess smiled to see Cameron sitting in the middle of them all, lapping up the attention and with Tara's hand on his leg.

Rusty was poring over a photo album with Patty and Jeff, and for once, much to her delight, Jess didn't feel jealous. People don't have a finite amount of happy memories they can hold on to, and she was thrilled at the sight of her parents joyfully reminiscing – her mum's laugh was the loveliest sound in the world.

Bryony, who had made it – Jess hadn't seen her since before lunch – was pinning Harvey against the wall and they were recreating *The Love Boat* for anyone to see.

And then there was Céline, standing on her own with a glass of fizz.

'What's she doing here?' hissed Leo, but Jess put a hand on his chest.

'I invited her. I'm going to go and talk to her.'

'All right, weirdo,' said Leo, and with a kiss left her to it.

Jess approached Céline, handing her a fresh flute of champagne. Céline eyed it with suspicion, which Jess ignored.

'Thanks for coming,' she said.

Céline took a sip of the ice-cold bubbles and a flicker of happiness crossed over her face. 'Why did you invite me?' she asked, fingers clasping the glass. 'Are you planning to throw me overboard or something?'

'Of course not ... not any more.' Jess met her eye and smiled, then both women turned and looked out at the calm water. 'Look, think about it like this: why did you come?'

'Because of, I don't know ... seizing the day, as you say. Because how could I turn down a party on a yacht when this kind of experience is so rare?'

'I know. You have to take opportunities like this when you can, huh?'

Céline nodded and sipped her champagne.

'I invited you,' Jess continued, 'because I realised we're not that different.'

'Really?' Céline raised her eyebrows and gave Jess a quick up-and-down glance.

'Yes, really,' Jess said firmly. 'I think we both just want to stop being on the outside looking in. And therefore I think you were jealous of me – yes, jealous, don't roll your eyes – because you feel I stepped on your toes. I got on the inside, so to speak. Am I right?'

With a shrug, Céline downed the rest of her fizz. 'I was with Leo, you know, before you came along.'

'With him?'

'Well . . . friends with him.'

Jess breathed a sigh of relief, while inadvertently running her eyes over Céline's perfect physique.

'We did some business together last year,' Céline continued. 'Nothing illegal, he bought local seafood through Noix de Coco to serve on the yacht. Anyway, we were friends, I liked him a little bit, and then he was gone. So when I realised he was back, and with *you*, this total nobody—'

Thanks.

'—I was a little, tiny little bit green-eyed monster. Okay?'

That must have been hard to admit, and despite everything, Jess knew exactly how it felt for this lonely girl who just wanted to experience a bit of the magic of the Cannes Film Festival. She was willing to come aboard a yacht occupied by someone she had a crush on, and his new girlfriend, whom she disliked, just to avoid missing the experience. That took guts.

Jess grabbed them each a fresh glass from a passing waiter. 'I like your eyeshadow,' she said, sensing they'd said all they needed to and it was olive-branch time.

'I like your dress,' replied Céline.

Bryony appeared and grabbed Jess's elbow. 'Could I talk to you for one second?'

Jess excused herself from a slightly more peaceful-looking Céline and allowed herself to be steered away to the opposite end of the yacht.

'So? What happened to the fight-back?'

'Are you okay? You look ... drunk, but without being drunk.'

'I'm, um, giddy.'

'Why?'

Bryony giggled to herself. 'Because there's something

kind of unexpectedly fun about the freedom of having no job.'

'Bry, what are you saying?' Jess put down her drink and pulled Bryony into the relative quiet of the lounge.

'I quit. I quit *Sleb*. I called Mitch and said he was a sexist, homophobic old dickhead, and that I didn't want to write for his publication any longer.' Bryony knocked back her drink.

Jess gasped. 'You quit?'

'Yep. Homophobic. Old. Dickhead.'

A snigger escaped her. 'What did he say to that?'

'He called me a homophobic old dickhead back, so I said, "Good one, Mitch, do you need a bit of time to come up with your own insults?" and he made a weird growling sound.' Bryony looked positively ecstatic about the whole thing, so Jess squealed and wrapped her arms around her, upsetting Bryony's glass and sprinkling gin and tonic all over the place.

'Good for you! Do you know how many people would love to have your courage and say that to their bosses? You are so ... Erin Brockovich, or something.'

'Well I don't know about that.' Bryony fluffed her hair theatrically.

'You are; you stood up for yourself and your princi-
ples. I for one may have found a new idol.'

'Now, Meems, don't you dump Marilyn for little
old me.'

Jess poured them both a celebratory bourbon. 'So
he's not going to publish the Veronica story?'

'Oh yeah, he will. He claims it's his property as
I was working for him, which is probably true from
a legal point of view, I'd have to check my contract,
although it'll be under his byline now, which he's even
more thrilled about. But it won't come out until next
Monday, soooooooo . . . I sent it to *The Times*.'

'You sent it? To *The Times*?'

'I sent it to *The Times*.'

'Really? You sent it to *The Times*?'

Bryony blinked. 'Am I pissed or do we keep saying
the same thing to each other? I spent four solid hours
this afternoon writing it how I wanted it to be written,
and then just pressed send. I sent it off. I thought,
bugger it – I might as well try. I even said they could
just have it if they wanted it, no need to pay, as long
as they were able to publish it ASAP.'

Jess was so proud of her friend. Whatever happened, whatever the outcome, Bryony had done the
best she could, risking everything she'd worked for.
Right now, she was all about the freedom, but where

did it leave her? She pulled Bryony into another hug and gave her an enormous squeeze. 'Do you think they will print it?'

'Probably not, but at least I'll have tried. At least when I see the cover of *Sleb* next week, and every time I see Veronica on TV for the rest of my life, I'll feel a fraction less guilt knowing that I *tried*.'

'Was he angry about you quitting?' Jess asked.

'Who cares? I don't even want to think, or talk, about it any more. I just wanted you to know. So, enough about that, it's time for you to bleat to your heart's content. You're back together – did everyone forgive everyone?'

'We're back together,' Jess confirmed with a grin, at which Bryony squealed loudly. 'There was a lot of forgiving, apologising, realising how silly we'd *both* been, and some kissing … *but* I don't know what's going to happen after tonight. He leaves tomorrow and so do we.'

'How do you feel about him?'

'I like him.'

'No shiz. But how do you really feel about him, right now?' Bryony spun Jess round by the shoulders to face Leo, who was visible out on the deck, talking with Harvey. Behind them, the daylight was fading and Cannes was coming alive with a thousand lights.

Jess took a breath, a moment to concentrate on her thoughts. 'It's hard to focus on anything else when he so much as walks across my vision,' she started. 'It's like he's the only face in the crowd, and I don't need to wait for glitz and glamour, or flashy parties or even these fireworks, because it's all dark compared to him. That's how I feel.'

'And you're not drunk?'

'No, just happy, I think.'

'All right, then. So what are you going to do about it?'

'I don't know. Tonight might be it.'

Bryony gave her a gentle shove toward the cool outside. 'Then what are you doing talking to me? Go and start making some adventures of your own.'

Time ticked by, the night seeping in faster than it should, like the evening was on time-lapse. The sky was now dark, and the sea air had cooled rapidly. Jess and Leo hadn't left each other's sides and stayed curled in each other, everybody else just a blur.

'I still can't quite believe my luck that you came back,' Leo said, tenderly brushing her hair off her forehead.

'I can't believe you took me back so easily. You ended up in handcuffs because of me.'

'Hey, it was you taking me back. I never gave you away.'

'What are we going to do?' she whispered to him.

Leo gently took her glasses off and leant his forehead against hers, and they breathed together for a moment.

Suddenly, long arms wrapped around her, pulling her away from Leo. Jess laughed as she was spun around and Bryony's chest smothered her face in a tight hug.

'What are you doing?' She looked up as best she could and saw Bryony with tears pooling in her eyes. 'Bry, are you okay?'

'What's that Marilyn Monroe quote you told me a couple of years back, when we were on that hen do at the casino, the one about rules?'

'"If I'd observed all the rules I'd never have got anywhere"?'

A grin spread across Bryony's face, and she whispered, 'I got somewhere.'

'With Harvey?'

'No!' Bryony laughed. 'With *The Times*.'

'OHMYGODYOUDIDN'T!' shouted Jess, pulling away from Bryony and jumping up on a sofa.

Bryony jumped up beside her. 'I just had an email from them. From someone called Daniel Kravitz. Or Daniel Klein. Hang on . . .'

'It doesn't matter. What did they say?'

'They said they really liked my story on Veronica. They want to publish it, tomorrow, with my name on it.' Bryony trailed off and stared past Jess into the distance. 'I'm going to be in *The Times*. My story, published in *The Times*.' She turned back to Jess, her eyes reflecting all the twinkling lights of Cannes harbour. 'Veronica's story is going to be in *The Times*! Ahhh, it's like this huge weight has just been lifted off me. A weight the size of this damned superyacht.'

'Are you going to be in trouble with Mitch, and with *Sleb*?'

'Probably, but it was worth it. Sometimes you just have to get in trouble.'

Sometimes you just have to get in trouble. Jess paused, thinking it over. It was true; sometimes you needed to get into trouble to be able to move forwards with your life, and to get what you need. That summed up the last two weeks pretty perfectly.

Jess kicked off her heels and wobbled across the sofa to her tower of a friend, giving her the biggest hug around the waist that she could manage. 'I'm so pleased for you; I knew you'd do it.'

'Wait, Meems, I haven't told you the best part: *The Times* guy said they'd be interested in adding me to their freelance database. They want me to work for them.'

'*Holy Monroeny*, this is incredible! We must celebrate.'

'No.'

'No?'

'No. You must go back to Leo, he's waiting for you.'

Jess looked at Leo, standing with her family, laughing with Cameron. The sea breeze tousled his hair and she found herself smiling, as she always did, at his smile. She turned back to Bryony. 'Nope, let's get a drink or make an announcement—'

'I don't want that, really. You and I can celebrate when we get home. We'll go for dinner, we'll take *The Times* with us. For now, you're going to celebrate my news by spending every last second with your very own Leo DiCaprio, and I'm going to celebrate ...' She hopped down, smoothed her dress and slapped on her best, most confident Olivia Pope smile. 'I'm going to celebrate by getting me some. *Oh, Harvey ...*'

Making her way back to Leo, Jess heard words she'd heard a hundred times before coming from Cameron.

'. . . so then this monk gave me the stone and said, "You earned it."'

Instinct would usually have caused Jess to roll her eyes and cut him off, but for the first time she found herself laughing along, enjoying how happy and relaxed Cameron was sharing his stories with an enraptured audience. She felt a bubble of pride for her big brother the showman, the storyteller.

'Cameron,' she interrupted. 'Have you told Leo about the elephant you rode in Thailand?'

Cameron met her eyes and smiled at his little sister, before turning back to Leo. 'Maybe another time, hey, Leo? For now, I need another drink. Mum, Dad – join me.'

With that, they were gone, and Jess was alone with Leo again.

'Good news for Bryony?' asked Leo. 'And for Harvey, I guess.' Jess followed his eyes to where Bryony was leading Harvey inside the boat, a mischievous smile on her face.

'Very good news. Now—' She moved back into Leo, holding him like she wouldn't let him go, like she couldn't let him go. 'Kiss me. Before we're out of time.'

A loud pop startled them apart and the sky lit up with blue, gold and red stars. *Pop, pop, pop.*

The revellers quietened and moved closer to loved ones or friends as the grand fireworks display signalling the end of the Cannes Film Festival lit up the sky and was mirrored in the water.

Leo wrapped his arms tighter around her and accidently squeezed a tear out of her eye, which she blinked back furiously. There'd be time for crying after he was gone, not before.

As she gazed up at the fireworks she felt someone touch her arm. 'Same time next year?' Richard asked with a grin.

Jess laughed. There was always next year, and the year after that, and the year after that. Would she come back?

How could she not?

The fireworks continued for what seemed like for ever, but also for no time at all, and then it was done; silence in the sky, clapping, guests yawning and Jess holding on to Leo because it couldn't be the end.

He looked down at her, allowing himself to look blue for the first time. 'Will you stay with me tonight, on the yacht?'

'I don't know. All the crew are back now, it might be weird ...'

'Please, Jess. Even if we don't do anything, please stay with me because I don't want to have to imagine, yet, what it's going to be like not sleeping next to you.'

'Okay.' It wasn't a hard decision to make. She'd stay up all night if she had to, just to avoid missing even a second with him.

And that, nosy reader, is exactly what she did.

The sun was still rising when Jess and Leo stepped onto the marina the following morning. Her flight was leaving Nice in a few hours, so it was time for Jess to leave him and go back to the hotel to pack.

'Can I walk you back to your hotel?' Leo asked, holding her close, both of them blurry from lack of sleep, but soaking in their last minutes together.

'No, I want to remember you here, on your boat. And I need time to pull myself together.'

Leo nodded, his cheek against the top of her head. 'I'll see you again, right, Jess? This isn't actually good-bye at all. Maybe I could sail over sometime.'

'Yes, you have to,' she choked. 'Thank you for an amazing two weeks.'

'Thank *you*. I'll see you soon, okay? For more amazing weeks.'

'Okay.' The tears were running free now, as much

as she tried to wipe them away with the sleeve of his T-shirt.

'I'm going to miss you,' he sighed. 'You're the best one ever.'

'*You're* the best one ever. Don't miss me, just come and see me, okay?' She pulled away and it hurt, and with a final, aching kiss she stepped back.

'Definitely. Soon. Love you, socialite.'

'Love you, billionaire.'

Epilogue

'Excuse me, Marilyn Monroe-a-like, do you know where I could get something Nutella-based?'

Jess put the dome back over the cake stand covered in salted caramel brownies and felt excitement bubble up inside her like a freshly popped champagne bottle. For a moment she stared at the photo on the wall, a framed picture sourced by Bryony from one of her photographer friends of Jess in the background of some celebrities on the red carpet. She took a deep breath – he was here – and spun around. There he was, two days earlier than expected, standing in her café and wearing – for crying out loud – a naval officer's uniform whiter than a Hollywood smile.

Jess leapfrogged over the counter – health and safety be damned – and jumped into Leo's arms. He was more tanned than usual, his hair lightened still further by the Caribbean sun. Other than that he was the same: big smile, warm eyes, warm arms, toweringly tall – and *hers*.

'Manpreet,' said Jess, not taking her eyes off Leo, 'can I—'

'Yes, go! I don't want to see you back here for two weeks.'

'I can't believe you're here already!' Jess grinned, dancing around Leo as they left the café and turned right, walking through the October drizzle, heading towards her house on the hill. 'What happened?'

'Rusty decided he couldn't miss the Queen concert happening in London, so cut short the trip. Luckily this little beauty had already arrived.' He gave her a twirl.

'You look delicious, every bit the captain.'

'Thank you. I know you like it when I keep it real.' He smiled as she let him into her house, which immediately felt more full and more alive with him in it. This was his third visit to Cornwall since they'd left each other in Cannes, and each time they swapped a little bit more of their hearts. It was hard, not being with him whenever she wanted, but it was worth it for the times they were together.

Later that afternoon, Jess and Leo huddled together on the rocks on the beach. The rain had gone and the low autumn sunshine was dipping towards the horizon. Leo pulled Jess in closer and she could have been wearing an electric blanket, she felt so cosy.

'So, I booked it.' She turned to him, eyes sparkling. 'I hope you still want to go.'

'You booked it?' he cried, beaming from ear to ear. 'Our first adventure together!'

'Yep, we arrive in Los Angeles on the third of April, and we're staying in a little condo in the Hollywood Hills.'

Leo kissed her. 'I'm so excited. Jess, you're going to put your handprints in Marilyn's.'

'I know.' She couldn't wait. An adventure of her very own.

'Do you know what?' Leo asked suddenly, gazing back out at the pale pink sky. 'I could get very used to coming home here.'

Jess's skin tingled. 'I could get very used to that too ... what do you mean, exactly?'

'I mean, I think maybe it would be nice to move here. What do you think?'

'But don't you love living at sea?'

'What do you call this? It'd be nice to have a proper base, with you, to come home to whenever I'm on a break from work.' His hands shook as he pulled a piece of folded paper from his pocket. It was a printout from an estate agent's website of a tiny blue beach house.

'I know that place,' Jess exclaimed. 'It's just at the end of the beach, near the lighthouse.'

'Well, it's no superyacht, or Hollywood mansion, but I thought maybe – if you wanted to, if you didn't mind living with a smelly boy – we could think about renting it together? You know, using my drug money.'

Jess laughed, nodded, laughed some more and could only stop her ecstatic giggling by pressing her lips against Leo's. When they broke apart, he rested his forehead against hers and they touched their cold noses together.

And her adventure began.

Acknowledgements

ME AGAIN! I'd like to raise a cold glass of rosé and a sticky Nutella crêpe to the following people:

Manpreet: Hey, do you fancy going to another Beyoncé dance class sometime? Sorry, off topic. Thanks for your extreme patience and wise words, and for being World's Best Editor x

Everyone else at Little, Brown: THANK YOU Marina and Zoe, Jennie, Clara, Sarah, and Ella. Also Sian Wilson and Emma Graves who created the perfect ice-cream covers and thanks to Bekki for the complete novel cover that's so azure I just want to dive in!

Brilliant Agent Hannah: You complete me kitchen x

Husband Phil: 10/10 xx

Emma: I heart you. Thanks for your help and thoughts, once again x

SJ, Sarah, Al and Ellie: Thanks for offering a foot-long of help with some difficult words ;-)

Mum and Dad, my family (P, L, R, B, D, M, R, J, E, P), my friends (K, R, L, K): xoxoxoxoxoxoxoxoxoxoxoxoxoxo

The amazing authors and Twitterati, who every day offer encouragement and kind words: One day I will meet you all and shower you with smooches. Like it or not.

Benedict and Andrew (Moriarty): Thanks for the near-kiss on Sherlock, very inspiring *fans self*

Myself: Thanks for finally pulling it out and getting the book done. You want to try procrastinating less next time, for crying out loud?

And to the beautiful, relaxing location that is Cannes: I love you and one day I'm coming back. I shall summer with you on my superyacht. Just let me sell a few more copies first . . .

If you loved *Catch Me If You Cannes*, turn
the page for an exclusive extract from
Lisa Dickenson's hilarious new novel.

Prologue

Emmy shifted in her seat, the hard plastic as unforgiving as her hangover. 'Come on, Jared, you know we haven't done anything wrong.'

'This is clearly a case of Ciderwood bullshitery,' Rae scoffed next to her, peeling fragmented pigments of last night's lip colour from her mouth and dropping them on the table like a pink pile of ash. 'This town ain't big enough for the three of us.'

PC Jared Jones mirrored Emmy's shuffling, uncomfortable under the gaze of the three sisters. 'How can I not bring you in for questioning? The misdemeanours are just stacking up against you.'

'Please tell us exactly what we've done wrong?' prompted Noelle, who sat up straight, business-face on, the knowledge of the law behind that unwavering smile.

Emmy pushed her hair away from her face, and feeling something against her fingers, pulled a small leaf from the tangles. She met Jared's eye for a second.

He refocused on his paperwork, a blush creeping out from under his collar. 'I've had reports of theft, criminal damage, threatening language, antisocial behaviour, disturbing the peace, breaking and entering, devil worship, kidnapping—'

'*Alleged* kidnapping,' Noelle sang out.

'It's all alleged,' sighed Emmy.

'Then help me out here, ladies,' said Jared, sinking his face into his hands. 'You can't keep up this silence. Where is she? Where's the mayor?'

Chapter 1

Rae pounded the car horn with her fist outside Emmy's house, hollering '*Sissyyyyyyy*' out of the driver's seat window.

Emmy flung open her front door. 'Would you shut up?' she cried into the dusk. It was only early evening but the autumnal sun had already dipped, and the street upon which Emmy lived was quiet and peaceful, up until the appearance of her older sister.

Rae jumped out of the car and headed round to the boot, squishing her belongings to one side. Two months' worth of luggage fit Tetris-style into her raspberry-coloured KA.

'I'll be two minutes,' Emmy called, backing away from the door and into the house. 'Do you want a coffee or anything?'

Rae appeared at the door, grabbing Emmy and demanding a tight hug, while thinking how she'd missed these bony shoulders, this freckled face. Time apart from her sisters was always too long. 'Nope, we'll break up the journey with a coffee stop at a service station. Let's hit the road, asshole. Are these all your cases? What's in the cool box?'

'Just stuff from my fridge that needs using up.' Emmy

looked back down the hall into her home. Two months away. It wasn't that long, and if she really needed space from her sisters, or from Ciderwood, she just needed to jump on a train and come back to St Albans for a couple of nights. Noooooo big deal.

Emmy, her older sister, Rae, and their younger sister, Noelle, hadn't spent this much time together in years. And more importantly, they hadn't been home to Ciderwood in Devon for more than fleeting, house-bound visits since they were at school. Until now. Now, apparently, they all thought they were Kirsty Allsop and at their mother's request, while she was away on another of her world cruises, the sisters were heading south to renovate the family home. Their mother, Coco, had become quite the adventurer since their father passed a little over a year ago, and no longer needed a huge, crumbling house in the woods to herself. So the idea was that the girls would have a clear-out, spruce the place up, and whack it on AirBnB for all those months of the year that Coco was sailing up the Nile, or trekking the Himalayas, or drinking mimosas with billionaires at the Beverly Hills Wiltshire (true story).

'How did it feel stepping away from the lab for two months? Did anyone give you a leaving present? Did you feel like you were heading off to have a baby? I don't think I've ever known you to take more than a week off at one time.' Rae fired questions as she swooped around collecting up Emmy's neatly stacked bags, a coat from the coat rack, a TV guide from her living room.

'It felt fine; they'll barely even notice I'm gone, to be honest. It's only a short sabbatical.' Emmy was distracted, trying to remember if she'd prepared her house for its lonesome spell. Was the heating off, but not *too* off so that the pipes wouldn't freeze if winter came early? Was the compost bin empty? Were there conkers in the corner of every room, because she didn't want to come back and find a family of four thousand tarantulas had taken up residence? 'How about you? I bet your voice is looking forward to a break.'

Rae, though you'd never have guessed it from her potty mouth and Harley Quinn-on-a-day-off style, was by night a highly regarded opera singer who'd performed everywhere from Covent Garden Market to the Royal Albert Hall, and the Royal Opera House. 'Actually, about that . . . '

'What? Wait – don't tell me you haven't taken the time off. We all agreed—'

'No, I have, I totally have. I just have one performance I have to come back to London for, all the way in November, at least six weeks away. We'll be coming to the end of doing up the house then anyway, and I'll only be gone for the weekend.'

'Are you also going to be coming back and forth to visit Finn?' Emmy asked, finally stepping over her doorstep and into the cold night air, locking her door behind her, lingering on every clack and pop of the latches as if she was leaving a part of her safely inside.

'Nope, he's about to start a huge project at work and will be travelling loads for it anyway. He's going to come and stay, if he can, for a weekend sometime mid-way.'

Rae felt a wash of aloneness. Finn, her husband, her big bear, her electric blanket. But she shook her head, evaporating those thoughts. She'd be fine. She and Finn were solid as a rock and a few weeks apart was a chance to bring back that closeness with her sisters. It would be fun.

She hoped. She strongly suspected Ciderwood might be exactly as she remembered.

*

Apparently Rae's voice wasn't planning to take any kind of break, as she'd sung loudly along to every track on the eighties rock anthem playlist in the car. But two hours into the journey and Emmy was zoned out, staring at the taillights and headlights that ribboned across the inky motorway.

'Where are you?' asked Rae, muting Aerosmith.

Emmy looked over. 'Hmm?'

'Where's your head at? You've barely sung along at all, and you're not even eating the Haribo.'

'When my road trip buddy is a professional singer, the road trip is more enjoyable for everyone if I don't join in.'

Rae picked up a jelly cola bottle and leaned over, forcing it into Emmy's mouth. 'Talk to me, Emmaline.'

Emmy took a breath. She hated herself for being in this funk – she already felt like a teenager again and she wasn't even over the Devon border. She wanted to do this, she really did, so she mentally slapped herself out of it. Another Haribo would help. 'Sorry. Right, how about a game of twenty questions?'

'How about you tell me what's on your mind?'

'How about a game of snog, marry or kill?' Emmy tried.

'How about … okay, snog, marry or kill and then you have to talk to me properly. Snog, marry or kill: me, Noelle and Finn.'

Emmy laughed, 'Oh my god. Really?'

'You *have* to do it.'

'Marry Noelle—'

'Why Noelle and not me?' Rae cried.

'Because she's all earthy and makes soup and she has pretty hair so we'd have pretty-haired children.'

'Well that's gross and incest, and you're not her type anyway.'

'Snog Finn—'

'*Bitch!* Stop snogging my husband!'

'And kill you, for making me answer this awkward question!' Emmy concluded. 'Okay, snog, marry or kill . . . um . . .'

'Let's talk about you now,' interrupted Rae.

'Why? I get to do a round.'

'What's going on? Is work okay? You didn't let another gorilla escape, did you?'

Emmy chuckled. 'Only a few.' Emmy worked as a zoologist for the Zoological Society of London, working partially on lab research and partially curating at London Zoo. But, unlike her little sister Noelle, earth goddess and lover of all creatures great and small, she still hated spiders and didn't want them in her house, thank you very much. 'It's just . . . aren't you nervous?'

'About going home?'

'Yes.'

'A little, but it's not like we haven't been home for ten years or anything, we were back at Easter.'

'But fleetingly. It's always fleetingly. This time it's *lastingly.*'

'What are you so worried about?'

Emmy paused, flicking her hair above her lip like a moustache while she collected her words. 'I'm worried that nothing will have changed.'

'Everything's changed. We've all changed. It's been fifteen years or whatever since we lived there, I'm sure it's going to be very different.' She was so *not* sure.

'Yeah well, you better hope that's the case, because the villagers of Ciderwood hated you,' Emmy stuck her hand into the bag of Haribo.

'They hated you too, dork.'

'My point exactly.'

Rae ripped open a second bag of sweets using her teeth. 'Look, if it's that bad we'll just paint the house in reds and blacks and market it on AirBnB as a great location for group sex parties. That'll show 'em.'

With a yawn, Emmy nodded, thoughts of faces from her past dancing in her mind. 'That'll show 'em,' she agreed. She could see it now, the Lakes sisters returning to their hometown like a tornado, shock blanketing the faces of the bullies and the judgemental. Her mum wouldn't be too happy to find the house overrun with swingers, so that might not be quite the right approach, but a little revenge did sound oh-so-sweet.

Chapter 2

Eventually, at close to ten p.m., Rae crunched the car over the rough gravel driveway, creeping through the blackness towards the front of the house. Their home was surrounded by woods; tall pine trees that stretched towards the sun during summer and cast feathery shadows upon the gnarled oaks that curled beneath them. It sat on the outskirts of the small town of Ciderwood, at the end of an unkempt driveway that strangers often veered off, finding themselves having to reverse back through tight gaps between tree trunks. *Spotlights*, Rae thought to herself, the idea of tiny bulbs at the foot of the trees, lighting the way for their future guests who might arrive after dark.

Of course, the girls knew the road like the back of their hands. Years of running up and down, pretending to be horses or space ships or Olympians, and later, first kisses and stolen cigarettes, away from the eyeline of the house. Shielded from the traffic on the main road, and as loud as they liked all the way out here, this was their playground.

'Wake up, snooze-face,' coaxed Rae, and Emmy lifted her head from where it leaned against the car window. She hadn't been asleep, just lulled into a sensation of going through the motions; her body returning to Ciderwood, her mind gone onto a screensaver.

Emmy squinted into the dark, trying to make out the house among the trees, until there it was, right in front of her. Tall and wide, raised a little off the mulchy ground and confronted by a vast decking area with steps leading up the centre. With the moonlight slicing through the gaps in the trees and highlighting the peeling paint and broken bannisters, Emmy felt more than ever that it really did resemble the houses in American horror films from the seventies.

On that happy thought she spotted a small figure sitting on the steps surrounded by paperwork, shielding her eyes from the car headlights, a grin visible on her face. Emmy's heart blossomed at the sight of her little sister, and it was as if it was twenty years earlier, and Noelle was doing her homework out on the decking, where she always found it easier to concentrate, there among nature.

Rae shoved the car into Park before it had barely come to a halt, and leapt out to throw her arms around Noelle. Emmy too jumped from the car, her legs stiff but slightly shaking, and she ran to Noelle, wrapping herself around both sisters in a three-person embrace. *Home.*

'How are you here before us? I thought you had to work late tonight, otherwise I would have picked you up!' asked Rae, detangling herself and wandering to the boot as she talked. She opened it and one of Emmy's suitcases tumbled out onto the dirt below.

Noelle, one tiny arm still wrapped around Emmy's waist, moved them both towards the car to help unpack. 'I thought I'd be there for hours finishing things off – someone in Weston-super-Mare was claiming they owned the seabed and wanted to start work on a submarine restaurant, and . . .

well anyway, turns out they didn't and that was the end of that, so here I am. *But*, I don't have any keys.'

'How long have you been waiting for?' Emmy asked, dropping her arm from Noelle to retrieve her suitcase.

'Oh, not long. I was sat in the car for a while but it got a bit stuffy, so I moved to the porch and all the little bugaboos helped me finish up my legal briefs by the light of my phone.'

Noelle loved everything about nature, from creepy crawlies to the way the wind blew, and she adored being outside. She suited being born in a house in the woods – from as soon as she could, she would run barefoot for what seemed like miles, playing games in her head (when her sisters grew too old for make-believe), and scrambling into dens between trees. Her hair was long and curly and sun-kissed, and her limbs small but strong. She used to think she was Mowgli. She still did, in a way. Noelle was an environmental lawyer in Bristol, but not a day would go by without her taking a couple of hours to go climbing, or for a run in the rain, or to practice yoga in the middle of her garden in full, unashamed view of the neighbours who surrounded her terrace house.

The three of them emptied the two cars and hauled their belongings up the steps, dumping everything on the decking before the front door.

'Home, bitches,' said Rae, philosophically.

'Two whole months back in Ciderwood,' murmured Emmy.

They stood awkwardly, looking up at the house, which creaked in hostile response to the wind that fluttered the weakest of the summer leaves off their branches. Homecoming was a funny thing, and none of the sisters quite knew what to expect.

'The three of us don't spend nearly enough time

together,' Noelle broke the silence. She picked up the nearest bag with one hand, and Emmy's cool box with the other, and smiled towards the door with determination, demanding her sisters get on board. 'I'm looking forward to being back in the nest with you guys.'

Rae turned the keys in the locks and pushed open the heavy wooden door, disturbing a pile of post on the carpet below, highlighted by moonlight peeping through the curtains. She stepped over the threshold, dumped the bag she was carrying in the way of Emmy and Noelle, and felt along the wall for the light switch.

As the hallway illuminated, Noelle stepped around her sister and plonked down her first load, removing her coat and dumping it on the stairs like she'd always done. 'It's really quiet here without Mum.'

'I wonder what she's doing right now,' said Emmy, stepping carefully into the hallway and looking around. She felt off-kilter, like she was in someone else's home. She grew up in these walls, but for years now she'd only thought of it as 'Mum and Dad's house', and then 'Mum's house', when their father passed away.

Noelle stooped behind Emmy and picked up a postcard from the floor, partially obscured by junk mail and bank statements. 'It's from Mum! She says, "*Spawn, welcome home! Thank you for undertaking the house spruce-up while I'm away. Don't let those 60 Minute Makeover people in, I don't want everything replaced with MDF.*"'

'Pretty sure it's mostly MDF anyway,' Rae remarked.

Noelle continued reading. '"*Help yourselves to anything of course. No parties!!! PLEASE make your rooms presentable and no longer like shrines to your teenage selves. This is not an excuse to snoop though all my stuff!*"'

Rae interrupted again. 'Um, excuse me, this is the *perfect* excuse to snoop through all Mum's stuff. She's right about our bedrooms though. Emmy, your shelf of Natural Collection toiletries is probably poisonous by now.'

'And finally she says, "*Currently in Peru, thinking about doing the Inca Trail, not sure I can be bothered. See you (and the new improved house in the woods!) in a couple of months. Kiss kiss kiss, Mama Coco.*"' Noelle looked at the front of the postcard, which was a close-up of a llama wearing rainbow tassels from its ears.

'I wonder how this place will look in two months,' Emmy mused, pulling in a few more bags from the porch. 'Where do we even start?'

'We start, little sisters,' Rae said, dumping the last of the bags down and locking the front door behind her, 'with a drink.'

'I brought some wine,' offered Noelle, unzipping a suitcase in the middle of the hall.

'And I have beer,' Emmy said, carrying the cool box towards the kitchen.

'No, no, no, I'm talking a "Mum and Dad's drinks cabinet" drink.' Rae ushered them into the living room and opened the dark mahogany corner unit. Jewel-coloured bottles containing various levels of silky clear and amber liquids sparkled at them. Aged whiskies, brandy, Vermouth, an open Baileys that should probably be chucked, gin (three types) and, bizarrely, a bottle of Sourz Apple. Rae poured the three of them brandies into chunky crystal glasses. Her mother was not the type to have things like actual brandy glasses.

The sisters took their natural spaces in the living room, facing a fireplace that wasn't lit. The air was cold and a little musty, but they'd figure out how the boiler worked tomorrow, and open a few windows in the morning.

Noelle curled cat-like onto the rug in front of the unlit fire, propping cushions around her, and swirled her drink round her glass. Rae flopped across the length of one of the sunken-seated sofas, exhaling like the weary traveller she was. And Emmy climbed into her dad's old leather armchair, her feet under her bottom, and stroked the worn arm where he used to dig his thumbnail absentmindedly into the material, while he watched movies.

'It really is quiet without Mum barking and singing and hollering at Noelle to pick up her crap, isn't it?' said Rae.

Emmy nodded and swigged at her brandy, which was like foul-tasting fire in her throat. 'I wonder if this is how she felt after Dad died. Just . . . like everything was quiet.'

'I miss Dad,' said Noelle, lying back against the cushions, her glass now balanced on her chest. 'And I miss Mum. Do you think she's lonely, Emmy?'

Emmy's chest tightened with guilt while she searched for an answer. Why didn't she know if her mum was lonely? She considered her words, mindful of her sister's feelings. 'I'm not sure if she's lonely, or she's bored. I do think living all the way out here in the woods, in this house, which basically hasn't changed in thirty years, must be a pretty quiet existence now.'

'When she goes on holiday now she always chooses group tours, or cruises.' Noelle continued to stare at the ceiling. 'She must want some company. We should make more effort with her.'

'I think she's probably okay with being on her own,' Emmy countered. 'Mum's always been very independent. But I think she does like noise and action and life.'

'It's true,' added Rae. 'Mum would hate being referred to as lonely. But she loves to people-watch, and is the nosiest cow I know. Remember that PTA meeting where she spent most of the time asking us to point out everyone who'd ever been mean to us out of the other kids, and then telling us snippets of gossip about their families?'

Emmy smiled. '"*Don't you dare repeat this, girls, this is for information only. Knowledge is power, and nobody can ever harm you if you have power over them – and they never even have to know you have it.*" I remember getting that speech more than once!'

Laughter hiccupped out of Rae. 'I *always* repeated it. Mum was constantly furious at me. "*Spawn of mine does not gossip!*"'

'But she is such a gossip,' said Emmy.

Noelle sat up again, the sombre mood lifted for now. 'No, no, no, don't forget; "*It's not gossip when it's within the family, it's awareness.*"'

'So we have two months, sisters,' said Rae, pulling them from their reflections. 'What are we going to do with this old house?'

Noelle laughed, lightly. 'I can't believe we live here again. Sort of.'

'We should drive to B&Q tomorrow and buy a load of paint tester pots,' said Emmy. *What was wrong with her? Why was she finding this so much harder than her sisters seemed to be?* 'I think every room is going to need to be freshened up, don't you?'

'Definitely,' Rae agreed. 'Freshened, and lightened. No more dark purple or maroon red, please. We need new carpets, the bathroom and the loo need redoing, I wanted to talk to you about spotlights—' she took a yawn break '—and I guess we should think about if we want to change the structure of any of the house. Like, knocking down walls or adding en-suites or anything. Whatever, let's talk about it tomorrow.' Rae stopped talking and closed her eyes.

Noelle stood up, finishing her drink and twirling her hair up into a high bun. 'Agreed. I'm going to bed. I can't wait to catch up with both of you properly, though,' she said, holding her arms out until Rae and Emmy raised themselves up and gave her a goodnight hug. 'I'm so excited to have two whole months back with my big sissies.'

'Me too,' agreed Rae, flicking Noelle's bun. 'Ciderwood might be the armpit of the world as we know it, but we're going to have fun.'

Emmy bid goodnight to her sisters and they climbed the stairs, taking a handful of belongings with them, and parting ways on the landing. Their three rooms were arranged in a row, with their mum's bedroom, the master bedroom, watching over them all at the end of the corridor. Noelle's room was next to Coco's, followed by Emmy and then Rae on the end, next to the bathroom. Rae's bedroom overlooked the conservatory and had always been the perfect escape route if any of them had somewhere to be; somewhere they shouldn't be.

Emmy closed the door to her bedroom and let the silence fill her ears. No, not silence. Muted noise. The type of silence you get when you live with roommates, which she hadn't done for a while, where things in the house just stir and shift and there are creaks of drawers and steps going towards the bathroom and sneezes at unexpected moments.

She walked around her room once, barefoot, making an effort not to add to those small noises beyond the walls. She wandered past her dressing table, running her hands over the old pots and bottles – the pencil pot filled with glitter pens had long-since dried up – and felt ... disconnected. This could all go in the bin. Maybe not tonight, but tomorrow. Lining the walls were posters of pop stars with frosted eyeshadow or floppy curtain hairstyles. She had so loved those boys with the floppy hairstyles. They were clean and safe and they sang to her with sweet, high voices about taking it slow and loving her forever and never breaking her heart.

They didn't really make her heart flutter any more. Maybe a tiny bit. Maybe just that one from 5ive.

Emmy took her clothes off and left them on the floor, standing for a moment in just her underwear, imagining what teenage her would have thought of her grown-up body. She would have pretended she didn't care about the lumps and the thread veins, the breasts that had never grown any bigger. She would have pretended she didn't care because she also pretended that she didn't care that she'd never had a boyfriend, and she pretended she didn't care that she was called a saddo and a science nerd, and that people made fun of her for living out in the woods, and the fact that she once said in an English class at thirteen, without realising she was supposed to have grown out of them, that her current read was a Point Horror.

The Emmy of now really didn't care whether boys paid attention to her. The Emmy of now could see very clearly that her science-nerd ways had landed her a corker of a job, and she was independent, she liked her body (as much as anyone does), she liked her book choices, she still liked Point Horror, dammit, and she liked who she was. She *didn't* like the Emmy of her past. Past-Emmy was a reminder of how she'd felt embarrassed to be herself and how she'd been close to throwing it away just to try and fit in.

Emmy pulled herself from her thoughts and dragged on a T-shirt, a musty Mickey Mouse one she found squashed into the top of her chest of drawers, and climbed into bed.

For a while she lay still, looking at the room, trying to remember what it must have felt like to be a teenager in these walls. Lonely? Confused? Desperate to change? A tear, followed by a few more, rolled down her face all of a sudden. Why didn't she feel any fondness for the place she grew up? How was that *fair*? Emmy didn't feel at home in her own home, and the realisation crushed her. How could she spend two months back in this town, when it never wanted her here in the first place?

She flipped off the light switch on her bedside lamp and the room went black, momentarily, before her eyes adjusted to a ceiling full of stars – hundreds of them, glowing in the dark and carefully positioned to recreate as many of the constellations as possible. Emmy laughed out loud, despite the wetness on her cheeks. She'd forgotten this ceiling. How was she ever going to go to sleep with all of this beaming down at her?

But her eyes closed soon enough, and as Emmy rolled onto her side, a small light, no bigger than one of the stars on her ceiling, opened up inside her, and Past-Emmy was there, smiling with happiness as N*Sync sang her a beautiful lull-aby. Even if she wasn't ready to believe it yet, she was home.

Join the fun online with
Lisa Dickenson

@LisaWritesStuff
/LisaWritesStuff
www.lisadickenson.com